# BLACK FLOWERS

## Steve Mosby

An Orion paperback

First published in Great Britain in 2011
by Orion
This paperback edition published in 2012
by Orion Books Ltd,
Orion House, 5 Upper St Martin's Lane,
London WC2H 9EA

An Hachette UK company

1 3 5 7 9 10 8 6 4 2

A CIP catalogue record for this book
is available from the British Library.

ISBN 978-0-7528-8442-4

Typeset at The Spartan Press Ltd,
Lymington, Hants

Printed and bound by CPI Group (UK) Ltd,
Croydon, CR0 4YY

The Orion Publishing Group's policy is to use papers
that are natural, renewable and recyclable products and
made from wood grown in sustainable forests. The logging
and manufacturing processes are expected to conform to
the environmental regulations of the country of origin.

www.orionbooks.co.uk

*For Lynn and Zack*

## Acknowledgements

Thanks, as always, go to my agent Carolyn Whitaker, and to Genevieve Pegg, Natalie Braine, Gabby Nemeth and all the other people at Orion who have worked so hard on this book and the others. Thanks also to my friends and family, and to all the readers who have been in touch over the last few years with kind words about my writing. Also to *Spinetingler* magazine for inviting me to write the short story that gave me the idea for this novel.

Most of all, thanks to Lynn for putting up with me and to Zack for being wonderful: this book is dedicated to both of you, with love and appreciation for everything.

It does not happen like this.

If there's one thing that Detective Sergeant Michael Sullivan has learned during twelve years in the police force, it's that little girls do not simply appear. In his experience, the world does not work that way; all he has ever seen, and all he continues to see, is the opposite, the slow disintegration of things that are good and right.

People vanish – especially children. Sometimes they disappear in gradual increments, the decent, hopeful parts of them casually chipped away. Other times, those parts are poked out, suddenly and violently. And occasionally people simply vanish entirely. But however it occurs, those people do not come back, especially the children. Or at least not in any way you would want them to.

No, the world as Michael Sullivan knows it – it only takes.

It is early afternoon, September 1977. Faverton is a sprawl of a holiday town on the east coast. The old village on the hilltop spreads down cobbled streets all the way to the sea front, with its penny arcades and cafés. The road here is embedded with brown, metal tramlines. A slatted wooden promenade stretches along the front, dotted with curled, green benches, wire-mesh bins and beige ice-cream vans. Families stroll slowly along, sometimes approaching the waist-high stone wall and looking out over the beach. The sand is packed flat and hard, broken by occasional fluffed-up patches where a child has dug. In the distance, the grey sea crumples and folds beneath a white sky bevelled with gulls.

It is an ordinary day with no hint of magic to it. And yet, in spite of Sullivan's experience, it happens like this.

There is an empty stretch of promenade. A tram trundles past. It is so old, and the metal carriage so frail, that you would expect the antennae above, where they track the overhead electrical cables, to crackle and spark, but in fact the only noise is the continuous weary crunch of the metal discs the vehicle grinds through town on. It is mostly empty, and reminiscent of a butler going about daily tasks in a household where all the children have left. The driver, behind the smeared front window, is holding the controls with stiff, unmoving arms, while a conductor waits at the open back corner of the tram, a ticket machine strapped to his chest like a tiny accordion.

The tram does not stop. Nobody gets on or off. But when it has passed, the stretch of promenade is no longer empty.

A little girl is standing there.

She has long, dirty-blonde hair, pulled into rough bunches that rest to either side on her tiny shoulders. She is wearing a blue-and-white checked dress and delicate shoes: both look like something a doll would wear. Her eyes are ringed with darkness and sadness. In front of her, she clasps a small handbag. It is pale brown, leather, and far too large for her – an adult's bag – but she clutches it tightly, as though she has somehow had it for a very long time and it is intensely important to her.

The little girl stands there.

Waiting.

And that is how it happens. She appears on the promenade as though from nowhere: as if the world shifted in its sleep, then woke with an idea so important, which needed to be told so desperately, that the idea became real. And now that idea is standing there, waiting to be discovered.

Waiting for someone to claim it.

2

Sullivan squats down in front of the little girl. His starched trouser leg forms a sharp contour up from his knee and over his thigh. Her small eyes follow him down. Their faces are now at the same height, and he smiles at her, trying to be reassuring.

'Hello there. What's your name?'

The little girl does not respond. The expression on her face is like a shield. She is far too serious for a girl her age and Sullivan knows immediately that something isn't right here.

He looks away for a moment. The woman who noticed the little girl and alerted him is standing, slightly hesitantly, to one side. She is middle-aged, holding her own handbag in much the same way as the girl. Sullivan nods his thanks to her – It's okay; I'll take care of this – and then turns his attention back to the child as the woman walks away.

He doesn't know, at this point, that he'll need to talk to the woman again and attempt to establish the exact circumstances of the girl's appearance here. Although he recognises something is wrong, the idea hasn't quite settled and become real. He's still thinking: she's lost her parents. That's all.

'My name's Mike,' he says. 'What's yours?'

Again, the girl does not reply. But after a moment of staring back at him, she breaks his gaze and looks away, off to one side. And she does say something, but he can't make out what. It's as though she's talking to a ghost, or asking advice from an imaginary friend.

Can I talk to him? Is it safe?

'What was that?' he says.

She keeps looking away. Listening now.

Christ, Sullivan thinks – because he's just realised something else: it really does look like her. Anna Hanson, the little girl who was murdered last year. They are both a similar age, about six years old, and Anna had the same straggly blonde hair. The recognition, coupled with the oddness of the girl's behaviour, makes Sullivan shiver slightly. He has the odd sensation that this could actually be her, returned to her grieving, terrified parents.

Of course, it can't be, not least because Anna Hanson has already been returned. Her body washed up on the beach: tiny, grey and empty. The similarity is genuine, though, and he feels a sudden and urgent need to look after this little girl and keep her safe.

She looks back at him. In all his twelve years of experience, he has never seen such despair.

'It's okay,' he says. 'I'm a policeman. Have you lost your mummy and daddy?'

'My daddy.'

Her voice is impossibly delicate.

'Well, I'm sure we can find him quickly—'

But he stops. From the flash of terror that appears on the little girl's face, it's obvious that this is not what she wants to hear. Her small body begins trembling slightly.

Instinctively, without considering how she'll react, Sullivan reaches out and rests a gentle hand on her shoulder, feeling the rough fabric of the dress against his palm. The little girl almost flinches, but doesn't. The fear is overridden by an innate, desperate need to be comforted. It is as though she hasn't been touched with kindness or reassurance for quite some time, if ever, and it requires bravery – a leap of faith – for her to believe such a thing is even possible any more.

'It'll be okay, honey,' Sullivan says.

Again, he glances around. There are a few people watching the scene, but most are simply going about their business, either oblivious or confident that nothing is wrong. After all, a policeman is in control of the situation. It is his job to look after people, and he will. That is the assumption.

Sullivan is about to turn back to the little girl and try to do exactly that, when he sees the man and instead he goes still.

Clark Poole.

The old man is walking awkwardly along the pavement

across the street, on the far side of the tramlines. He is slightly hunched, and his cheap coat is stiff with grease over the slight hump of his spine, as though age is gradually forming his whole back into a boil that's soft and wet at the centre. His head is bald and pale, but thin white hair clings to the side, while his face, out of sight now, is wide and unkind. Poole walks with a bound wicker cane that Sullivan suspects, but can't prove for sure, the old man doesn't really need.

Tap tap.

At first, Sullivan doesn't think Poole has seen him. But the old man pauses outside the café, then turns to stare back at him. Poole smiles and gives Sullivan a nod – as he so often does; as he so enjoys doing – before turning back and continuing on his way. Tap, tap. People move for him, more from instinct than manners, and Sullivan fights down the familiar urge to dash across and grab hold of him. If he started shaking the old man, he knows he would never be able to stop.

So he forces himself to watch the old man amble away. Was Poole involved in this somehow? It seems unlikely. After all, he didn't return little girls, did he? He took them away, carefully and precisely, so that it was possible to know but impossible to prove. Regardless, Sullivan knows where the old man lives. He searched the flat after Anna went missing. But there have been times since when he has parked up a little way down the street, in the early hours of the morning, and spent time wondering what he might be capable of doing to the old man.

Sullivan turns back to the little girl.

He notices the handbag again. It is far too grown-up for her. It looks dirty now, as though it has been left outside somewhere, but he has the sense that it might once have been expensive.

'Can I have a look in there, please?'

She hesitates.

'I'll be careful,' he says. 'I promise. You can have it back again afterwards.'

Still unsure. But she does pass it to him.

5

'Thank you.'

The zip is stiff: as he suspected, crumbs of dirt block the teeth. When he finally opens it and looks inside, he is expecting to find a small purse, handkerchiefs – keys, perhaps – but the handbag is almost entirely empty.

Except for . . . a flower.

Sullivan reaches carefully in and lifts it free. The stem is fractured and half broken; the petals, which at some point have been pressed, are grey-black.

His fingers tingle.

And there is that feeling again, only now far stronger than before. Something is wrong here. Sullivan looks at the girl's dirty hair, the odd dress. For the first time, he notices there is the slightest hint of a bruise on her cheek.

The little girl says, 'Jane.'

'Is that your name?'

She shakes her head, then motions almost imperceptibly at the flower.

'That's Jane. She doesn't talk to me any more.'

Sullivan stares at her. He does not understand what she means, of course – not yet – but the answer is strange enough to send a chill shivering across his back. The next tram is rattling down the street; he can hear it growing louder. And in front of him, the little girl's fragile resolve finally disappears entirely and she begins to cry.

She says, 'Please help me.'

# Part One

# Chapter One

My father was a writer. I wanted to be one too, so I would have been thinking about him that day anyway, even without what happened later. But for most of the morning, I'd been thinking about goblins and changelings.

Well – and students too, obviously.

It was nearly lunchtime now. I walked round my desk and raised one of the slats in the blinds. Outside, an angle of midday sunlight cut across the flagstones below my office. A stream of new students was flowing past. They looked almost impossibly young. The boys all seemed to be dressed for the beach, wearing shorts and T-shirts. The girls wore floaty summer dresses, enormous sunglasses and flip-flops that slapped at the stone. It was Freshers Week 2010, so the whole campus was one big party. For most of the morning, I'd been able to hear music thudding from the Union building, more of a constant heartbeat than an actual song.

I allowed the slat to click down, then returned to my desk. In comparison to the bright, carnival atmosphere out there, my office was small, drab and grey. The air in here smelled of dusty box files and the rusted metallic radiator that underlined the window. I'd wedged the door open. Ros – my boss – was down at the sports hall handling module admissions, and the common room was deserted. Aside from the thump of the music, and an occasional muffled bang echoing down the corridor, the only real sound in here was the electrical hum of my old monitor.

Right now, I had two files open. The first was the student records database I'd been stringing out for weeks now, pretending it was far more difficult to construct than it actually was, while the second was the short story I'd been working on all morning instead.

I scanned through it again now.

By my standards, it had turned out pretty weird. At the beginning, a young guy finds out his girlfriend is pregnant. It's an accident: they just got carried away in the moment, then grinned about it afterwards. 'That was stupid, wasn't it?' they say. 'It won't happen to us.' But it does happen to them.

The girlfriend decides she can't have a termination and the guy accepts that, even though it's not what he wants. He tries to be good, but as time goes on he resents her decision more and more – and then he starts to notice hooded gangs huddled on street corners. They're watching him, following him. He gradually imagines the existence of a shadowy crime lord – a kind of Goblin King figure – who is reaching out to him. Like the goblins of fairy tales, these urban equivalents will be more than happy to steal his child away: all the man has to do is wish for it to happen. Eventually, selfishly, he does.

For two days afterwards, nothing happens – enough time for him to doubt it was real – and then the pregnancy mysteriously disappears.

The story ends years later, with the main character encountering one of the hooded minions on a street corner and recognising enough in the boy's face to know it's his son.

*Pretty weird, Neil.*

It was, but I sort of liked it. And anyway, I was procrastinating too much. Weird or not, successful or not, it was as done as it ever would be. So I saved the Word file, and opened a quick email to my father.

Hi Dad

Hope you're okay – I know it's been a couple of weeks, so I'm guessing everything's going all right? Meant to be in touch. Failed miserably.

Got some news, but in the meantime I wanted you to have a look at this. I don't know whether it's any good or not, but maybe you can have a read if you get the chance? I'll give you a bell properly soon and we can chat.

Love always,
Neil

I took a deep breath and pressed send.

Oddly, I felt nervous. My father had published twenty novels over the years and was always honest about the technical side of my writing – that was why I sent him things in the first place. It wasn't that; I wasn't quite sure *what* it was. Just that, as I watched the email indicator circling, I wished I could take it back.

Then it changed to a tick.

That was that. My story had gone out into the world.

*Forget about it.*

When I checked my watch, it was close to twelve. So I minimised the email program, locked up the office and headed out.

Ally was working at Education now, but today she had a conference on at the Union Hall building. It was on the far side of campus, so I had to follow the throng of students right through the thudding heart of everything.

The combination of sunshine and the time of year made it feel like the first day of a festival. Outside the Union, the grass was bright and sunlit, and everyone seemed to be sitting around with plastic glasses of foamy beer. The tarmac around the steps was a multicoloured carpet of discarded flyers; speakers were balanced on the upstairs window ledge, pumping out music. A skinny boy in sunglasses and a pork-pie hat was standing up there with his foot on the ledge, shouting what sounded like static and occasional words through a megaphone, haranguing passers-by.

Despite not being a part of the carnival, I knew there were a million worse places to work. Not only was it relaxed enough for me to wear jeans and trainers to the office, there were also lots of times like today when I could sneak some writing in. Technically speaking, I was even being paid for it. But there's nothing like working at a university to remind you how old you're getting, even when, at twenty-five, you actually aren't. It got worse every September, with the arrival of a new and even more fresh-faced cohort. You feel like a bunch of old flowers, maybe not quite past your sell-by date yet, but already beginning to wilt in the corner, and nobody's choice.

All I'd ever wanted to do was write. My father made only the vaguest of livings from it – his books skipped across too many genres, the publication dates a few too many years apart – and, growing up, I was dimly aware of our relative poverty in comparison to other kids' families. That didn't really matter. I was brought up to love books and stories: we always had plenty of the former, and, with my father around, an infinite number of the latter. There was never anything else I'd wanted to do except be a little bit like him.

But I wasn't.

Since coming to work here, I'd submitted four books to publishers, and all of them had been knocked back with the solid wooden *tock* of a well-hit baseball. Fine. But as much as you tell yourself you need to learn your craft and serve an apprenticeship, all those bleary early mornings and late nights . . . they start to get to you. You have to take it seriously, so it's basically like working two jobs. And for me, trying to fit real life around that was getting hard. Maybe it was starting to get impossible. Maybe I was going to have to start facing facts.

Ally was supportive, of course, but it still felt like there were too many plates to keep spinning and that pretty soon I was going to have to let something fall. It wouldn't be my relationship with her. I loved her far too much to let that go. So maybe it was writing that would have to get shelved. It was a depressing thought.

But I would do that for her. I really would.

She was already outside the Union Hall, waiting for me on the steps. It was easy to spot her amongst the students – she had dyed-red hair, for a start. But she'd also made an effort for the conference and was wearing a smart black dress and heels. Away from work, she wore baggy jeans, trainers and T-shirts, and normally looked somewhere between a punk and a Bash Street kid; you'd half expect to look down and see her holding a skateboard. A casual observer right now might nod and say she scrubbed up well, but a smart one would realise she was beautiful in anything. Either might wonder what the hell she was doing with me.

'Hey there, you,' I said.

'Ah. *Finally*. Keeping me waiting, Dawson?'

'Keeping you on your toes, more like.'

She went up on them now to give me a kiss, putting her hands on my shoulders. At first glance, Ally looked small and fragile. She was actually slim and muscled, the kind of girl that might surprise you at arm-wrestling, and would certainly try. The first time we'd ended up in bed together, a year ago now, both of us as drunk and surprised as the other, I'd barely have been able to escape if I'd wanted to.

'Come on,' she said. 'I'm starving.'

'Can't have that.'

We went to The Oyster Bar in the Union. It was called that because the bar was down in the centre, glistening with mirrors, then surrounded by rising, circular ridges of white seats and tables. We found a space, and, while we waited for the food to arrive, chatted about our mornings over the mingle of conversation around us.

As time went on, though, it was obvious that she was distracted: not entirely interested in the small talk. She was asking questions but didn't seem to be listening to the answers, and answering mine without saying much. But then, it's difficult to do small talk when the shadow of big talk is looming over you both.

'Okay,' I said eventually. 'What are you thinking?'

'Nothing.'

'You're thinking something.'

'All right then, I am. Maybe I'm building up to it.'

'About the baby?' I guessed.

But our food arrived, so I leaned back to allow the waitress space to slide the plates onto the table. Ally hooked a strand of hair behind her ear and picked up her knife and fork.

She said, 'I've made a decision.'

'That you're keeping it.'

'Yes.' She nodded around the bar. 'I know it's not wonderful fucking surroundings for this conversation, but I wanted to tell you as soon as I was sure.'

I did my best to smile.

'I already knew,' I said.

'I just don't think I could *not* go through with it.'

She looked at me now, and it was like an armed conflict was going on behind her eyes.

'I know,' I said. 'I love you.'

'I love you too. But it's going to change everything.'

'It'll be okay.'

I did my best to sound convincing. Even though I'd been sure what her decision would be, hearing it out loud still made it feel like the bottom had dropped out of my fucking world. Obviously, I wasn't going to tell her that.

'It'll be okay,' I said again. '*We'll* be okay.'

'Promise?'

How can you promise anything like that? We'd only found out a week ago, and I'd barely had time to get my head round it.

The idea still wasn't real; it was impossible to imagine what *everything changing* was going to involve for me, for her, for us. Even so, I reached out and rubbed the back of her hand. Around us, the clinks and clatters in the bar seemed to have faded away almost to nothing.

I promised.

Back home later, I took a sip of ice-cold white wine, and stared at the screen of my laptop. Below my makeshift desk, the printer *chittered*. Paper stuttered out of the front, landing face up on the floor. The story I'd written, printing out in reverse order, the end working its way steadily back to the beginning. If only everything in life was so simple to undo.

My front room was my bedroom. Outside the window beside me, I could see the familiar neon row of late-night takeaways and off-licences across the road. I lived in a converted house, which had been divided by the landlord into two studio flats. The entire second floor – all three rooms of it – was mine. My neighbour had the first floor: he was an Argentinean student who didn't seem to do much besides listen to action films very loudly at random times of the day and night. We shared the stairwell and the communal front door, which was squeezed in-between a newsagent and a hairdressers. As I arrived home after work, I could usually hear the blow dryers through the thin wall and smell, just faintly, scorched hair.

It wasn't great. It wasn't even particularly safe. Round the back of the building, the door to the cellar was half broken. If you were determined enough to push through the rotting litter there, and then the broken furniture in the basement, you could get all the way up to my personal front door without busting a lock. Fortunately, I didn't have anything worth stealing. There was only my cheap laptop, which normally lived in a drawer beneath a pile of T-shirts – surely beyond the imagination of any thief.

The printer *chittered* to a halt, and I was left with the

gunshots and explosions from below. They were in full effect tonight – the floor vibrating beneath my feet. It was possible to imagine an actual war was occurring down there. I sipped the wine, then picked up the pages, tapped them into line on the desk, and read them again.

Pretty weird.

And pretty harsh too.

But stories are allowed to be, so long as they're honest.

For example, my father's last book was called *Worry Dolls*. It was about a small village, and a lonely young boy with a father who beats him and his mother. A doll maker teaches the boy how to make a worry doll – a little figurine fashioned from pegs and coloured cloth. At night, you tell the doll all your fears and place it under your pillow where it looks after them on your behalf, so you can sleep soundly. The boy makes a monster. His doll has used matchsticks poking from its back like burnt wings, and toenail clippings for claws. And that night, when the father is drunk and going to kill the whole family, the creature comes to life and rips him to shreds.

That story works on its own terms, but the book's about much more than that. The narrator of *Worry Dolls* is a very old man who witnessed the events first-hand. His wife was very sick at the time, and the doll maker taught *him* how to make a worry doll as well. The man created it in the shape of his wife, and told it that he was terrified of dying alone. In his case, the magic didn't seem to work, because his wife died anyway. And yet, on his deathbed at the end of the book, he realises the ghost of his wife has been sitting beside him the whole time, waiting for him to finish, and when he dies she takes his hand and they leave together.

Dad began writing *Worry Dolls* two years ago, when my mother was fighting cancer for the final time. It was the last battle in a long war, and he finished the novel just after she died.

At one point, the doll maker tells the boy:

*It doesn't really matter how tatty or incomplete it is. All that matters is that it's yours.*

And to my father, stories served exactly the same purpose as worry dolls, except he confided his fears and troubles in words on a page. That book contained all the emotions he would never have said to my mother out loud. Rather than breaking down and confessing his own pain – that he was scared of living and dying without her – he had concentrated on looking after her. Being selfish in his writing had allowed him to be the opposite in real life.

That was what I'd done. My story was a dumping ground for all the miserable, negative shit I was feeling deep down: the stuff I knew wasn't fair and which I would never say out loud to Ally. Obviously, this was going to be way harder for her, and require at least as many sacrifices and compromises as it did for me. So the guy on the page could seethe with stupid, childish resentment on my behalf, and I could get on with being a supportive partner, a good person. Close as I got to that anyway.

I finished the wine.

Even so, it did seem harsh – and I had another idea. I picked up a pen and scribbled at the end of the last page:

*Regret.*
*Maybe guy changes his mind and has to fight to get child back?*
*A descent into hell?*

I stared at that for a moment, thinking it through.

Maybe that would end up better. More satisfying.

More wine. I stood up. The night was young, after all, and fuck it – if you couldn't get drunk on the day you find out you're going to be a father, when could you?

I was heading through to the kitchen to explore that question more thoroughly when my phone rang. It was the landline: chirruping away in the corner by the bed. It surprised me; I'd almost forgotten it was there. Nobody ever called on it. My friends were all texters or emailers.

I put the empty glass down by the computer and walked over.

'Hello?'

'Hello. Is that Neil?'

It was a woman's voice, but not Ally.

'Yes.' I sat down on the bed. 'This is Neil.'

'Oh good. This is Marsha Dixon. I'm your father's agent.'

It took me a second, but then I thought: *Ah, yes*.

I'd met Marsha a handful of times, and found a mental picture of her now. A woman in her fifties, with grey hair in double plaits, like a schoolgirl. Very bohemian. When I was much younger, my father had explained to me that a lot of the people in publishing were *flamboyant*, and for a while I'd imagined he meant some weird variety of exotic creature, distantly related to flamingos. The last time we'd met, Marsha air-kissed me to either side, and smelled of strong perfume and wine. All of the book-length manuscripts I'd finished had passed – anonymously – across her desk and been returned. I'd actually held one of them up to my nose, checking for perfume. Nothing.

'Hi Marsha. What can I do for you?'

She paused, then sounded distraught:

'It's your father, Neil. I'm afraid he's missing.'

# Chapter Two

Dad still lived in the same house I'd grown up in.

We'd had one quarter of an old, converted, gothic mansion, set back down a winding, white-tarmac driveway. It was a flat, really, since aside from the staircase up to it, it ran along on a single level, but the building as a whole was enormous and imposing: soot-black, and built from bricks that, when I was younger, seemed bigger than I was. From the outside, it looked grand and desirable, but it wasn't. During my return visits there as an adult I'd had two separate realisations.

The first was how genuinely ramshackle my home had been. There was something threadbare about the place; if it had been a jacket, it would have smelled of mothballs and had patches stitched on the elbows. The walls inside were freckled with damp, and the old carpets curled up against the dusty skirting boards, no longer nailed down. In some ways, it reminded me of my own flat – and that brought home to me just how much my father dominated my parents' marriage. This was the house that he, a struggling, intermittently successful writer, would *always* have lived in, regardless of my mother's presence. Rather than them forming a new life together, it seemed she'd been content to be a passenger in his.

The second realisation cancelled that out. After my mother's death it struck me just how *empty* the house felt with her gone, and how diminished my father was in her absence. But I thought

I understood. My father had been driven to write, and writers need readers. It's a partnership, and although it might not seem equal on the surface, it actually is. Just because one person appears content to listen, it doesn't mean the other – the speaker – doesn't need and rely on them being there for the whole thing to have meaning. Love can be the same.

I'd never been worried about him though. Over the last year, I had watched him age before my eyes, as though my mother's presence had kept an older man at bay, one who was now free to appear. With every passing week, he seemed smaller and more fragile than he had the week before. But after the tears had dried up, and he'd begun to adjust his life to fit around the shape of his loss, my father did what I knew he would, what he always had. He began writing.

So I'd never been worried.

And there was no reason to be worried now. Marsha was just being melodramatic. Despite the vague niggling feeling in my chest, I kept telling myself that, as I sat on the bed and listened. My father hadn't been in touch about a new contract, she said, and he wasn't answering his phone or returning her calls, and that was *so unlike him*. Which wasn't true. In fact, from everything she said, it sounded like Dad had been behaving very much like Dad.

'I'm sure he's okay, Marsha. You know what he's like.'

'Oh, I'm sure he is too. It's just with your mother passing last year. And I'm so sorry about that, darling. So sorry.'

'Thank you.'

The niggling feeling began curling slowly into an itch of irrational panic. When was the last time I'd spoken to him? It had been over two weeks ago, I realised – actually, that *was* longer than normal. And, looking back, he'd seemed even more preoccupied than usual. As though there were far more serious things on his mind . . .

But you can think yourself into all kinds of worries.

'I'm sure it's nothing,' I said. 'He's not the type to do anything stupid. Obviously, he took Mum's death hard, but he'll be channelling it into his writing.'

It sounded stupid, spoken out loud.

Marsha wasn't reassured. 'Do you think you could check up on him for me, Neil? Honestly, it would set my mind at rest.'

I rubbed my forehead. There had been no reason to worry before, and there was no reason to now. I could repeat that to myself over and over, and it wasn't going to make the slightest bit of difference.

'Yes,' I said. 'I will.'


It was a half-hour's drive across town, but I weighed up my general state of sobriety and found it a little on the light side. After trying my father's home phone and mobile, the next call I made was for a taxi. Just before eight, it pulled up outside my father's house. The engine puttered to itself while the driver stuck the light on in front to consult his plastic charge sheet.

After I'd paid, I walked down the drive, and into the garden. My mother's old washing line was still strung across, hanging loosely in the middle, as though weighed down by invisible clothes. Old pegs were clipped on by the wall. All my father's windows faced out this way, apart from the kitchen which was round the corner. Looking up now, the ones I could see were curtained over and dark. Either he was in bed – unheard of at this hour – or he wasn't here.

I had my own key.

'Hello?' I called up the stairs. 'Dad? It's just me.'

I was met by silence. The corridor at the top was dark and quiet, and everything beyond it felt still. The house seemed empty, and there was a musty smell to the place, as though the front door hadn't been opened in a while.

I closed it behind me and went up the stairs. Walking around, I clicked all the lights on. However irrational it was, my heart thudded every time I stepped into a room and flicked the switch – each time revealing nothing.

He wasn't here.

I was surprised by how relieved I felt.

*Where is he then?*

The window in the kitchen was old, held shut by a metal arm that hooked over a nub in the base and clenched the frame tight. I opened it, letting in a hush of night air, and peered out. The garages for all four flats were directly below, and my Dad's car wasn't there.

I stayed with my head out of the window for a moment, thinking. My father didn't go out much on an evening, as far as I knew, and if he'd gone away I thought he would have told me.

I closed the window and walked halfway back down the corridor. Stepped into his office.

This had been my bedroom as a child. It still held wisps of memories now, like cobwebs in the corners, but he'd changed so much around that it was barely recognisable; to picture the room I grew up in, I had to rely on the mental equivalent of dents in a carpet that showed where furniture had stood.

On the right, where my bed had been, the wall was now entirely covered with shelves. The bottom one contained reference materials and box files; the rest, all the way up to the ceiling, were filled with what looked like hundreds of copies of my father's own books.

I stared at those for a moment. There were all the English editions, and it was easy enough to pick out the hardbacks and paperbacks of each, with updated editions studiously slotted into place. The foreign copies were harder to decipher, but they seemed to have been grouped together by title as well. Had he kept one of everything? I glanced here and there in wonder. The books, along with various anthologies, appeared to be arranged chronologically – *autobiographically*, I thought – so that *Worry Dolls* was at one end of the top shelf, clean and fresh and new.

What must it be like to have your life's work on display like this? The number of spines visible was impressive enough, never mind all the pages and words contained inside. You could practically hear the pages whispering.

I turned around and walked over to the desk. When it was my room, there had been an enormous wardrobe here, and a standing lamp with an old feathered shade. My father's desk looked even older than the wardrobe had been; it was made of pitted wood, the texture of a desk in a school science lab. The lamp had been replaced by an angled metal contraption. The only other things on the desk were a battered old paperback and dust. But there was a clean, laptop-shaped space in the middle. So, wherever he'd gone, it looked like he'd taken his computer with him.

I looked up. There was a calendar on the wall, with photos of sports cars; this month's page had caught a blurred red Ferrari in the act of cornering on a racetrack. Below the picture, various days in September were blocked out. Last Friday, he'd written *Haggerty A*. Saturday was marked *Ellis F ??*

And then, underneath that, *Southerton Hotel, Whitkirk*, with an arrow running across all the days until tomorrow.

So that was that. He'd gone away after all.

It pissed me off a bit that he hadn't let me know but then, he was his own man, and it wasn't like I'd been in touch myself. If it was work-related, it was possible he'd been so distracted that it just hadn't *occurred* to him to tell anyone.

What was he working on?

I looked again at the book. It wasn't like my father to sit and read in here; he was a front-room, armchair reader. I picked it up. A novel, and an old one at that. It looked like it had been left out in the rain, or found in a field – or maybe just thumbed through so many times that it had begun to fall apart, like some ancient map.

The title at the bottom was embossed, and had once been gold, but most of the colour had flecked away over the years.

## THE BLACK FLOWER

And in smaller letters underneath:

ROBERT WISEMAN

The cover image above was strikingly horrible. It resembled a rose, except the petals were black, and the centre had been twisted to form a woman's face contorted in agony. Sharp thorns curled upwards from the stem, drawing beads of crimson blood from the petals.

I flipped it over and read the sparse description on the back:

This is not the story of a little girl who vanishes. This is the story of a little girl who comes back . . .

A little girl who appears on a promenade, clutching a bag. Inside, there is only a mysterious black flower. She has no name, no identity, and nobody knows where she came from. What she does have is a terrifying and disturbing story to tell.

The policeman who finds her is determined to discover the truth. Because the girl's tale is surely too horrific to be real. But if it is true, then her life is in danger. And she is not alone.

I started to flick through it without thinking. The book immediately fell open in the middle. Where, pressed inside the pages, there was a flower.

The remains of one anyway. It looked half fossilised. The stem was reed-thin and crisp; the petals, dried and flat, their colour paled almost to grey, with tiny black veins visible in the surfaces. It reminded me of the skin of a very old lady.

A *black flower*.

I wondered if maybe it was some kind of promotional thing but that couldn't be right. Because the more I looked at it, the more I felt there was something wrong with the flower. It was *ugly*. And certainly not something you'd normally choose to keep. I closed the book and slid it back across the desk, deciding I'd ask my father about it when I saw him.

Walking back through the house, clicking the lights off, I

finished in the living room. In one corner, by the television, a small red light was pulsing on the answer machine. Messages. I walked across to see a red '7' on the display. Were they all from Marsha? I pressed play and listened.

The first two were, indeed, from Marsha, recorded three days apart and still – at this point – relatively calm.

The third was someone I didn't recognise.

'Hello, this is Barbara calling, with a message for Christopher Dawson. About the interview? Give me a ring back if you're still interested. You've got my number.'

Beep. A journalist then. My father would be thrilled.

The next three messages were all from Marsha, growing increasingly anxious in tone. The last of them, left this afternoon, told him she was going to try getting in touch with me to make sure he was all right.

Again – he would be thrilled.

The final message on the machine had been left an hour ago. Another woman's voice that I didn't recognise.

'Hello,' she said, 'I'm trying to reach the family of Christopher John Dawson. My name is DS Hannah Price of the Whitkirk constabulary. If anyone picks up this message could they please phone me back on oh one—'

I scrabbled for a pen, then played mental catch-up with the number.

'It's very important,' she said. 'In the meantime, I'll be trying to reach you by other means. Thank you.'

*Beep.*

I stared at the machine for a moment. Why were the police calling my father? *Whitkirk*. That was the address of the hotel he'd listed on the calendar. The Southerton.

Something began crawling in my chest.

*I'm trying to reach the family of Christopher John Dawson.*

His family. Not him.

So why ring here?

I picked up the phone, then slowly tapped in the number

she'd given in the message. As it rang, the crawling sensation became worse. The dark house behind me seemed to throb harder and harder with emptiness.

And a minute later, I learned that my father was dead.

# Chapter Three

Five tiny crosses, the colour of blood.

*Which you will not think about.*

Instead, DS Hannah Price opened the drawer below her office desk and took out the photograph album. She was waiting for Barnes to arrive for the briefing on Christopher Dawson's death, and there were a hundred things she could be doing in the meantime – a pile of reports on other cases to be written and filed, contacts to be chased – but she'd been finding it difficult to concentrate on work recently. Or, in fact, to do much of anything at all. Even sleep. When she'd looked in the mirror that morning and been faced with a pale, hollow-eyed junkie, she'd thought: *you look like you should be haunting someone.* But then, maybe she was. If it was possible to reverse the usual order of things, and for the living to haunt the dead.

Hannah glanced up at the door.

Outside, she could hear the *clitter* of typing from the secretarial support workers. Above the door, the wall clock ticked away the passing time. For some reason, the sound unnerved her.

Her emotions were all over the place recently, but the thing she felt most was this displaced sense of fear. *Dread*, almost, as though something terrible was going to happen to her. Ever since her father's death, she'd alternated between that and sadness. Sadness was natural enough, of course, but even that emotion seemed heightened, far too intense. Just a few hours earlier, Neil Dawson had identified his own dead father's belongings, and while he'd been doing his best to stay in control, she'd still practically caught the anguish and grief from him. It had taken her back three months, and there had been an ache of connection, like the answering call of a ship on a dead sea. *Oh God, yes, I know what you're feeling.* Hannah had almost broken down herself.

She opened the album.

There was some kind of comfort here at least; the book told a familiar story, one which steadied her. It contained photos that charted her life from birth to . . . twenty-two? She couldn't remember when she'd joined the police. Her father had pasted the photos two to a page. The first showed her as a baby in her mother's arms. Her mother looked weary and beaten but also proud: both of the baby she was holding and herself for what she'd been through.

*How things changed.*

The bottom photograph was her favourite. It showed her cradled in her father's arms, in the same hospital setting as the one above. Where her mother had been facing the camera, though, her father was looking down at the baby he held. This was his first and only child – and Hannah was so fragile here, so tiny, red and bruised from birth – and yet Colin Price looked totally at home in his new role as a father. This photo reassured her about two things. The first was how capable and confident he had been, the strong, reliable type of man who could do most things he turned his hand to on the first attempt, and the second was that he had loved and protected her from the very beginning.

Which was something to cling to, wasn't it?

Or at least it should have been.

Hannah worked her way through the album. In another of her favourites, several pages on, her father was wearing his dark blue, starch-straight uniform, bent over at the back of the shot, a delighted smile on his face. The focus of the shot was on Hannah, who had an equally delighted smile on hers. She was riding her bike without stabilisers for the first time, still convinced her dad was helping her keep upright when, in reality, she was now doing it all by herself.

*You are Hannah Price. Daughter of DS Colin Price.*

*And that means you can do anything.*

That mantra was the oldest memory she had of him. Not only had he always made her feel safe, he'd also encouraged her – and convinced her that she could achieve whatever she set her mind to, that there was nothing to be afraid of. Often when she'd felt nervous or scared as an adult, she'd repeated it to herself. That feeling of security was partly what she was trying to recapture by looking through the album now.

With each turn of the page, the spine creaked.

The final photograph had been taken on her first day in a constable's uniform. *Seventeen years ago now?* God. She hadn't changed much physically – still tall and slim; same ratty-blonde hair she mostly kept tied back – but something in the face was certainly different. She remembered how proud her father had been that day. He was often proud of her, but on that day in particular there was also this: his daughter had been able to do anything in the world, and what she had chosen to do was be like him.

DS Hannah Price, daughter of DS Colin Price.

Her eyes threatened to blur, but she shook the emotion away.

*Must not cry. Not here. Especially not in front of Barnes.*

Although it was the last photograph in the album, the images she had of him continued in her head. The older man, his skin slacker. Salt-and-pepper stubble. Lines kissing the corners of his eyes. Quicker to laugh but slower to stand.

And last of all, a king.

Three months ago, Hannah had arrived at his house, letting herself in as usual, and then walked into the front room to find former DS Colin Price in his comfortable chair, slumped, head bowed, with vomit staining the front of his shirt. His hands were clutching the nubs of the chair's arms, so that her first thought was of a sleeping king, refusing to leave his throne.

She'd felt an initial whump of panic, as though the air had been sucked from the house by an explosion in a world skewed centimetres from this one. But she'd been very calm as she approached him, probably because, at that point, she'd presumed he was dead, and that kind of knowledge always takes time to settle. It wasn't until she caught the desperate flutter of his pulse that the panic had flared – the explosion arriving in this world now, blasting her into action – and she'd gone scrabbling for the phone.

*A king.*

There were later images, of course, but none she wanted. He'd suffered a massive stroke, the doctors said, and there was nothing she could have done. But she was there during his days of dying in the hospital, as his body yellowed and shrank down, in search of its final colour, its final shape, pulling the bed covers closer as it went. She was there until the doctors asked her a question for what felt like the hundredth time, when she closed her eyes, considered it for an infinite moment, and said yes, turn the machine off now please.

She tried not to think about that, because in those final days he'd seemed to lack the nobility of every other image she had of him. She wanted to remember her father as DS Colin Price, strong and decent.

That was also why she wouldn't think about the other thing.

*Five tiny crosses, the colour of blood . . .*

The thing she'd discovered a few days ago, in his attic, which threatened to undermine everything she knew about him. About herself too. That was the problem, wasn't it? In relying on other people and using them as a foundation for your life?

When the floor breaks, you fall.

\*

'Are you all right, Price?'

DCI Graham Barnes closed the door to the office behind him.

'Sir?'

'You look like you've been crying.'

Damn it. Hannah had snapped her make-up mirror away in time; she'd thought she looked okay.

'No, sir. I'm fine.'

'Glad to hear it.'

Barnes was a small, pointy man: with the exception of his little round glasses, everything about him was angular and waspish; even his grey hair had receded up his forehead in sharp-edged triangles. He was nearing retirement age now, and was probably the only officer in Whitkirk who'd worked with her father during his time here. Colin Price had transferred to the department at Huntington, a few miles away, years before Hannah joined the police – a move for which she was eternally grateful. She imagined anyone who'd known him would either have been too easy on her as a result or else far, far too hard – Barnes was the latter – and she had been glad to have had the chance to prove herself on her own terms.

'Dawson,' Barnes said now. 'Dead.'

'Yes, sir.'

'Run me through it then. Ah – PowerPoint. Delightful.'

The briefing was set up to display on a pull-down screen at the side of the room, currently showing a black square with the case number in the corner. She forced herself to ignore Barnes's sarcasm.

*Just do this. Get it over with.*

Hannah stood up and went straight into it.

'Yesterday morning, we received a call from an anonymous female, placed from a phone box on the seafront. She claimed to have been jogging in woodland between Whitkirk and Huntington and spotted what she believed to be a man's body by the river.'

'Name?' Barnes said. 'Address?'

'The jogger?' It was typical of Barnes to latch on to that. What part of anonymous didn't he understand? 'She left a message with the switchboard clerk, so we don't have that information. The details were passed through and I visited the scene to investigate the report.'

Hannah clicked the button, and the screen changed to show a Google satellite map of the area. Three yellow circles had been drawn on it, linked by a snaking red line. The first, labelled (1), was on a main road; the others, (2) and (3), were close together in the middle of a dense green area.

'I approached along this dirt track, which joins the Huntington Road at point (1) as indicated. It's an old path, not signposted from the main road. At location (2), I encountered this vehicle.'

Another click. The screen displayed a photo of the car she'd found: an old blue Escort positioned against a dark background of trees and thick undergrowth. The driver had pulled in at a section where the track would be wide enough to turn round again.

'The vehicle was unlocked. I performed a check on-site and learned the vehicle was registered to Christopher John Dawson. Subsequent enquiries have revealed Mr Dawson was staying at The Southerton Hotel here in Whitkirk.'

As always, she felt a strange disconnect to find herself talking about the man in such an impersonal way, especially after his son's reaction. The physical mess of death didn't bother her in the slightest, but she'd never achieved that casual, emotional distance cops were fabled for. *Dawson. Dead.*

She clicked the button.

This photo had been taken from the end of the path, facing out along the disused viaduct.

It was creepy in itself: an old, rusted bridge in the middle of nowhere, extending thirty metres out over space towards a line of trees at the far side. Every rivet was black with age, and the floor was coated with several autumns' worth of leaves and dry mud. What the photograph didn't convey was quite how unworldly and forgotten the location had felt in real life: how lonely and humming with threat. The only real noise was the uncaring rush of the river, seventy feet below, but it had felt like that might be masking other sounds. Hannah was as rational as they came, but the place still seemed like some half-remembered childhood nightmare. The kind of dangerous fairy tale place you only found by taking the paths your parents warned you not to.

'This is point (3) on the map, a short distance further on from the vehicle. The body was below the viaduct on the riverbank.'

Hannah stopped the commentary and clicked through a series of images that required no explanation.

The first showed the body in situ: taken from where she'd first seen it. The man was lying far below, in the centre of the image, his top half in the river, his legs spreadeagled pitifully on the muddy bank. He was fully dressed, although his clothes were wrenched oddly on his broken frame, as though someone had tried to reverse them without taking them off.

There were more photos from the riverbank below. Closer now, you could tell the man was lying on his back, his head turned sideways. His cheek was a flat, pale stone visible just below the surface of the water. One white forearm stuck up like a tree branch, and his abdomen appeared to have flopped back towards the shore, distended enough to stretch open the buttons of his shirt. Out of the water, one thigh was already bloated tight inside the suit trousers.

'We don't have an exact time of death yet,' she said. 'Most likely, he'd been dead between two and three days at time of finding.'

Click, click, click. Finally, a sad close-up of Dawson's mottled face was replaced by an overhead shot from inside the mortuary that showed the clothing and possessions cut from his corpse.

'Due to the deterioration of the body and the availability of other corroborating evidence, we decided not to obtain a formal identification from Christopher Dawson's son. However, Neil

Dawson identified these items of clothing as belonging to his father. Also, the keys you'll see in the bottom right-hand corner match the vehicle we found, and the wallet contains a credit card in his name.'

Barnes's gaze hadn't left the screen the whole time.

'A positive ID, then.'

'Yes, sir.'

'Cause of death?'

'We're still waiting for the coroner's report, but it appears that Mr Dawson died as a result of a fall, presumably from the viaduct above. The injuries I observed on scene are consistent with that.'

'A jumper.' Barnes nodded. 'That's what we have.'

'It looks that way,' Hannah said.

Clearly, he'd already made up his mind about the case, which irritated her, even though he was right that all the evidence pointed directly to suicide. Neil Dawson had told her about his mother's death the previous year, and Hannah had found prescription drugs for depression in Christopher Dawson's hotel room. So it was what she would have concluded herself, if it wasn't for . . .

*The other thing.*

Barnes picked up on her indecision. 'But?'

*You should leave this.*

She said, 'But I have some doubts.'

'Oh?'

'Well, for one thing, there's the car. Dawson parked it in a spot where he'd be able turn around, which obviously suggests he intended to drive away again.'

'People are creatures of habit,' Barnes said. 'And suicide is an extreme course of action, isn't it? *Obviously* he hadn't fully committed at that point.'

'Yes, sir.' Again, she could leave it there. And yet she found herself plunging on anyway. 'But there's something else.

34

Christopher Dawson was a writer. His son believes he was working here in Whitkirk. And his laptop is missing.'

'His laptop, DS Price?'

'His computer.'

'Yes,' Barnes said slowly, 'I know what a laptop is.'

She swallowed his sarcasm. 'It's not at his home address, sir. It wasn't in the hotel and we didn't find it in the car.'

'So he took it with him when he jumped.'

'Yes, sir. That's what *has* to have happened. But we haven't located it, when all of his other possessions have been accounted for.'

'We wouldn't. I'm familiar with that river, DS Price. It's very deep and very fast, and it flows straight into the sea a little way down the coast. Do you know what that means? It means we're lucky a small child didn't trip over Christopher Dawson's corpse on the beach.'

'Yes, sir.'

He was right, and it had been stupid to press the point. As it happened, the laptop didn't interest her in the slightest; it had just seemed like a convenient hinge on which to swing open an investigation.

One she wasn't even sure that she wanted.

'What about the woman?' Barnes said.

Hannah shook her head. 'Sir?'

'The anonymous caller. This woman said she saw the body while jogging, but called from a phone box on the seafront. That's strange, isn't it?'

'Is it?'

'Of course it's strange. For one thing, it means she was out in the middle of nowhere without a mobile phone. But then she came all the way to Whitkirk to use a payphone.' He stared at Hannah. 'So have we got an image of her? Is she on CCTV?'

'I've not checked whether that phone's covered, sir.'

'Well do that, then. Let's see how anonymous she stays.'

He headed for the door.

'In the meantime, coroner's report, as soon as it arrives. Then let's draw a line under this.'

'Yes, sir.'

'All of this.'

The door rattled shut in the frame behind him.

Hannah sat down, frustrated. As irritating as Barnes could be, she was more annoyed with herself. What was she doing? Vaguely pushing to extend the investigation, when she should have been trying to forget all about it.

But the truth was that, however much she tried not to think of *the other thing*, she couldn't do anything but. Five tiny crosses. They had knocked a hole in her life, and when something like that happens you can only tiptoe around the edges for so long before peering in.

She caught herself reaching for the drawer. Stopped.

It wouldn't help; it wouldn't solve anything. Looking through it was just storytelling, really – repeating a fiction in the hope it would become true – whereas what she'd found at her father's house was reality, there whether she looked at it or not.

*I've not checked whether that phone's covered, sir.*

She had, of course. Hannah might have been terrified half the time and grieving the rest, but she wasn't an idiot. No cameras. That was why she'd picked that particular payphone to place her anonymous call from in the first place: no cameras. Although she wasn't going to tell Barnes that. *Obviously.*

She sighed to herself.

If her emotions hadn't been so shot, though, she might have come up with a better cover story than pretending to be a jogger.

Hannah sighed to herself and tapped the mouse. The monitor had gone to screensaver, and it came alive again now, showing Christopher Dawson's belongings.

*Why there?* she asked the dead man.

*Why did you have to choose* there *of all places?*

Because anywhere else and she wouldn't have this problem. What Hannah had found had led her to the viaduct – but if she hadn't spotted Christopher Dawson's body lying on the river-bank below, she wouldn't be faced with the predicament she was in now: wondering why Dawson had ended up there out of all the places he could have chosen to end his life, and whether his death was connected to what she'd discovered in her father's attic.

Whether it was connected to his crosses.

# Chapter Four

Cartwright could feel himself dying.

In one sense, that was nothing new. Ever since he was a boy, he'd been aware the world was different from how ordinary people saw it. Normal people packaged life up with a beginning and an end. They used words like *birth* and *death*, as though a person's life was linear and contained: something that started in one place and then stopped, later on, in another.

His father had taught him that was wrong, and helped him to see the truth: that life was not something that began and ended, but ever-present. It was the forms life took that rose and fell. But before Cartwright was born, he had existed as something else. His matter had been spread far and wide, and it was just happenstance that it had come together now in a form capable of understanding that. The atoms of his body were a crowd, summoned briefly into a room. After his death, that crowd would disperse to different places. That was all any form of life was. Just the universe at play, making shapes with its hands.

Of course, his current form was very old now. And while he had always been aware of the continuum, like a constant rush of wind in his mind, this sensation of dying, right here and now, was different. This was what ordinary people meant by the term.

He looked around the café.

It was even smaller inside than it had looked from the street:

barely the size of a living room, with seven tables cramped in so close together that the wicker chairs were pressed back to back. Oak beams were exposed across the ceiling, and dark wooden shelves lined the walls, covered with old tea tins and ancient toy cars.

Most of the clientele appeared to be elderly ladies in flowery blouses, their waists thick as barrels and their conversations either murmured or simply dispensed with altogether. There was a crutch leaning against one wall. The loudest sound was the *tink* of a teaspoon tapping round a china cup.

If he was dying, then, he had chosen the right place.

But it was other circumstances that had dictated his choice. Cartwright had managed to secure the window seat. To either side, the curtains were rolled open, as thick and soft as cushions. On the glass itself, the name 'Flanagan's' curled in reverse. Across the road from the café, there was a row of exhaust-blackened cottages. They were nice, he thought. Homely. Each had its own individual character; each looked like it had a story to tell and wanted to do so. One had an old wooden cartwheel, painted a glossy black, bolted to its outside wall. That was the one he was watching.

'Would you like a refill, sir?'

He looked up to see the owner had come from around the counter and was offering him a fresh pot of tea. Cartwright had not formed a very positive opinion of her. She was middle-aged and astonishingly happy with herself: as polite and insincere as he had been led to believe air hostesses were. In her conversations with the other patrons, he'd heard her employ the same sing-song voice each time, as though she was talking to children.

'Yes,' he said. 'Thank you.'

'*Not* a problem.'

She put the pot down and picked up the old one.

'Surfing are we?'

'I'm sorry?'

She nodded at his computer. 'Silver surfing, I think they call it. Terrible term. I know the library is having a big push at the moment though.'

'Oh yes.' Cartwright forced a smile, and tried to sound as doddery as she expected. If that was how she saw old people, then he didn't want to stand out and be remembered. 'I can't recall. Perhaps I did see something about that.'

She smiled back. He was far better at acting than she was.

When she'd returned to the counter, he poured himself a fresh cup of tea. Energy dissipated in the form of steam and in the sound of the slight rattle as the cup filled.

A faint heat.

The aroma of the leaves.

Everything shifting constantly.

But as he placed the teapot back down, he felt it again: a jab of pain in his side, which set off a chain reaction of smaller bursts across his stomach and through his chest. It was excruciating, but he didn't let it show. Anyone watching would just have seen an old man pouring his drink. Nobody would sense the multitude of cancers blooming inside him: so many by now that they surely half filled him, pressing against his skin like flowers overgrown behind glass. He could practically smell the pollen in his sweat.

Cartwright sipped his tea. A tube of heat materialised at his centre, and the pain gradually subsided.

Despite the discomfort, he appreciated the tumors for what they were: just a stage in his change. His body was transforming itself. New life was blossoming within. It was nothing to be afraid of, really, this ordinary version of dying. He had only two real regrets. The first was the question of what would happen to his family when he was gone. They were not as capable as he was. For the most part, they never left the farm and they lacked the necessary familiarity with the outside world to survive in his absence. He knew he should have prepared them better.

There was nothing to be done about that now.

The second regret, though, was a different matter.

On the far side of the street, the door to the cottage opened. Cartwright sipped his tea and watched with interest as the woman emerged. She was in her mid forties and very beautiful, with a sweeping rush of brown hair and a slim frame. But she had aged considerably in the year since he had last seen her. The thinness had become unhealthy; he could see her hip bones jutting below her dress. Her face had weathered too, so that she looked far older than her years.

*It will be all right*, he thought.

*You'll see.*

She did see – or, at least, she spotted the envelope on her doorstep. He watched as she stared down, then crouched to retrieve it, picking it up a little too quickly. He turned away just in time as she looked across at the café. Out of the corner of his eye, he saw her looking up and down the street, cars flashing past in-between them.

When he risked looking back, the woman had retreated inside. That was disappointing: he'd hoped to see her open the envelope. She looked so very sad, and Cartwright liked pleasing people. He liked helping them to understand.

He turned back to the laptop, open on the table in front of him. It was a battered old thing, the kind of device that most people would have thrown out and replaced by now, but it served its limited purpose adequately enough. It was also the only useful thing they'd salvaged from the debacle at the bridge – beyond the fleeting glimpse of *her*, escaping into the trees. That glimpse had only made things worse. It was his second regret. Cartwright hoped he might have what he wanted most in the world before this ordinary way of dying had finished. Even after all these years, he just wanted his daughter back where she belonged.

In the meantime, he had what was before him right now. One of the benefits of seeing the world properly was noticing the beautiful echoes the universe produced, seemingly for its own pleasure. Patterns created for their own sake. Reading what was in front of him, Cartwright knew that people could do that too, unwittingly or deliberately, and that there was joy to be had in hearing the chimes of coincidence and adding to them. Just as the universe played, so could he.

He read the story again.

Goblins. Changelings.

Cartwright liked the story, and he liked the idea of bringing it to life, especially as it might help him to do so. And the best part of all? His son wouldn't even need a mask.

People would be terrified enough of him already.

# Chapter Five

My flat was too small to store lots of books, so I didn't have copies of all my father's work, but I did have *Worry Dolls*. Like all my books, it was stored in a pile on a shelf in the wardrobe. I slid it out now, and opened it gently to the dedication at the front. The spine creaked: a soft, comfortable sound. It made me think of an old man sitting down on leather upholstery.

> *For Laura.*
> *I never want to be without you. I tell you every day in person.*
> *This is to tell you in print.*

I noted the present tense, although I also knew my mother died before the book was published and would never have been able to read it. Even so, he'd addressed it to her as though she could hear, as though she was still with him. *I tell you every day in person.* I believed that. My father had been repeating the words that defined him, no matter that the person they were directed to was no longer able to hear.

*Obviously he took Mum's death hard, but he'll be channelling it into his writing.*

What I'd said to Marsha on the phone that night sounded so stupid to me now. On top of the guilt it conjured up, it also made me feel like a fucking idiot. As a kid, I'd absorbed all his romantic ideas about the power of writing, and as an adult, I'd begun to build my life on their foundations. But when it had mattered, those ideas had been shown for exactly how empty and meaningless they were. *He'll be channelling it into his writing.* Except he wouldn't, because writing was just writing, not magic. And so I felt naïve – like I'd spent my life believing in the Tooth Fairy.

I closed the book and caressed the cover once, as though sealing it. *Worry Dolls.* The story of a man who was terrified of living and dying alone, whose wife came to hold his hand as he passed away. *I never want to be without you*, my father had written. It didn't seem so wrong to hope that maybe, in those last few moments, he hadn't been.

'Hey there, you.'

I almost jumped as Ally walked into the room. I hadn't heard the front door open: the echoing booms and bangs from the flat below had obscured it. In fact, I hadn't even realised it was after five now and work was done with for normal people. Time had just . . . passed. Despite everything, it kept doing that. When something awful happens, you half imagine everything should slow down respectfully to take note, but of course it doesn't work like that. The days just disappeared around me.

'Hey.' I put the book back. 'How was your day?'

'Crap.'

She let her handbag fall down her arm onto the bed, then sighed to herself. I sat back in front of my laptop, and a moment later she walked over and put her arms around me from behind. The smell of her perfume was a shock after being on my own all day. Her chin jutted against the side of my neck as she spoke.

'The usual crap, to be more precise.'

'No excitement?'

'Ha! No. Although Ros phoned. She wants to know when you're coming back. She's sympathetic, but stressing out.'

'Monday,' I said. 'Probably.'

'Yeah, I told her. But you know what she's like.'

I reached up and ran my hand over Ally's forearm: over the

fine hairs there that she hated but I loved. There's something especially comforting about being hugged from behind. Maybe because, by definition, you don't ask for it, so it always feels honest.

I hadn't had to ask for anything these past few days. It must have been obvious to Ally how badly I needed her right now, and so she'd just stayed, looking after me in imperceptible ways ever since we'd returned from Whitkirk. Food would appear. Phone calls and arrangements would have been made without my noticing. All the things that could easily have been overwhelming – that might have caused me to buckle – I'd emerge from my dazed state, begin half panicking about them, and then realise she'd already done them.

'I don't know what I'd do without you,' I said.

'Me neither. Good thing you don't have to worry about that.'

As I rubbed her arm, it occurred to me that she and my father had never met, and now never would. He hadn't known he was going to become a grandfather.

Would it have made a difference if he had?

Would anything?

The handful of newspaper reports I'd seen on his death all mentioned *Worry Dolls* and my mother's death, placing heavy emphasis on the latter. I still found it hard to believe, but the facts were the facts. He'd lost his wife and had a vague history of depression; his car had been found in an isolated spot by a bridge; his body was recovered from the riverbank seventy feet below; and police were not currently looking for anyone else as part of their enquiries. The word 'suicide' didn't appear in the newspapers, but it emerged unspoken through the details, between the lines. I couldn't avoid what he'd done even if, most of the time, I also couldn't quite believe it.

A number of journalists had called or emailed, asking me to comment, but I didn't acknowledge them. What was the point – what did they expect me to say? Maybe that I hadn't cared enough to make sure he was okay? Or that I was having trouble accepting he'd killed himself – and that a part of me still didn't, not really? There was nothing sensible for me to tell them. The result was that, in the reports, I was generally reduced to a footnote.

*He is survived by his son, Neil, 25.*

There was an enormous chatter of gunfire from below.

Ally sighed and moved away from me.

'Excuse me for a moment, babe.'

'No worries.'

This time, I heard her open the front door – and then several large *bangs*. A moment later, the noise from the television below fell silent. There were no raised voices. After a few more seconds, Ally came back up the stairs, my door slamming pointedly behind her, and the television downstairs did not resume.

'That's *much* better,' she told herself. 'I'm going for a shower.'

She whistled on her way down the corridor, and I managed a half-smile before turning back to the computer. There was a new email I needed to respond to.

The messages had all started on the day the obituaries began to appear in the media, and then increased in volume as the news of my father's death spread across the blogosphere. I don't know how they found me, but they did. My father's friends, colleagues and fans, expressing their shock and sending their condolences. All contained variations on the same themes.

*I had the pleasure of meeting Christopher once.*

*His work was an inspiration to me.*

*He was a wonderful writer, a wonderful person.*

*I'm so very sorry for your loss.*

A few of them sent personal anecdotes – usually stories about their encounters with him at conventions or signings. That was the strangest part, actually: the tales of late-night drinking, draining hotel bars dry, falling over furniture at six in the morning; the adventures in foreign countries, winding streets, late-night taverns and hidden drinking dens. They made my father sound exotic and exciting, as though he'd lived the life of a spy, and I found it hard to square their version of Christopher Dawson with mine.

But as strange as the stories seemed, they helped. They were comforting. Reading them created an odd combination of sadness and happiness: they tightened knots in my heart and my throat. Every novelist wants to be read, of course – what's the point of speaking if nobody listens? But, to my father, there had always been a difference between saying the thing you know people want to hear, the bestselling thing, and saying what *you* want to – what you *have* to – and then hoping someone likes it enough to listen. That was what Dad had done all his life. And it was clear from all these emails now that people had listened.

From the bathroom, I heard the hiss of the shower starting up, and then the *whump* of the boiler kicking in.

I hit the reply button and started typing.

Dear Mr Cartwright

Thank you for your email. My father's funeral will be held at Longwood Crematorium at 1.00 p.m. on Friday 24 September. If you would like to attend, please do come. There will be a reception afterwards at The Regency. Directions to both are attached.

Donations, in lieu of flowers, should be made to Cancer Research UK.

Thank you, and I'm sorry for your loss too.
Neil

Flowers.

It reminded me briefly of the book I'd seen at my father's house, the one with the pressed flower secreted inside its pages.

As I transferred the email from Joseph Cartwright to the folder I was keeping all the messages in, I scanned down the list of names there. No reason to expect it, of course, and it wasn't there. None of the people who'd emailed me was Robert Wiseman.

I dreamed I was four years old again and scared of the dark.

My bedroom was halfway down that long corridor. Every night, after tucking me in, my parents would flick off the light switch and go back to the living room at one end, and close the door. I would lie there, the covers drawn up to my chin, hearing the dulled sound of the television and the throb of silence coming from the *other* direction. From the empty part of the house. Except, the more I listened, the less empty it seemed. It felt as though something was forming in the shadows down there, and then creeping closer along the hallway. I'd stare at the doorframe, the whole time waiting for fingers of some kind to wrap slowly around it. For a face to peer in at me. And when it did, I knew my parents would be too far away to reach me in time.

Other times, I'd manage to drop off to sleep, only for something to startle me awake again. This was one of those nights.

Something had woken me up.

Something had happened.

'Dad!' I shouted.

Then I listened intently, my tiny heart thudding. Normally, I would hear hushed conversation from the front room – *was that Neil?* – and eventually the door opening. But not tonight. Instead, I heard silence for a few moments, the sound of someone holding still, and then quiet footfalls as that person made their way to my bedroom. For some reason, one of my parents had already been in the corridor.

It was my father. He appeared in the doorway now, still carrying whatever book he was reading, and then walked over and switched on the feathered lamp. His voice was quiet, soft.

'What's wrong, Neil?'

'I don't know,' I said. 'There was something.'

'A noise?'

'Maybe.'

He glanced back at the hallway.

'Do you want me to go and check?'

I shook my head; I knew enough by that age that checking wouldn't solve anything. Logic didn't work. There might not be anything there *now*, but that didn't mean there wouldn't be something there *after*. Children's logic, perhaps, but, deep down, my father understood this too. He certainly never got impatient or angry with me.

He sat down on the chair beside my bed.

'Do you want me to read to you?'

I thought about it. 'Yes please.'

'Okay.'

He put his book down on the floor. The one he'd been reading to me recently – *Archer's Goon*, by Diana Wynne Jones – was on the nightstand. It was resting face down, splayed open, creased. Despite being a writer, my father had always been careless with books. *It's the stories inside that matter,* he would tell me. *You can't bend them back.*

But he didn't pick that one up. Often, instead of returning to a story we'd been reading, he'd make something up instead. When that happened, he always started slowly – tentatively – but, as he went on, the story would gather pace and flow more quickly. I would watch his eyes glint with excitement, and I'd believe, in my naïve, childish way, that the story he was telling was something magical: that it had been there all along, waiting to be discovered and claimed.

He rubbed his hands together slowly now, as though washing the ordinary world from them.

And said, 'This is not a story about a little girl who vanishes.'


And I woke up with a start.

The bedroom was dark; the main street outside was quiet and empty. It was still the dead of night. I turned my head and saw Ally asleep beside me. She was lying on her front, her naked back shifting slowly and gently as she breathed, her face peaceful and clear. As far as I could tell, after lying still for a few more moments, nothing was wrong or out of place. It was just the dream that had woken me. And yet my heart was punching as hard now as it had when I was a little boy, scared of darkness and silence.

*This is not a story about a little girl who vanishes.*

I remembered that from the back of *The Black Flower*, but everything else in the dream might as well have been pulled straight from my childhood. Had my father ever said that? It was impossible to know; I couldn't remember what had happened in any of the stories he'd made up. The content was never really the point: it had always been more about filling the silence, warding off the darkness, for a while.

So why did Wiseman's book keep cropping up in my mind?

I put my hand behind my head and stared at the blue-grey ceiling. Maybe it was natural to keep thinking about it: I'd looked at the book just before speaking to the police, after all, so it made sense that the two things were linked in my head. Not to mention that creepy fucking flower. But it felt like there was something more to it than that.

I lay there for a few minutes, half-heartedly trying to get back to sleep, but it wasn't happening. For whatever stupid reason, I was wide awake.

Quietly, so as not to disturb Ally, I slipped out from under the covers and went through to the kitchen, my bare feet *tacking* on the plastic tiles. The timer on the oven read 4:58. Absurdly early, but I put the kettle on anyway, then sat down at the circular wooden table. Rested my elbows on it and rubbed my temples.

It was more than just the timing of finding the book and the flower inside. It was also the fact that it was right there on my father's desk, as though he'd been looking at it, consulting it even, while he was working. It was also the thing I'd said to Marsha about my father's writing. Regardless of my own naïvety, he *had* been distracted by a project of some kind – and there were things scheduled on his calendar, for Christ's sake.

Haggerty. Ellis. Did it make sense to arrange appointments, to go on what looked like a research trip, if he was planning to do what he had?

No. It didn't really make sense to me.

And if he was going to kill himself, why go to Whitkirk to do it? Maybe it held some meaning or resonance for him, but I'd never heard of the place before. And while I could understand him not wanting me to be the one who found him – wanting to spare me that horror, if nothing else – it didn't require driving across the fucking country.

Which meant he'd been there looking for something.

*Why, Dad?* I thought. *What's there?*

What were you working on?

The kettle burbled louder and louder, until it seemed like it would boil over, the plastic rattling in its stand, and then it clicked off. I didn't stand up yet though. I sat there, still thinking, still slowly rubbing my temples, as the kitchen fell silent.

Except . . .

Not quite silent.

There was some kind of noise from outside: a gentle *puttering* sound. The kitchen window looked out over the alley behind the building. I stood up, raised one of the slats in the blind and peered down.

There was a van there. The puttering sound was its engine idling.

It was an old one too. The metal looked rusted. I couldn't quite make out the colour, but guessed it was red or brown. The lights were all off, but the engine was running. A streetlight from the end of the alleyway just reached it, so that a dagger of amber rested across the windscreen, revealing the driver was inside, but not much more. The figure was broad enough to guess it was male, and he had what looked like a large moon printed on the front of his chest: a pale, distorted circle.

The circle ducked suddenly backwards out of view.

*Shit.*

I let the slat go with a sharp click. That had been his *face*. He'd been leaning forward, staring right back up at me through the windscreen.

Outside, the tone of the engine changed. I looked out again, and only just caught the back end of the van as it rolled out of view, slow and steady. There was no chance to see the license plate from this angle, and a moment later I was left with the purr of the vehicle turning onto the main road and the roar as it accelerated away.

My heart had started up again.

*That couldn't have been his face.*

Whatever – what the fuck was someone doing out back at this time of night? A burglar, scoping the place? Maybe. If so, then I'd seen them, they'd seen me, and now they'd gone and wouldn't be back any time soon. Burglars were opportunists, after all – no point making life hard for themselves.

And no point me jumping at shadows.

But I kept looking out – and listening too. The back street remained empty; the world stayed silent. When that happens – when you're an adult, anyway – it's easy for your nerves to settle, and for you to start down-playing how odd something was. Growing up turns your fears inside out.

It took a while though. When I finally lowered the slat in the blind and went over to make myself that coffee, I touched the plastic on the side of the kettle and needed to put it on again.

*Nothing to worry about*, I was telling myself as it boiled.

*Nothing at all.*


That morning the weather was blustery and indecisive, the clouds vague white swirls on grey steel. Overcast and drab. Ally and I pottered around, drinking coffee and lazing in bed watching television – or trying to in my case, as my thoughts kept wandering. In the afternoon, we walked down the road to the supermarket in town, then trailed back up lugging plastic bags, with leaves skittering across the pavements and whirling through the air overhead like birds.

I'd almost forgotten about the van by then; the incident in the night, whatever else it was, felt a long time ago now, the way things do when you've not slept since they happened but probably should have. Regardless, Ally and I didn't talk much. My mind kept returning to my father, and every time it did my chest grew tight. Inside, I could tell, I was building to a crescendo. My heart had already decided what I was going to do, and it was just a matter of my head catching up; the longer it took, the more impatient my subconscious was becoming. Eventually, after we'd unpacked the shopping, the emotions reached fever pitch, and I said:

'I think I'm going to go out for a while, if that's okay.'

'Of course.'

Ally sounded like she'd expected it. She didn't even ask where, and probably already knew, but I said it anyway, as much to myself as to her.

'To my father's house.'

# Chapter Six

The CCTV monitoring suite for Whitkirk was based in a small room at the back of the station. The room itself was old and in need of refurbishment. There was paint flaking on one wall, and a number of the polystyrene tiles in the ceiling were cracked. One, in the corner, was missing entirely, revealing a network of pipes in the gloomy space under the floor above. When the radiators came on, they clanked and thunked, and the dusty grilles on top made the air smell of slowly simmering rust.

At least, the surveillance equipment was state of the art. A bank of monitors, six across, four down, was built into a wooden casing that curled slightly back against one wall and then out again as it reached the ceiling. Each screen showed a static image of a street or junction. On the desk in front, which was built into the wall unit, there were further screens where on-duty officers could bring an image down for sharper focus, manoeuvring the live camera itself with a joypad, zooming in and out.

Hannah was viewing a separate monitor, sitting at a desk on the other side of the room. Going through older footage. The archives.

'No joy so far?'

'Nope.'

She didn't turn around to look at Ketterick. He was the only officer on duty, a broad-backed Sergeant. Whitkirk was a tourist town, so most of its crime was shoplifting, bag-snatching, pick pocketing, and there wasn't much of that to cope with. Later on, as the pubs got busy, another officer would probably come on to help. She hoped so, if she was still here then.

Ketterick chuckled.

'Well, you're determined. I'll give you that.'

*And that's all you'll give me.* He'd already said it to her twice; she wished he'd just shut up and leave her alone. There was nothing worse than people talking for the sake of it. And, apart from anything else, the footage she was watching was running at one-oh-five speed, and turning round for small talk she didn't want might cause her to miss something she did.

*What* might she miss exactly?

She still didn't know.

Officially, it was the pretence of locating the anonymous caller that had got her in here, but obviously she had no interest in undertaking a futile search for herself. Unofficially, she was attempting to track the final movements of Christopher Dawson. Hannah knew why *she'd* gone to the viaduct. Now, she wanted to get a better idea of what Dawson had been doing here in Whitkirk, and why he had chosen to go *there* of all places to die. Was his choice of suicide spot just a coincidence, or did it have some connection to her father and his crosses?

It was harder than she'd anticipated.

She knew Dawson had been staying at The Southerton and that he'd ended up at the viaduct. But she didn't know when he'd gone there, or where exactly he'd left from. Maybe he'd gone to other places first. Following him was tricky, as well: since the CCTV coverage was restricted to certain parts of the town centre, the bastard kept walking off the footage. Every time that happened, unless she caught a lucky glimpse, she had to return to the camera covering the hotel, hoping and waiting for him to reappear.

She'd zoomed into the image as much as possible without losing the detail. Right now, she could just about make out the faces of the people walking towards her outside The Southerton, the profiles of those entering and leaving. Last week, when this was live, Dawson had been inside.

'Get you anything?'

'What?' This time she did turn around, although she immediately wished she hadn't. Ketterick was standing up, leaning back over his own belt as he stretched his spine.

'Just running to the men's room.' He stopped stretching and thumbed at the door. 'Passing the drinks machine on the way. Get you anything?'

'No. Thanks. I'm good.'

'Okay. Give me a shout if World War Three breaks out.' He winked. 'Somehow, I don't think it will.'

'Yeah, I'll hold the fort.'

The door sealed shut as he closed it behind him. Hannah turned back to the screen, pissed off. She reached for the jog-shuttle, intending to rewind the footage, but then—

*Ah, there you are.*

She knocked the speed down to one and watched as Christopher Dawson emerged from the hotel. He was a tiny figure on the CCTV, but she could tell it was him. He was dressed in the clothes they'd found him in: the overcoat; the V-neck pullover with the shirt and tie beneath. All memorably old fashioned. He stopped at the bottom of the steps in front of the hotel. Hannah zoomed into the recorded image as far as possible, stopping when his body filled the frame, then watched as he turned this way, then the other.

Looking for somebody?

A thick black line curved around his shoulder. She waited as he looked around . . . waited . . . and there it was. A black bag on his back.

The missing laptop? It seemed likely.

So: this was probably close to the moment he set off on the journey to the viaduct. She felt a slight thrill – just as Dawson vanished from the frame.

*Shit.*

The scroll button on the console rattled round as she reversed the zoom, panning back as much as she could – and there he was again, crossing the street. He headed to the left of the screen, clearly with intent, and then disappeared off the edge.

Hannah rolled the scroll button in frustration. It was a pointless gesture as this wasn't live footage. History was set: the camera had pointed where it had, and there was no way of changing it now. She was about to try one of the other feeds when she remembered his car. She could have kicked herself: he had *driven* to the viaduct. And the entrance to the car park, just past the hotel, remained in the frame.

She watched the random stick figures moving soundlessly about the frame and waited. A minute or so later, Christopher Dawson reappeared. He walked back across the street towards the hotel. But now, there was someone beside him.

Hannah zoomed in.

A woman.

She was on the far side of Dawson, so it was impossible to see much detail: all Hannah could really make out was that she was wearing a puffy black coat and blue jeans. She had skinny legs, dark hair, and was a little taller than Dawson. It was hard to tell what age she was. One thing that *was* clear was that the pair of them were talking to each other: walking side by side, with their heads turning in conversation. Dawson had crossed the street to meet her and now they were heading back across.

Hannah watched as they walked up the side of The Southerton, then disappeared. She sped up the film again. A moment later, Dawson's battered old Escort nosed out of the car park, backed up slightly, then spun out and disappeared out of shot.

This time, she was sure, Dawson wasn't coming back.

# Chapter Seven

Inside my father's house, the familiar hallway was grey and dim.

I stood at the top of the stairs for a moment, feeling the profound emptiness all around me. It was stronger than before. Nobody had been here since my last visit, and nobody would until my next, and my presence didn't seem enough to leave a mark.

I stared into the shadows at the end – listening to the silence that had scared me as a child, not so much now – and then went down to my father's office, my childhood bedroom, and opened the curtains there. A spread of dismal late-afternoon light fell reluctantly into the room. Motes of dust turned lazily in the air. I sat down in the office chair with a thump that sent it rolling slightly, then rubbed my fingertip slowly across the surface of the desk, through the dust, and stopped in the clean centre.

I tapped the desk once.

Where was his laptop?

At some point, I had to pick up his belongings from the police station in Whitkirk. But that was just his car, and the clothes he'd left in the hotel room. The laptop was missing. If I was to believe the police, it was lost for ever – either heavy enough to be lodged below the surface on that riverbed, or else swept away downstream into the sea, maybe smashed against the rocks – and, either way, nobody was going looking for it.

Except I couldn't imagine him clutching it as he jumped. Why would he do that? Despite the ways writing might have failed him, I still didn't think he would have deliberately destroyed something he was working on . . .

*But you can't imagine him jumping at all.*

No, I couldn't. Which felt like a dangerous idea because there was such an obvious emotional convenience to it: if he hadn't, I couldn't be responsible for failing him; there wouldn't be anything I should have done. So I kept rolling that thought around, making sure I was thinking it for the right reasons, and not just through guilt.

It wasn't just guilt.

I glanced up at the calendar on the wall in front of me. Assuming the things he'd written there were names, my father had gone to see 'Haggerty A', and possibly 'Ellis F', before heading to The Southerton. And then whatever had happened in Whitkirk had happened. It was, very clearly, a schedule, and the question from last night came back to me now. Why make appointments to meet people if you were planning to kill yourself afterwards?

Who were they, I wondered, and what had he been working on? Something to do with *The Black Flower*? Wiseman's book was at the back of the desk where I'd left it. I rolled the chair slightly closer to reach for it – and, as I did, my knee hit the single drawer built in below the desk.

I leaned to one side and stared at it, then reached down. It opened with a scrape. A smell of old wood emerged, like pencil shavings, revealing a single item inside: a black book. *A diary*, I thought but then realised it was too small. An address book.

Almost as useful.

The cover was rough leather, and a sheet of paper was feathering out at the back: folded up and tucked into a lip in the cover. I took that out and put it on the desk, then flicked through the pages of the address book itself. My father had clearly had it for a long time, as some of the contacts were faded away almost entirely. They'd been recorded with pens, pencils, felt tips in all different colours – clearly just whatever had been to hand as he scrawled the entries.

I glanced at the calendar again, then checked through.

Nothing for 'Ellis F' under either E or F. But 'Andrew Haggerty' was there, listed under H in bright black ink – a fairly recent entry, by the look of it. There was no phone number for him, just an address, but the postcode wasn't far away – south of the city centre. Seeing it there almost gave me a small thrill. That was my father's first contact located then. I might not know who Andrew Haggerty was or why Dad had been interested in him, but I did know where to find him. Which meant, if I followed this up, I could ask.

What about the paper then?

I picked it up and found there were actually two separate things: an A4 sheet, and a newspaper cutting that fell out as I unfolded it. I looked at the sheet first, which my father had printed from the Internet. The Wikipedia entry for Robert Wiseman.

That pretty much confirmed he'd been working on something to do with that book.

I read:

**Robert Nigel Wiseman** (1947–1993) is the English writer of three detective novels. He is presumed deceased, having been missing since 1993.

**Early career**

Educated at St Bartholomew's College, Chichester, Robert Wiseman expressed an intention to become a writer from an early age [1]. Following a number of short stories, his first novel, *An Excellent Death*, was published in 1986 at the age of 39. Before then, he worked as an advertising executive, and continued to do so until the publication of his second novel, *Dangerous Times*, in 1988.

**_The Black Flower_**

*The Black Flower* was Robert Wiseman's third novel. Published in October 1991, it immediately outsold his previous titles, and was eventually to become a bestseller, reaching number five on the UK sales charts, and selling well in Europe and the United States. Rights to film the story were sold, but never came to fruition.

The plot concerns a little girl who appears as if from nowhere on a seaside promenade. When she tells the story of where she came from, it leads the police officer in charge of the investigation into danger. Critical opinion was mixed [2,3].

### Death of wife and subsequent breakdown

Prior to the publication of *The Black Flower*, Wiseman had become estranged from his wife of eight years, Vanessa [3]. Some reports suggest a series of infidelities was responsible for the dissolution of the relationship, but the two remained in contact [3]. On 5 November 1992, the pair met in Whitkirk. Directly after this encounter Vanessa Wiseman was killed in a car accident. Following his wife's death, Wiseman withdrew from public life and began drinking heavily, with many sources commenting on his increasingly fragmented mental state [4,5,6,7].

### Last known sighting

Robert Wiseman's withdrawal from public life culminated in his ultimate disappearance. He was last seen at approximately 7 p.m. on 6 September 1993 while leaving The Southerton Hotel. Wiseman had been resident in the hotel for four days and was rumoured to be working on a sequel to *The Black Flower*. On the morning of 7 September, Wiseman's car was found parked on a cliff near Whitkirk Abbey, which was the last place he had seen his wife alive. Despite an extensive police investigation, Wiseman's body has never been found, although he was pronounced legally dead as a result of presumed suicide in 1998 [8].

After I'd read it through once, I did so again.

*Holy shit.*

And then a third time – so I was sure I wasn't imagining it. But no, the connection was plain and obvious. Nearly twenty years ago, Robert Wiseman had booked into The Southerton, allegedly working on new material, and killed himself – apparently anyway. And that wasn't the only similarity to my father either. Wiseman's wife had died the year before too.

I read the entry a fourth time, but it didn't help. I was tingling inside, both excited and scared. This couldn't be a coincidence, but what did it mean? Had my father been trying to *emulate* Wiseman for some bizarre reason? Or had he been investigating the man's history and then something else had happened? I needed to get online and look the entry up – make sure the details were right – and then get in touch with the police. There was something going on here. Something that people weren't seeing.

The other piece of paper.

I picked it up carefully; it was yellow and brittle, and felt dusty beneath my fingertips. A quarter-page clipping, torn from a newspaper: the Whitkirk and Huntington Express. The date in the top corner said 6 November 1992.

## VIOLENT CRIME WRITER
## TALKS VIOLENT CRIME
### BARBARA PHILLIPS

Robert Wiseman has made a very successful career for himself by writing about murder. His latest novel, *The Black Flower*, has sold to 10 countries and spent 8 weeks on the bestseller lists earlier this year. Its graphic killings and grisly subject matter appear to have struck a chord with audiences, but how does the author himself feel about violence?

Speaking to me in nearby Huntington, Mr Wiseman is unmoved.

'You have to remember that we're not talking about real people doing horrible things to other real people. They're fictional characters. Nobody actually gets hurt.'

Fictional or not, the subject matter of *The Black Flower* is dark indeed. When a little girl, eventually named Charlotte Webb, appears on a promenade, she brings death and destruction in her wake. The detective who finds Charlotte must protect her from her father, who is hunting her down, while at the same time dealing with his own demons. So far, you may be forgiven for thinking, so familiar.

'No, the book is different from many other crime novels,' Mr Wiseman asserts. 'In most books, you have a murderer hunting and killing people. But *The Black Flower* isn't like that. It does have a serial killer, and a particularly horrible one at that, but it's more about the little girl who escapes. Who is she? Where did she come from? And I like that the act of her telling her story is what sets events in motion.' He is unable to suppress a smile. 'That idea was hard for a writer to resist. A man becoming haunted by a story that may or may not be true.'

However, when asked about perceived similarities between his novel and real crimes that took place in the 1970s, Mr Wiseman is reluctant to comment directly.

'Ideas are everywhere,' he tells me. 'I grew up on a farm. I have friends who are borderline alcoholics. I'm a writer, after all! No, it's not where the ideas come from that matters – it's what the writer does with them through his work. You need to put a lot of effort in to transform ideas and experiences into a story. Think of it like wine. Ideas are the grapes, while the book is the finished bottle.'

His eyes glitter at that. You get the feeling he would love to have said champagne instead.

*The Black Flower* is out in paperback this week.

It was a strange little article, I thought – as though it wanted to be a hatchet job, but the journalist hadn't quite had the heart to unload on him. Was that because of the date? If the wiki page was right, this article had been published the day after Vanessa Wiseman's car crash. Maybe the writer had tempered it down slightly, out of respect.

*Barbara Phillips.*

The name rang a bell – and after a moment I remembered why.

The message I'd heard on my father's answerphone: a journalist called Barbara, asking about an interview. I'd assumed she wanted to interview him, but perhaps I'd got it the wrong way around. Given she'd written this article, then, if my father had been working on something connected to Wiseman, maybe it was him who'd asked to speak to *her*.

*You've got my number.*

I flicked through the address book to P, and yes, he did. So I could ask her too, or else the police could. I read through the article again, my attention catching on one line in particular.

*Real crimes that took place in the 1970s.*

What crimes?

The book's cover struck me again, out of the corner of my eye this time. The woman's face, roughly transposed over the centre of the flower, screaming in pain as the thorns drew blood. What kind of real crimes could that be based on? I picked it up and allowed it to open where it wanted, on the page with the flower pressed inside it. It was my imagination, I was sure, but the petals seemed even more fragile than last time – flat and thin and weak – while the flower itself looked more obviously deformed. But it wasn't my imagination that it bothered me a hell of a lot.

I turned back, all the way to the beginning of the book. There was no prologue, no indication of chapter number. It just started.

*It does not happen like this.*

I read the first few pages of the book.

And then I carried on.

**Extract from *The Black Flower* by Robert Wiseman**

As soon as Sullivan enters the office, before anything has even been said, he knows that DCI Peter Gray does not believe him. Or – more accurately – that Gray does not believe the little girl's story but antici-pates the fact that Sullivan will.

The first is obvious from his superior's body language. Gray is visibly tense, but nowhere near as tense as he would be if taking the girl's story as truth. The second is clear in a different way. After what happened to Anna Hanson, everyone in the department knows that DS Michael Sullivan cares very deeply when it comes to children, that he will not let a cry for help pass him by again. He has acquired a professional blind spot, one that potentially occludes his judgement. Even Pearson, his partner, believes that. Gray thinks the same.

The plastic-glass door rattles in its frame.

Gray motions to the chair.

'Sit down, DS Sullivan.'

He is all business: determined to get this out of the way as quickly and with as little discomfort as possible. Sullivan resists the urge to leap straight in and argue his case, and instead does as he is told, pulling the thin chair back with a scrape and sitting down across from Gray. From behind him, even with the door closed, he can hear the clatter of typewriters, the whirr and bing.

For a moment, neither of them says anything.

Sullivan glances around. Gray's office has a truly appalling colour scheme. The walls are painted an unpleasant shade of pea-green, the carpet is beige, and his old desk is made from dark-brown wood, chipped and hinged, like something you'd see folded up beneath the window in a pensioner's bedsit. With the rusted, screeching filing cabinet and the cobwebbed potted plant on the windowsill, the office has the feel of something assembled in desperation from the last vestiges of a jumble sale.

The foam tiles in the ceiling were originally white, but over the years they have been stained with amber bruises from the cigarettes Gray constantly smokes. His sharp, smart cap rests on the desk beside a glass ashtray filled with orange tab ends and ash. Sullivan's report lies between them.

Gray lights his next cigarette, exhales a plume of smoke, then slides the file towards the middle of the desk.

*Take this back*, he seems to be saying.

Sullivan says, 'I've checked out some of the details, sir.'

Gray raises his eyebrows slightly. *Of course you have.* The gesture makes it clear Sullivan's words bother Gray in a small way, but surprise him in no way at all.

Already, Sullivan has no real hope – Gray's demeanor makes that clear – but there is an urgent curl of anger in him, like the light you get in your vision after staring at a bare bulb. It had been there since the interview with the little girl.

'Jane Taylor,' he says. 'She disappeared on the fifteenth of March last year from Brookland. She was last seen playing outside her house.'

He leans forward.

'Now, there are conflicting witness reports, but two people saw a similar rusty red van to the one described in the file. And she was twelve years old, which is about the same age as the "Jane" our child describes playing with underneath her house.'

*Our child.*

Even as he says the words, he regrets them but it doesn't matter. Gray is not really listening; he is simply following formal procedure and waiting for his chance to speak. At which point he intends to add a full stop to the conversation, whether Sullivan likes it or not.

'What I'd like to do, sir,' he says, 'is present her with a photograph of Jane Taylor for verification. I have it in the file.'

Gray makes no move to check; of course, he has already seen it. Instead, he takes a drag on the cigarette. A second later, the air between them fills with derisory smoke.

'Do you believe her story, Sullivan?'

*Yes*, he thinks. *I do.*

'It's possible, sir. I think it would be—'

Gray holds a hand up.

'*Possible*.'

He says it as though musing, but Sullivan knows exactly what he is thinking. Everybody in the department believes that what they are dealing with here is a runaway child, scared to tell the truth and face the repercussions.

Everybody, that is, apart from Sullivan. But again, he knows what people think of him. After the death of Anna Hanson, he is too biased, too haunted, too primed to believe whatever comes his way. Of course, they all sympathise. A child's death is supposed to affect you; there would be something wrong if it did not. At the same time, the unspoken rule is that you're not supposed to dwell. A balance must be struck between empathy and strength; it must only affect you *so much*. A year on, Sullivan is now in breach of that unspoken rule. He has been since Clark Poole lodged his first complaint.

'Lots of things are *possible*, aren't they?' Gray says. 'To me, this has the feeling of a child's invention. Something she's made up after watching an unfortunate movie.'

Sullivan does not reply. Gray certainly has a point: the child's story is the most horrific thing he has ever heard. But that does not, to his mind, mean she must have invented it.

Gray taps away some ash.

'Have you found this farm?'

'No, sir. There was no obvious way forward there.'

During the interview, the little girl told them that she had grown up at an isolated farmhouse. To her, of course, it was not isolated, because it was all she had ever known. She had a younger brother, a mother – and the father. The only time she ever encountered the outside world was on days like yesterday, when her father drove the family in his rusted old van to different places. Sometimes the journeys would take hours. And on many of those occasions, they returned with a new friend. Sometimes a child; sometimes an adult. Sometimes more than one.

But that, as awful as it sounded, was not as terrible as what happened to the victims once they arrived back.

'It must be easy to find a farm,' Gray insists.

'Sir?'

'If you look hard enough, I mean.'

Sullivan shakes his head, confused.

Gray spreads his hands. 'If you look for a farm, you'll find one. The same way that if you look for missing children called Jane, you will likely find several.'

'I'm not following you, sir.'

'What I'm saying, DS Sullivan, is that *our child* could have invented any name at all, and away you would have gone and found a missing child to match. They all have names, you know. Unfortunately, there are enough of them to cover all the names under the sun.'

'You think she invented it? Why would she?'

'I don't know. Why would I? The workings of young girls' minds are a mystery to me – probably as much as they are to you. What about the handbag?'

'We've identified the manufacturer. It's a common brand.'

'And it's not a *little girl's* handbag, DS. So she must have stolen or found it somewhere, yes? It certainly didn't belong to this Jane Taylor, did it?'

'No, sir.'

But again, this is all in the file, which rests between them on the desk. The little girl never claimed the handbag belonged to her or to 'Jane'. She said it belonged to one of the other women her father had brought to the farm, whose name she never learned. One of the many.

Gray taps the end of his cigarette over the chunky glass ashtray but then thinks better of it, and stubs it out altogether. Sullivan realises he has been allowed precisely the amount of time it took his superior to smoke it.

Gray says, 'If you want to continue this foolishness in your spare time, that's your own business, Sullivan. At least it will keep you away from certain people's houses. But from what I hear, you would be better off spending your time at home.'

'Pardon, sir?'

Sullivan leans forward. He's not sure whether to be alarmed or

68

angry. What had his wife been saying? And to whom, in what circumstances? It is no secret between them that things have become complicated and difficult, but this is the first time he's heard his personal problems referred to at work, even as obliquely as this.

'But that isn't my concern,' Gray says, ignoring the question. 'And in the meantime, what we have, effectively, is a missing child, only in circumstances far more fortuitous than normal. Parents tend to want their children back. They are not usually difficult to find.'

Sullivan remembers the look of panic on the little girl's face.

'Sir—'

Gray holds up a hand.

'Be quiet. We need an appeal, DS Sullivan, don't we? Rather than further attempts at authenticating a fairy tale, we need a photograph for the newspapers. Rather than believing in horror stories, we need a press conference. We need information for the television. We need to get this girl's image out there.'

Sullivan feels deflated. There is nothing he can say, and he knew this would happen as he walked in, but even so.

He also feels afraid.

*Parents tend to want their children back.*

That is the impression he got from the interview, and it is exactly what the little girl is afraid of. That her monstrous father is going to want her back very much. That he will not stop looking until he finds her and takes her home again.

'Is there a problem, DS?'

'No, sir.' Sullivan stands up. 'For the record, I think this is a mistake.'

'That is *possible*, Sullivan. We shall see, won't we?'

Finally, now that the meeting is over, Gray picks up the file. He still doesn't open it, but he stares down at the cover with a slight frown on his face, as though – beneath the bluster – he isn't quite sure what to make of the details inside after all.

'We shall see,' he says again.

Sullivan walks back through the typing pool towards his desk, half imagining a slight pause in activity at each station he passes. But he does not care.

He is remembering Anna Hanson, and the one time they met. Last year, he and Pearson visited the primary school to talk to an audience of enraptured, cross-legged children; she pulled him aside timidly afterwards, and told him she was scared someone was watching her house. But Sullivan had not listened carefully enough and not believed sufficiently. Preoccupied with his marriage, he had heard only a child's *inventions*. He had not even known her name. Weeks later, he had recognised her face in the missing persons report, and the next time he saw her had been on the beach, where she was tangled in strands of black seaweed, her small grey hand resting on the rocks.

He thinks of the little girl on the promenade. How brave she has been; how much courage it must have taken for her first to run away, and then to trust them with her story. About her father, who will do anything to have her home again. Who will never stop.

Whatever anyone says, he *does* believe her and he *is* going to protect her. Because in a world that only takes, in a world filled with lost little girls who were not believed in time, someone has to.

# Chapter Eight

I drove home too quickly.

*There's nothing to worry about.*

I kept telling myself that. It didn't help; I'd told myself the exact same thing after Marsha's phone call, after all, and been wrong then. There was no rational basis for how on edge I felt, how nervous, but that didn't help either.

Robert Wiseman's wife had died in an accident. A year afterwards, he checked into The Southerton, where he was rumoured to be working on a sequel to his most popular book, but instead of doing that he disappeared, and was presumed to have committed suicide. Twenty years later, my father had done the same: gone to the same place, possibly writing a book of his own, and now he was dead too. *Something* was happening. Something still only half visible between the lines.

As I drove, pushing as hard as I could through the traffic, connections and implications kept flickering in my head like ghosts, forming and dissolving, but it was one set in particular that was strongest. Wiseman had written: *Two people saw a similar rusty red van to the one described in the file . . .*

And the journalist interviewing Wiseman had referred to the book being based on real crimes that took place in the 1970s.

That was a hell of a long time ago, so there was nothing to worry about. Certainly no reason to make any kind of connection with what I'd seen last night out of the kitchen window.

As irrational as it was, I couldn't shake it.

I parked up in front of my building. It was after six now, and it was the weekend, so the pub across the street was busy. Groups of men were planted outside on the tarmac, leaning back over their heels. Some of them, drinking from their pint glasses, looked as though they were trying to get the whole rim between their teeth. As my car door slammed, laughter echoed across, more aggressive than it usually sounded. None of them were paying me any attention. From down the street, I could hear the rhythmic *thump thump* of music from a parked car.

I opened my front door.

The uneasy feeling didn't go away as I stepped inside. The downstairs hallway was dark and empty – although at least I could hear the thuds and explosions echoing down from my neighbour's flat. For once, that was weirdly reassuring. But there was something else that wasn't. Something different. Standing there, it took me a moment to work out what.

A smell.

It was unpleasant. I breathed in, trying to identify it. Rubbish, maybe, or rotting vegetables. Only slight, but definitely there. Cool air too. A draft was delivering the smell here from . . .

I stared along the downstairs hallway.

At the far end, it doubled back and stairs led down to the cellar. I'd only been in there once, to check the meter when I first moved in; the rooms under the house were filled with broken furniture, mostly impassable. But I remembered an outline of daylight where a fractured door faced out up rubbish-strewn stone steps into the alley behind.

That was where the smell was coming from. A breeze was working its way from the alley, through the cellar, then coiling up the stairs and reaching me here, bringing that stench with it. Because . . .

Because someone had broken in.

Above me, the artificial bangs and booms continued.

*Ally*. I took the stairs two at a time. When I reached the first floor landing, my neighbour's television was louder than ever. There were shrieks coming from inside. I turned the corner, up the stairs to my flat, and—

At the top, my front door was hanging open against the white, woodchip wall. Not broken, just open.

My heart was beating too fast. *There's nothing to worry about*, I told myself, walking inside. Maybe she'd gone out. Not closed the door properly on her way.

'Ally?'

I half stepped into the front room – but then held still in the doorway. It seemed even smaller and more crammed than ever, because my few items of furniture had been scattered around. The coffee table was over by the wall on its side, one leg buckled outwards. The TV was on its face. The wires, and the weight of it, had pulled the stand over too. The bed was angled to one side, the mattress half hanging off. Sheets of paper littered the carpet.

The floor below me was vibrating.

And at first, I couldn't make sense of what I was seeing. It looked like a burglary, but none of the drawers were open, nothing obvious had been taken.

*No*. The thought came with a chill. *Not a burglary*.

My gaze caught the corner of the coffee table, where the leg was bent. There was blood there. A smudge of it across the wood.

For a second it was all I could see. I stared at it, and it suddenly felt like I was metres closer, like I was seeing it magnified right before my eyes.

*It looks like a fight.*

'Ally?'

I moved quickly down the hallway, checking the bathroom and the kitchen. She wasn't here. Obviously she wasn't here. And there were no other signs of disturbance. In the kitchen, I peered down into the alley. Empty.

This was madness. My heart was thumping in my chest.

73

There were a couple of seconds where I didn't actually know what to do and just stood there uselessly, my fists clenched. Was I in shock? And then my phone began vibrating in my pocket. I scrabbled for it.

Ally Mobile

I answered it. 'Ally?'

For a moment, there was no reply. All I could hear was a crackle on the line. It sounded like traffic. Maybe she was—

'No.'

A man's voice.

'Who is this?' I said.

'You know who I am.'

I shook my head, said the first name that came to mind: 'Wiseman . . .?'

'No, not Wiseman.' The man was old, I thought. His voice was rich and textured, full of throat. 'But Wiseman knew me. He wrote about me. Wrote bits of me into being.'

Even though I didn't understand, even though it was all too strange to make sense of, everything inside me still went cold. Wiseman had written about this man? Wiseman had written about a serial killer, who lived on a farm. His book was nearly twenty years old now. This couldn't . . .

'Who is this?' I asked again.

'I'm your Goblin King.' The old man stopped, then let loose a great, hacking cough. 'I gave you what you wanted, didn't I.'

'What?'

'I liked your story.'

My story? I started to say that out loud but then realised: my father's laptop was still missing. Dad had never been much of a techie. When he logged into his Yahoo account, he probably checked the 'keep me logged in' button on the screen. So there was only one obvious way this man could have read my story.

'You've got his computer,' I said.

'My boy took it from the car after he made him fly.'

I hesitated. 'Why did that . . . why did you kill him?'

74

'Because he was in the way.'

The world was suddenly unsteady. I sat down at the kitchen table, my legs shaking.

'Where is she?' I said.

'Here with us. And that's where she's staying.' He said it decisively. 'She's part of my family now. We'll take good care of her. You'll forget her in time. Both of them.'

'You can't—'

'You asked for it to happen!' He snapped, suddenly angry. 'You *wanted* it.'

*All the man has to do is wish for it to happen*, I thought.
*Eventually, selfishly, he does.*

But that was . . .

'No, that was just a story.'

'There's no taking it back. She belongs to me now.'

I shook my head. What was happening was too surreal. I couldn't fit this into the everyday world and make sense of it.

'You can't get away with this,' I said. 'Whoever you are. I'll call the police, and they'll find you. Whatever it is, what you're really doing here, you need to stop it now.'

'Do it. Call them. They haven't found me yet, have they? Never have, never will. But let them try, if that's what you want – see if they believe anything you have to say, or have the first idea where to look. And then you'll never see this one again. Never get her back.'

'Wait,' I said.

'There is one way though.'

For a moment, I didn't reply.

'One way,' I said. 'One way to get her back?'

'That's right. She's mine now because you gave her to me. That means you need to give me something in exchange. You have to trade me. There has to be a *change* so we come out equal.'

'*Trade* you?'

'Fair's fair, isn't it? That's the way it works.'

75

'For what?' I said. 'Trade her for what?'

'For *my* little girl.'

I started to reply again – to say something, anything – but stopped. In Wiseman's book, the killer was determined to find his escaped daughter, whatever the cost. Barbara Phillips had implied the book was based on real crimes. *My little girl*. Was that what this old man was implying? That he wanted me to find a fictional character? Or rather, the real person a character might have been based on?

I repeated, 'For your little girl?'

'You know who I'm talking about?'

'The girl from Wiseman's book.'

'That's her.'

'But she's not real.'

The old man laughed to himself.

'She's as real as I am.'

'How am I supposed to find her?'

'I don't know, do I? If I did, the trade wouldn't be worth anything. Same way your father did. If you want to see this one again, you'll figure out how he did it. And you won't go to the police either. You won't tell *anyone* about me. You'll just find my little girl, and then maybe we'll trade.'

*Same way your father did.* I made the connection with what he'd said earlier: that my father had 'got in the way' at the viaduct. What had happened? Had he gone there with someone – with someone this man thought was his grown daughter – and then, when they were attacked, fought back long enough for her to get away? I remembered the pale, malformed face I'd seen peering up through the van windscreen: the bulk of the driver's body. My father was a small man, not a fighter. He wouldn't have stood a chance against most people, never mind someone as big as that.

He would have tried though.

'I'll give you a couple of days.' The old man laughed again.

'After that, she's mine for ever. This phone's going in the water now. But you keep yours handy. I'll be in touch.'

'Let me speak to her.'

'She's in no state to talk right now.'

I remembered the blood on the table leg, and panic twisted inside me.

'She's pregnant. For God's sake—'

'I know.'

'But—'

'Do you know how babies are made?'

I closed my eyes. *No, no, no.*

He repeated it: 'Do you know how babies are made?'

'Yes. I do.'

'No, you don't. They get half from their father, and half from their mother. You know that much. But I bet you didn't know this. A woman's born with all her eggs inside her already. She's got them as a baby. Got them in the womb. Isn't that amazing, eh?'

'Yes,' I said.

'You know what that means? It means half your baby existed long before you came along. She was born with that half already inside her. And her mother was born with half of her, which makes a quarter of your child. And her grandmother. And so on. All the way back, for ever and ever.'

I didn't say anything.

'Set in stone, long before you and I. That's beautiful, when you think about it, isn't it? A part of your child's been there forever. Women birthing women is one of the world's *continuums*. Most people don't see that. Most people don't want to.'

I still didn't say anything.

'Anyway,' he said, 'you don't necessarily need to worry, is what I'm saying. If it turns out to be a girl, we'll keep it.'

And then the line went dead.

# Chapter Nine

Hannah stood outside her father's house.

It was a large detached property a mile from the seafront, set back from the road behind railings and apart from its neighbours by a wall of trees. The downstairs windows were criss-crossed black; the ones upstairs were capped with wooden peaks. Dark paths ran down either side of the building, leading to the substantial garden behind. Her father had not been rich, but the house would probably be worth a great deal when she put it on the market.

*If* she did that.

Right now, Hannah lived in the centre of Whitkirk, in a small, run-down flat, and she knew a decision was required some point soon about what to do with this place. Move in and make it her own? Sell it and buy somewhere better? Both were huge acts, logistically and emotionally, and the last three months had seen her oscillating: putting the moment off.

*A big decision*, she'd told herself. *Don't rush into it either way.*

Now, given what she'd found, it was good that she hadn't.

The gate scraped across the tarmac drive, and she felt a chill, even though the air was still. It was a balmy evening; there was no breeze. The shiver came from that unfocused feeling of dread, amplified by the house in front of her.

This was the place Hannah should have felt safest in the

world. Growing up, she certainly had, and she was painfully aware how precious that was. In all her years as police, she'd met countless children who *should* have felt safe in their homes but didn't – kids with skinny shoulders, collarbones like skeletons, and hollow, wary eyes. But her father had loved her and taken care of her. Until recently, this house had reminded her of that, and, as an adult, there had always been that familiar feeling of warmth and security returning here. The gentle, rhythmic knocking of the grandfather clock in the hallway; the fabric of her father's coat, rough against her knuckles as she hung her own on top; the sound of wood spitting and cracking behind the copper guard on the hearth, where he would have lit a log fire regardless of the season, because he understood that a warm hearth was not solely about heat.

Walking into this house had always felt like folding herself into a comforting, familiar embrace. Somewhere she could allow herself to feel as small as she wanted and still be safe, because she could do anything.

Not any more.

She closed the gate behind her with a gentle *clink*, and it felt like a key turning: locking her inside a room with something that had once been good but was now soured and rotten, maybe even dangerous.

Hannah opened the front door and sensed it, hard as a shove.

*Go away*, the house was saying. *You're not welcome.*

She shrugged off her jacket, glancing through the open door to the living room. There was no fire burning in there this evening, of course; she'd never resurrected it. The ashes sitting in the grate were the ones from the evening she'd found him.

*A king*, she reminded herself.

*Whatever happens, hold on to that.*

She went upstairs and opened the door to his study. It was a small room, but a grand one. There was an ornate desk in the centre with a reclining leather chair pushed underneath on the far side. Behind it, a window ran along most of the back wall, covered by red velvet curtains that were thick and lustrous enough for a child to stand in the creases, turn around three times and be hopelessly lost in. The other walls held bookcases, broken only by the doorway she was standing in, and the old chimneybreast that her father had often talked of opening up but never had.

Hannah walked across to the desk and looked down, as she had so many times now, at what she'd found.

*The other thing.*

It had started a week and a half ago.

For some reason Hannah couldn't identify, she had started feeling that now familiar sense of dread. It was worse, though. She was actively scared: small and vulnerable and alone. At the time, this house had still felt like an embrace – albeit a sad one, like hugging someone goodbye – and so she'd returned here and done what seemed natural and harmless at the time. She'd come up to this room to feel closer to her father, to remember him, to try to regain a little of the reassurance and safety he'd always provided her with.

*You are Hannah Price, daughter of DS Colin Price.*

*And that means you can do anything.*

After a while, she'd realised there was something she wanted. Maybe it was stupid and frivolous, but the idea became impossible to shake. She wanted a book: one in particular. A simple story from her childhood that she'd always enjoyed her father reading to her. It reminded her of his quiet voice, and the clean, sharp tang of his aftershave. And she wanted those memories again. There was no harm in that, was there? Of course not.

Except she couldn't find it.

Which was wrong. All the *others* she remembered were on the shelf – even the ones that had never been favourites and which she'd barely read. There were books so old that their spines were bare and torn, like a child's attempt to skin a branch with a penknife. But the book she was looking for was missing.

It had been an idle search at first. And yet suddenly, from wanting to find and read it, it had become *needing* to.

The attic, then.

In contrast to the rest of the house, it was only a simple conversion: just boards laid down and a bare bulb installed, the cord wrapped in webs. The light was soft, the colour of butter, and the air smelled of sanded wood. At the back, she'd found cardboard boxes sealed with parcel tape, and cut them raggedly open with her keys.

Inside, stored away at random, there were hundreds more books. Hannah had sat cross-legged on the dusty floor of the attic, feeling the height of the empty house stretching down a giddy and precarious distance below her, and she had gone through each box methodically, book by book.

Her book had still not been there. That stopped mattering, though, because in the last box she had found the old carrier bag, and the things her father had hidden inside.

That bag – empty now – was resting below the desk, but it was so old that it had kept its shape when she discarded it, like an enormous piece of crumpled paper. Every now and then, it rustled to itself, gradually relaxing. She could imagine it doing that when she wasn't here, the noise brief and crisp in the empty house: the gradual breaths of something emerging from hibernation.

The two items she'd found inside were on the desk now.

The first was a folded map of Huntington county, which she'd spread out. It had the opposite instincts to the carrier bag, and kept trying to close itself. Hannah leaned on either side of it, resting her palms on the edges to flatten it down. The age was apparent from the stars worn through at each junction of creases. The veins and capillaries of Huntington were faded in places, totally obscured in others. But the things her father had added to the map remained clear.

Five tiny, red crosses.

One was over the middle of a residential street. Mulberry Avenue. The second was over the side of Whitkirk Park. A third was by Blair Rocks, a small, bare picnic area ulcering the edge of the woods. The fourth was close to a derelict cottage a short distance from there – again, by the woods. But the largest, this one with a circle drawn around it, was some way deeper into those same woods. Directly over the viaduct.

The map felt ominous enough by itself, but the second item made everything infinitely worse. Her father had given this second thing its own bag, as though he wanted to preserve whatever evidence was sealed away inside. She hadn't opened it because she didn't need to. Even through the opaque plastic it was wrapped in, it was easy to identify it by shape.

A hammer.

*You have a real fucking problem here, Hannah.*

Yes. She certainly did. Because even without understanding the exact details, she had no doubt what she had found in her father's attic was evidence of a crime. Perhaps a terrible one. One that, rather than being investigated by her father, had been covered up by him. Or possibly even worse.

Maybe even perpetrated by him.

Hannah ran her fingertip over the crosses, imagining she could feel the ink dyed into the paper.

What she should have done – straightaway – was put the map and hammer back in the box in her father's attic and forgotten about them. Maybe in time she'd even have forgotten them successfully enough to have the father she remembered back again: the loving, caring one; the strong, infallible man who'd made her feel safe.

Instead, the day after the discovery, she had investigated. Visits to the first four sites revealed nothing, as far as she could tell. It was something to do, though: a cursory look to reassure herself. *See – it was nothing. It meant nothing.* But then, at the viaduct, she had spotted Christopher Dawson's body. She hadn't been able to ignore that.

And now, after what she'd found on the CCTV footage this evening, hiding everything away again was no longer an option. She wasn't a perfect person; she could, and would, continue to lie about the anonymous call; and, because the past was the past, she could fail to disclose what she'd found up in the attic to anyone else. But a woman had been in the car with Christopher Dawson – a car that had ended up abandoned at the viaduct with Dawson lying dead on the riverbank below – and that was another matter entirely. A human being couldn't be boxed away and forgotten about. Hannah wouldn't have been able to live with herself. Professionally as police, or personally.

No, that woman urgently needed to be identified and accounted for.

Hannah had already left a message on Neil Dawson's home number, requesting him to phone her as soon as possible. Perhaps he would have an idea who she was. In a few minutes, she would leave her father's house and head to the viaduct to co-ordinate with the head of the dive team she'd requested. Had the mystery woman ended up in the water with Dawson? They would need to check. Depending on what they found, forensic teams would be required on-site as well. They would search the entire area. If there was anything at the scene connected to her father, it was likely they were going to find it. Whatever he'd done was about to come fully into the light, where she would now have no choice but to face it. She was Hannah Price, of course, daughter of Colin Price, and that meant she could do it.

That meant she could do anything.

Hannah looked at the little red crosses marking the map, and then at the bag of grimy evidence she didn't dare open.

*But what about you, Dad?* she thought.

*What the hell did you do?*

# Part Two

# Chapter Ten

I headed to the university. I didn't know where else to go.

Late evening on a weekend, the campus was busy. In the distance, towards the Union, I could hear the steady *thump* of a club night, echoing in the flagstones. It was ominous now, as though there was something huge out of sight below me, banging to be released. I passed clusters of shadowy students moving in that direction, and their laughter jarred. It felt like I was half asleep, even though my nerves were on fire.

What the fuck was I doing?

*You won't go to the police*, the old man had warned me.

And I wasn't going to the police – not yet. Because whoever the man really was, he was right that nobody would believe me. What could I possibly tell them? That twenty years ago, a man named Robert Wiseman wrote a novel that *might* have been based on a real-life serial killer? And that somehow, all this time later, the killer apparently remained active, still searching for his missing daughter? That he'd now kidnapped my pregnant girlfriend to blackmail me?

Right now, I didn't know how much of it I believed myself.

I walked quickly through the cold night air. Even the phone call I'd received seemed unreal: a world away now. If it hadn't been listed in the call log on my phone, I might have doubted it really happened. But it had. I'd tried Ally's number again a few times since, and each time it had gone straight to automated voicemail. So either the man had turned it off, or done what he'd told me – thrown it in the water.

Which meant that, even if the police did believe me, there was no obvious way of finding this man. They couldn't trace the phone. Maybe the van had been caught on CCTV somewhere, but maybe not. If this whole thing was really true, the old man had been operating for decades without being caught. He'd be careful about things like that.

*You won't tell anyone*, he'd told me.

*You'll just find her.*

Yeah, but then what? It was madness. I wasn't going to trade anyone for Ally – or at least I fucking hoped I wasn't. At the same time, the man's final words kept coming back to me, the implications filling me with fresh horror each time.

*If it turns out to be a girl, we'll keep it.*

I walked more quickly.

Worst of all was the knowledge that I'd contributed to this. Irrational, maybe, but the guilt was eating the inside of my chest. If I hadn't written that story, this wouldn't be happening right now. That was what it came down to, wasn't it? If not for me, this wouldn't be happening to Ally . . .

*God*, I thought. *Ally.*

*No.* I couldn't bear to imagine where she might be or what might be happening to her, or to deal with the idea that I'd caused it to happen. And that maybe she even knew I had.

I didn't wish you away, I thought. You or the baby.

My toes half caught on the flagstones.

*It was only a story.*

The building was deserted. I used the main key to get in through the heavy red doors, making sure they *cricked* shut behind me.

My footfalls echoed up the spiderweb of staircases that criss-crossed the centre of the building. I unlocked the door to our small common room, and there was something vaguely reassuring about hearing it *shush* closed behind me, then click tightly shut as well. It meant there were at least two locked doors between me and the outside world.

The first thing I did was look around the common room. It was pitch-black and still, but I checked the other offices to make sure I was alone – just glancing at the underside of the doors, searching for any slivers of light there. It wasn't unheard of for Ros to work this late, even on a weekend, but the rooms all looked dark and empty. That was good.

There was a row of flat comfy chairs over by the noticeboard, which I could sleep on if I needed to. As though there was the faintest fucking chance of me falling asleep.

I went into my office. Half of it was in darkness, but one end was illuminated with amber from the floodlights a little way down the concourse. I didn't bother turning on the lights. I just turned the lock behind me, then slid into my rattley old chair and booted up the PC.

As the desktop loaded, I realised I didn't feel safe at all. It wasn't about doors. The old man wasn't nearby. I almost wished he was: if he and his boy turned up here, at least I'd have something tangible to grab hold of – or try to. No, the worst thing was that they were probably miles away by now, completely out of reach, and that Ally was with them.

It didn't matter about me. *She* wasn't safe.

But I was going to find her.

How, though?

*Same way your father did. If you want to see this one again, you'll figure out how he did it.*

That was the key, I thought, whatever I decided to do afterwards. I had to get more information: try to understand a little better what was and wasn't happening here. Before I went to the police, if that was what I was going to do, I needed something more concrete: something conclusive they'd have to take seriously. I had to try to discover if the woman really existed. And if she did, I had to try to find her. While I wasn't going to trade anyone, she might at least be able to corroborate parts of my story. She might know something that would help me – help the police – find Ally and get her back safely.

And so whatever I did, I needed to follow my father's trail.

*Keep calm, Neil.*

Ridiculous, but I thought it anyway.

The first thing I did online was load up the wiki page Dad had printed. Robert Wiseman's biography. The references for the numbers dotted through the text were at the bottom of the page. I clicked on them one by one, but each time I was met by an error message on the new window that opened. I checked the 'History' tab on Wikipedia and realised the article hadn't been amended for years. The sources linked to it had probably been correct at the time of the article's last edit, but they'd disappeared from the servers in the time since.

After that, I hit Google. I wanted more information about *The Black Flower* – ideally something else about the *real crimes* it was supposed to be based on. Barbara Phillips was my natural contact there, but I wasn't sure about talking to her. Not yet. Because all I knew about her for sure was that she'd been in contact with both Wiseman and my father – and they'd both ended up dead. I would talk to her eventually, but I wanted something independent first. Something I'd be able to measure against whatever she told me.

The problem was I couldn't find anything much at all.

*The Black Flower* was supposed to have been a minor best-seller, but its success was all pre-Internet, and it didn't appear to have been a book that had lasted. Most of the links I found in the search engine went to auction and marketplace sites, where paperback editions of the book were being sold for tiny amounts of money. There were no reviews or essays to speak of. Aside from occasional mentions, nobody was namechecking *The Black Flower* online; it didn't feature in any genre retrospectives, and nobody was hailing it as an inspiration to their own careers. It wasn't some kind of forgotten masterpiece. It was just forgotten.

*Mostly* forgotten, anyway.

I did an image search next. Predictably, I got a long series of tiny book covers: screen after screen of small faces crying out in pain. I didn't want to look at any of them; that image started the panic rising in me. But after clicking through a little way, I managed to find a couple of photographs of Robert Wiseman himself.

Obviously, both were old. The first and then most frequent was a mannered head and shoulders portrait. Black and white. I guessed it was the publicity still Wiseman had used on his book covers. His hair was coiffed, curled at the front like a breaking wave, and he was looking at the camera from a slightly sideways angle. A handsome man who knew it. A bit arrogant.

*You get the feeling he would love to have said champagne instead.*

The second photograph I found was more interesting. It appeared on a much smaller number of websites, so I found the largest version and clicked through to that. This image was in colour, and it showed four men and a woman stationed around one side of a circular table. Wiseman was in the middle, his elbow on the table, his chin resting in the cup of his hand, looking at the camera with a roguish glint in his eye. There was a glass of wine on the table in front of him.

The woman was sitting beside him. She was much younger – perhaps twenty years old, at most – and pretty in an ethereal way, with dark hair that hugged the contours of her face. She was also staring at the camera, but with such an eerie intensity that her eyes had stolen Wiseman's thunder and become the focus of the shot. Two other men were sat on the far side of him, turned towards each other, engaged in private debate. And at the other end of the shot, on the far side of the woman, was . . .

*Dad.*

My throat tightened.

I hadn't even recognised him at first glance. He was a young man here, younger than I ever remembered him. Boyish and bleary-eyed – there was wine on the table in front of him as well. This was the Christopher Dawson from the emails people had sent me, rather from my own memories. He was wearing a slightly old-fashioned suit, with both forearms resting on the table, so that the sleeves were pulled back slightly, revealing a watch and dark curls of hair on the backs of his wrists. He was looking down at them, his mouth twisted slightly at one corner.

So: he and Wiseman had known each other.

It made sense, I supposed; they were both writers, both around at the same time. Maybe that was why my father had decided to write about *The Black Flower* in the first place, to investigate what happened to someone he had known.

Maybe.

The text underneath the photo read:

*Robert Wiseman (centre) and the gang.*

When had it been taken?

There was a 'back to photos page' link below it, so I clicked on that, and the screen was immediately filled by placeholders for thumbnails of images, a line of text written underneath each one. The top of the screen read:

*Carnegie Crime Festival*
*20 Years of Murder and Mayhem at The Southerton,*
*Whitkirk*

The Southerton.

Christ – another connection. An annual crime convention, held in Whitkirk: one that both my father and Wiseman had attended. And from the little I'd read, Wiseman's novel was set in a thinly disguised version of Whitkirk. If the book was based on something real, it was something that had happened there.

The tiny images loaded slowly, appearing one by one. Divided into sections by year. The images at the top of the page were for 2003 – presumably the last year that the festival had taken place – while scrolling down to the bottom revealed the first had been held in 1983. After the photos had all finished loading, I scanned through until I found the thumbnail with Wiseman and my father on it. It was from September 1989. I searched through the other photos for that year, but that was the only one either man appeared in.

I opened it up again, and, as before, my attention was drawn to the woman. She seemed to be looking straight into my eyes, across the years. Was it my imagination that, on one side of her, Wiseman looked intrigued, excited, caught out, like he'd just had an idea of some kind? Whereas my father, on her other side, looked concerned, anxious, uncomfortable: as though something was beginning to unfold at that moment, and he'd just had a glimpse of what the consequences might be.

And the woman between them, the centre of it all.

Wiseman had published *The Black Flower* in October 1991. So this was probably around the time that he'd started writing it. A book with perceived similarities to real crimes in the 1970s. Which would make the woman in the photo about the right age.

I stared at the screen for a few more moments: stared at *her*, wondering. Assuming she was real, could this be her?

It could be.

I sent the image to print.


Of course, I had no way of knowing if the woman in the photo was the woman I might be looking for. It could have been Vanessa Wiseman. For all I knew, it could have fucking well been anyone, and there was no way of tracing her anyway, who-ever she was.

Regardless, I couldn't find the slightest evidence online that *The Black Flower* had been based on real crimes.

It didn't help that I didn't even know where to start, coming at it from that end. In the book, Sullivan had talked about another victim – Jane Taylor – but if she was real then Wiseman would surely have changed the name. I checked anyway, and found nothing. I checked all the other names as well, but the result was the same. Nor did I find anything in archived news articles about serial killers who lived on farms or little girls appearing on promenades telling stories about them. If Wiseman's book was based on actual crimes, they hadn't been well-publicised ones.

So that just left me with my father's contacts.

Barbara Phillips.

I leaned forward and typed her name into a Google search. Predictably enough, there were thousands of hits, and most of them weren't for her, but I found a handful linking to articles from the Whitkirk and Huntington Express. They were few and far between, though, and on random, inconsequential topics. It was a free local paper and the website was correspondingly shit and incomplete. But then, maybe she didn't do much journalism any more. I didn't even know how old she was. Once again, all I knew for sure was that she was linked to two dead writers who'd stayed at The Southerton.

What choice did I have, though?

I took out my father's address book and found her number. No point hesitating if I was going to do it, so I just took a deep breath and dialed.

The number rang and rang.

Then clicked to voicemail.

'Hello. You've reached the Phillips residence. I'm afraid we can't come to the phone right now, but if you'd like . . .'

Frustration clenched up inside me but at least it was the same woman; I recognised the voice from my father's answerphone. After the recorded part had stopped, I left a message after the beep. I gave her my name and mobile number . . . then hesitated. Unsure how much to say.

'It's about my father,' I said finally. 'If possible, I'd like to meet up to talk about something. I'd really like you to call me back as soon as you can. It's really urgent. Thanks.'

I hung up, that frustration still tight in my chest.

Andrew Haggerty, then. That's who my father had gone to see first, before 'Ellis F' and his trip to Whitkirk.

*Let's see who you are, Andrew.*

I looked him up online, without the slightest expectation of getting a result. I didn't even know *how* he was connected to this. Was he another journalist? A writer – maybe one of the other men in the photograph? Maybe he and Ellis both were. It took a few minutes to combine the right search terms until I found him, but eventually I did.

And when I read the information on the screen, my father's interest in Haggerty became obvious. In the darkness of the office, something fell away inside me, leaving me with an ache in my stomach. In my heart.

*Oh God, Ally.*

Because suddenly, this was all very real. There was no denying it any more: these were real crimes I was reading about on the screen right now.

Just not from the 1970s.

## Extract from *The Black Flower* by Robert Wiseman

'Hello, Detective Sullivan,' Mrs Fitzgerald says.

'Hello again.'

He steps over the chipped wooden doorstop into her home. Mrs Fitzgerald is a foster carer: a plump, slightly stooped woman in her early forties, with hair so frizzy that it hangs around her head like rusty mist – or perhaps a halo. She lives slightly out of Faverton, further along the coast, in a property that backs onto the clifftop. The distance from town is the single concession to the little girl's safety that Sullivan managed to wring from DCI Gray.

'How are you this evening?' he asks.

'Oh, I'm fine. I'm always fine.'

Sullivan nods. Mrs Fitzgerald is always fine; it is a gift she has. He takes off his hat and stamps his feet on the wicker mat. A gloomy staircase extends up on the left. Ahead, at the end of a shabby downstairs hall, the worn carpet gives way to the old Formica floor tiles and cracked white porcelain of the kitchen. Out back, the garden ends where the cliff-edge allows it to.

The house is in disarray, and one day erosion will take even this from her. It hardly seems fair. Sometimes, when he visits, a clothes press is set up on top of the kitchen counter; Sullivan has seen Mrs Fitzgerald there, sleeves bunched up, feeding sopping wet clothes through the slick, pale-blue rollers, water dipping down into the sink. Her round cheeks will be red with the effort, the machine hot and grumbling, and Sullivan will wonder how she does all of this without a single complaint.

*I'm always fine.*

'Charlotte is in the front room,' she tells him.

He pauses, just as he's about to hang his coat by the door.

'Charlotte?'

Mrs Fitzgerald leans in to talk quietly. 'We talked about it last night after you left. We agreed that she needed a name. So I let her look at the bookcases until she found one that she liked. *Charlotte's Web.*'

'Charlotte.' Sullivan nods. It suits her. 'Can she read well, then?'

'Not as well as a girl her age should,' Mrs Fitzgerald tuts, as though this means anything in the light of what she has gone through, 'But certainly more than a little.'

Sullivan nods again, more thoughtfully this time. In his spare time, he has been reading about feral children, foundlings, children who have grown up in extreme deprivation or isolation from the outside world – sometimes even literally raised by animals, as part of a pack. One of the key features of the research is the impact of such an upbringing on learning. The consensus seems to be that if language is not learned soon enough, through companionship and interaction, it is not learned well, or even at all. Children who have been raised in such circumstances can often barely talk, never mind read or write.

But he has never read of anybody growing up like Charlotte has. According to her story, her father made an attempt to raise both her and her little brother – albeit in his own way and according to his own rules. And her mother had been present. Reading between the lines, it sounded as though the woman was very much a slave: a victimised subordinate. But she may well have taught the child to read.

'How has she been today?'

'She's been quiet, but she's eating better. And we had a little play earlier on.' Mrs Fitzgerald raises her voice slightly. 'Didn't we, Charlotte?'

Sullivan turns to see her standing in the doorway to the lounge.

Over the past week and a half, there has been quite a transformation. Mrs Fitzgerald visits second-hand shops every weekend and buys what she can, and many people donate their cast-offs, so the doll's dress has been replaced by blue jeans and a simple white T-shirt. Elsewhere, more personal wonders have been worked. The girl's tatty hair is now combed out straight and full, falling halfway down her arms in a golden sheen. The bruises have faded from her face, and any dirt has long-since been washed away. In many ways, she looks like a normal little girl. Except in the eyes, which are beautifully blue but wary, and in the blankness of her expression, which remains much as it was the first time he saw her.

At least now, rather than the handbag, she is clutching something more appropriate. A battered, old teddy bear.

'Hello, Charlotte,' he says. 'That's a nice name, isn't it?'

There is a familiar moment of coolness, of *not quite trusting*, but he has visited every night and she is more used to him now, so it only takes a moment for her to relax. Without saying anything, she reaches out a small hand. Sullivan walks across to take it and, while she is only capable of the gentlest of tugs, he relaxes his big frame and allows her to lead him into the lounge.

For half an hour, they sit in the front room playing.

Charlotte is cross-legged on the floor; Sullivan sits in an armchair, leaning forward and watching her, responding to her, talking as and when required.

Mostly, she wants to show him things. Mrs Fitzgerald keeps a long Tupperware box full of toys in the corner by the hearth, and Charlotte picks from it at random, scrutinising the toys one by one. Sometimes she cradles and talks to them; other times, she purses her lips, leans forward and gives them to him, then goes back to look for something new. She grows more and more bold, more playful, more *normal*. He accumulates the toys on the arms of the chair, or in his lap, or wedged next to the cushion, unsure on the surface what is required of him but understanding deep down that nothing is.

He wants to ask her about her father, but does not.

Instead, he quietly takes each toy she passes to him. Watching her increasing ease with a feeling akin to privilege. In some ways, by the time he leaves this house, Sullivan feels younger than she is: renewed in some way. *Charlotte*, he thinks. *You're going to be okay.* But it is not entirely clear to whom he is directing the thought: to her, or to the memory of Anna Hanson, the little girl he failed to save. He recognises this mistake even as he's making it but it is so easy to do, so very easy to do, and he lets himself do it night after night.


And so, every night, he arrives back home late.

His wife says little; they drift around each other in a carefully co-ordinated dance, subconsciously avoiding touching. They fail to find anything that needs talking about, beyond the perfunctory and the practical. She is drinking, although neither of them ever mentions it. Often he is as well. Recently, it feels as though their lives have schismed: been split in two, like a trunk by an axe, and they are now beginning to grow irrevocably in different directions, sprouting fresh buds destined never to touch.

*You would be better off spending your time at home.*

He tells himself there are two reasons he visits the girl.

The first is so he can make sure she is safe. Even though Mrs Fitzgerald has an enforced door and an unlisted address, he feels better seeing the girl for himself and making sure she is all right. He has promised to keep her safe, and he will.

The second reason comes on the journey itself, as he watches his rearview-mirror driving out to the foster home. Sullivan's name is the official contact for anyone coming forward on behalf of this little girl, and, while he does not expect the girl's father to contact him through official channels, he thinks it's possible the man will try to discover his daughter's whereabouts in more furtive ways. So he takes odd, winding roads, but so far he's seen nothing unusual behind him. Nothing follows him, certainly no rusting red van. Not the vehicle he imagines smoking and rolling, silhouetted against a setting sun, as though emerging from Hell itself.

There has been no official progress either. The relatively small amount of press coverage has resulted in little more than the expected fake phone calls and time-wasting counter visits. The cranks; the attention seekers. People who clearly know nothing about the little girl, her handbag, the flower, and are just desperate for attention, even of this low kind. Steadily, they have been weeded. And as the days have passed, Sullivan has become more and more anxious, more certain than ever of the girl's story.

Finally, other people feel it too. Gray's prediction has quietly begun to haunt the department. Parents tend to want their children back – and yet a parent has not come forward. What does that mean? Why does nobody want this little girl?

*Anna*, he thinks.

Except, of course, not Anna. Charlotte.

Lying awake in bed that night, he tells himself: *you're becoming too involved*. And yet he observes this fact with the same detachment with which he stares at the bedroom ceiling. His own workings are all too clear to him, the problem apparent. But he can't stop. Whenever he tries to remember Anna Hanson, it is harder and harder to conjure up her small face; but whenever he pictures Charlotte, it is Anna who appears instead. His heart throbs with alarm. He is afraid not just that something terrible is going to happen but that, when it does, it will somehow be his fault.

When he does sleep, he dreams of black flowers.

He is in the crawl space beneath a house. It is high enough for him to kneel up in. There is an awful, pale globe in the darkness before him: the slack features illuminated by cut diamonds of sunlight from the lattice surrounding them. The whole space feels strangely fertile. It smells of worms going about their business in the soil. It sounds like crickets, and the *click* of grass untangling from itself as it grows. The girl's head rests in the slowly turning soil, buried up to the neck. Something on the scalp is squirming.

This is Jane after she stopped talking. When she could no longer play. All around her, night-black petals flick open and closed, audible as blinks in the darkness.

# Chapter Eleven

*Audible as blinks in the darkness.*

It was one of Cartwright's favourite lines from the book, because it showed that Robert Wiseman had really understood. Even though they'd never met in the flesh, they had been connected: two separate waves resonating on a similar frequency. Cartwright had felt a kinship with him ever since finding the book, which had happened quite by accident. He'd been searching for clothes in a charity shop, spotted an almost-new hardback on the shelves and been drawn to it by the title. After he read it, he'd realised that Wiseman had taken his life and turned it into a different form. When people read *The Black Flower*, Cartwright came alive in their minds.

The notion had fascinated him immediately. He had always understood life was a constant ebb and flow of matter but he'd only ever considered it on a physical level. And he had always loved the fantasy world within books. But Wiseman had shown him that books constituted a whole other realm of existence, as the forms life took were transformed into ideas. This new world was like a vibrant tapestry that hung above our own. He pictured souls rising from the real world like mist, and ideas tumbling down from above, landing with a *thud* that sent seeds rolling away on the breeze. In the chains of cause and effect, every second link was made of dreams.

So Wiseman had written him and, in return, he had written

Wiseman. In his own way – just as with the story he'd found on Dawson's laptop. He'd sensed the connection that the new story had to real life, caught a hint of the soul that had risen below, and now the idea had landed back again with a *whump*. Cartwright had blown gently on the pollen. Started it spreading, and allowed it to bloom.

He stood up. There was another passage that came later on in Wiseman's book. He found it and read it to himself now.

Sullivan watches as the man pitches something white and flopping into the hole at the roots, then begins to shovel dirt back on top.

He liked that.

Yes, Wiseman had understood all right. Even back then.


Outside the farmhouse, he could hear the *tuck-tuck* of the chickens, and the occasional flap and crash as they reached the limits of their wire cages and scattered back in surprise. In the distance, the sun was threatening to rise; a yellow corona beginning to warm the horizon through the trees. Out on the fields, rays of light would soon flatten over the grass, and then the world would catch fire. In the meantime, the whole farm was coming alive in the softening dark. It was stirring in its sleep. Stretching and blinking like . . . petals.

'Gather the family,' Cartwright told the boy on the porch.

The boy scampered away to do just that.

None of them had out-loud names. That was one of the improvements he'd made on his father's teachings, after he realised that names effectively tied people and objects down. It was unavoidable for some things, of course; Cartwright couldn't take back his own, and needed it anyway for his dealings with the outside world, but none of the others knew it. Wherever possible, items were not itemised. The world on the farm was liquid rather than solid.

Cartwright walked carefully down the porch steps, and then round the back of the house. He was faced with a field of unkempt grass, patchy in places, like the unshaven skin of an adolescent boy. To the right, there was a pale concrete bunker; ahead of him, a row of apple trees at the edge of the wood. The bunker was lit up inside, and a skewed rectangle of light stretched out over the ground beyond like a carpet, the yellow fraying to pale.

He stood for a while, breathing in the air, listening without listening to the screams coming from the bunker. Without warning, the pain flared across him again. And then a second time: his organs blaring their alarm call at the intruders slowly strangling them. For a moment or two he couldn't breathe, and stars appeared above the small field like fairy dust. His heart galloped slightly, then halted, then galloped again, as though it was lost.

Cartwright waited.

Gradually, the pain subsided. His chest unclenched. As it did, he sensed his family congregating around him in the dirt. A bare handful of shadows and shapes in the darkness. There weren't many; there never had been. But he could see enough to know that one was missing.

'Where is she?'

The boy shrugged. 'I can't find her.'

Cartwright stared at him, and the boy flinched.

'I can't,' he said again.

'You checked under the house?'

'Yes.'

Cartwright looked back down the field, then sighed in annoyance. She would be somewhere in the farm buildings, he thought, pretending not to hear her brother's calls. Talking to her dolls. He would make sure she got the belt when she showed her face. He'd bury another of her dolls as well, just outside the fence where she couldn't reach it.

In the meantime, this couldn't wait. The sun would rise soon, and that was the hour to do it. When one day became another.

Cartwright whistled to indicate they were ready.

A moment later, the light on the lawn was broken by a

fractured dance of black shapes. Then the light flicked off altogether and the door slammed shut. His eldest boy carried the woman down the field in darkness. She was trying to scream, but the tape binding her head muffled the sound. She was also trying to fight, but even if she hadn't been weakened by the month of captivity, she wouldn't have stood a chance against his son.

The woman inside the bunker was screaming again. Obscenities, mostly. Well, that would change. The window on the far side was barred, but open to the elements, so she would be able to see what happened next. He imagined, if she was like the others, she'd shut up pretty damn quick. Certainly, the profanities would cease. They all became mice after a while, hoping against sense that that way they would not be noticed.

A breeze picked up behind the house.

Cartwright looked to either side to make sure his family were watching. They were. They were staring down the field with the usual dull expressions or looks of excitement.

He turned back.

His son had reached the trees at the bottom of the garden now. The hole had already been prepared; the spade was still leaning against one of the trunks to the side, next to a mound of churned earth and bones.

Five minutes later, as the sun came up and one day transformed into another, after the new woman's screams had dissolved into horrified silence, after the camera flash, Cartwright watched his son pitch something white and flopping into the hole at the roots, and then begin to shovel the dirt back on top.

# Chapter Twelve

The next morning, I left my father's notes and the printouts I'd taken from the Internet locked in the office, and set out on foot. Outside my building, I kept checking behind me, still nervous of being followed or watched, but it was Sunday morning and the campus was dead. Just a few students meandering around, and nobody paying me any attention.

I pulled my coat around me, tired from a miserable night's half sleep on the common-room chairs, and shivered slightly as I walked.

South of the centre, I crossed the bridge over the river, but stopped for a moment halfway over and leaned on the flaking green paint of the old balustrade. Twenty metres below, the water was thick and ripe, lapping against the mossy stone blocks along the bank. In the distance, the sky was lined with sleek glass towers and enormous cranes.

This area had all been industrial once: an old grey spread of factories and workshops. They had grown out of the trade and commerce brought by the river, and then fallen into disrepair. Bursts of money had been injected since, dabs of colour dropped onto the landscape, and redevelopments had bloomed – briefly. There were prestigious blocks of flats lining the far banks of the river, tapering up to penthouse apartments, their clean sides mirroring a fracture of clouds, but many of them were empty inside. A large number of developments had stalled, leaving empty apartments dotting the buildings. At ground level, trendy bars and boutiques opened and closed with painful regularity. This whole side of the city was faltering and half finished, ready at any moment to collapse back into disrepair.

Given what I'd read about him online, it felt sadly appropriate that Andrew Haggerty had ended up living here.

Across the bridge, I walked down a faux-cobbled street, then emerged into a central square with a gently trickling fountain at the centre. Haggerty's block was on the corner: five storeys of flats built above a green shuttered bistro and a newsagents. The front door was on a keycard system, but there was an intercom beside it. I buzzed for the flat number my father had written down, and waited.

A few moments later there was a crackle.

'Hello?'

It was a woman's voice, which surprised me.

'Hi,' I said. 'I'm looking for Andrew Haggerty?'

'Okay. Hang on just a moment.'

Another crackle, then silence.

Then a man's voice. 'Hello. Who is this, please?'

'Hi, Mr Haggerty. My name's Neil Dawson. I think you might have spoken to my father a couple of weeks ago. Christopher?'

Silence again.

'Mr Haggerty?'

'Wait there,' he said. 'I'll be down in five minutes.'

He was down sooner than that.

Andrew Haggerty was tall and bald, with small glasses and a salt-and-pepper goatee. As he emerged from the building, wearing dark-blue suit trousers and still pulling on a thin black coat, he looked harried and troubled. Older than his years. I'd done the maths and knew that he was only forty-five, but the last decade had clearly affected him. It was as though what had happened ten years ago had stretched time suddenly wide, and then it had contracted more slowly afterwards, leaving him baggy.

I felt a certain kinship with him. At the same time, it created a wrench of panic that I had to fight down.

*This is not how you're going to end up.*

*No matter what.*

'Come on.' He indicated with his head. 'Let's go this way.'

He led me round the corner of the building, down another short street, and into a new square. This one was smaller, with benches and bushes around the outside, and a bronze sculpture in the middle of three men playing bowls, one of them crouched down and peering beneath his hand into the distance. They were so uncannily lifelike that I half expected them to move.

'Here.'

Haggerty gestured at one of the benches with an open hand, and I wasn't sure whether he was showing me it or suggesting we sit down. There was a gold plaque in the middle of the wooden beams at the back that read:

*In Loving Memory of Lorraine and Kent Haggerty*

'The council were looking for donations. It wasn't much, but at least it's something.' His head was tilted to one side, staring at it. Then he smiled sadly. 'Come on. Let's sit down.'

We did. I leaned forward slightly, rubbing my hands together aimlessly. The plaque felt like a hot button behind me, something it would have been wrong to rest my back against.

'I'm really sorry.'

'Thank you.' He nodded. 'But it was a long time ago now.'

From the way he said that, I didn't quite believe it. Certainly, I couldn't imagine ever getting to the point when I'd be able to say something like that myself.

'Are you re-married now?' I said.

'No, no.' He half laughed. 'Or not quite anyway. I'm living with someone, but we're not married. Maybe one day.'

'I'm sorry to interrupt.'

'No, she's very understanding. That kind of goes with the territory of a relationship with me.' Another half laugh. 'But obviously, all of this upsets her a bit. That's why I've come out here. She knows it's important to me, and she doesn't say anything about it, but . . . well, it's nothing she needs to hear, is it?'

'No, I guess not.'

Again, there was an edge to his voice that suggested more than the words themselves did. It was nothing she needed to hear. *But it's something I still need to say.*

'My father wanted to talk to you about Lorraine and Kent,' I said. 'About what happened to them.'

'Yes. How is he getting on with his book?'

I paused.

'My father died.'

'Oh God. I'm so sorry.' Haggerty looked at me with horror, then shook his head, thrown. 'What happened? Was it—'

'An accident,' I said quickly. For the moment, it felt like the safest answer to give. 'It happened last week – and it had nothing to do with the project he was working on. Actually, until yesterday, I didn't even know he was working on anything at all.'

Haggerty still looked shocked.

'And that's why you're here?'

I nodded. 'This is for my peace of mind. I hadn't seen him for a few weeks and I felt very guilty about that. I suppose I just wanted to find out what he was working on. What he was doing.'

'I'm sorry,' Haggerty said again. 'Sincerely. He seemed like a lovely man.'

'Thank you. He was.'

'And I understand what you mean. When you lose someone, you ask yourself all those questions, don't you? Sometimes it helps and sometimes it doesn't.'

'You did meet my father?'

'A couple of times. He was working on a new book; that was why he wanted to talk to me. He hadn't decided whether it would be fiction or non-fiction. He was very polite, you know. Very respectful.'

I nodded. *Fiction or non-fiction.* With my father, of course, those boundaries had always been blurred. Except that, in the past, he'd only ever seemed to write about himself, whereas it seemed this time he'd also been mining the lives of others for inspiration.

'Part of his research was about your family. Is that right?'

From the news articles I'd found online, I knew a certain amount about what had happened to his wife and son. When it came to the basic facts, that meant I probably knew almost as much as he did.

'Yes,' he said. 'It was about Lorri and Kent. The family I used to have.'

Ten years ago, Andrew Haggerty had been a successful estate agent in a town called Thornton, which was a little further inland from Huntington and Whitkirk, but still close enough to be on the same page of the map. Andrew's wife Lorraine was a stay-at-home mum; their son, Kent, was four years old. They were a happy, ordinary loving family, until one Tuesday, after working late, Andrew returned home to find his wife and child weren't there any more.

The car was gone too – which was something – but there was no reason for them to be out so late, and Lorraine hadn't left him a note to say where she'd gone, which was very much unlike her. Andrew laboriously called round the various friends and family members who he thought might know where she was, but none of them did.

Finally, he called the police.

'They didn't take me seriously at first,' he said. 'Can you believe that?'

I could believe it all too easily. And it was a lesson, wasn't it? The police hadn't believed Haggerty's wife and child were missing even without him telling them the wild story I would have to.

Again, I fought down my emotions and tried to sound calm, natural. 'No,' I said.

'Because the car was gone too, you see? So I suppose it makes sense. They thought we'd had an argument and she'd gone off. That she'd come back home when she was ready.'

Haggerty shook his head.

'It turned out she'd gone to the supermarket. Not at that time, obviously, at some point in the afternoon. That was where they found the car though. It was the only one left in the car park overnight.'

I nodded.

Security footage from inside the store had captured the last known images of Lorraine and Kent Haggerty alive, and stills from that footage had appeared alongside a number of the articles I'd found online. They showed a woman and a small boy, dark and blurred and indistinct. They didn't look real. It was like they'd been scribbled on the film: shaded in with the side of a pencil.

There were no cameras in the car park itself, but, over the days that followed, a few reports and witness statements were gathered. A handful of people remembered separate small parts of an overall picture: an old van parked nearby, browny-red, the colour of rust; a woman complaining about something to an old man; hearing a little boy crying; a larger man with wild hair. They were all just impressions, of course, and none of them had been conclusive enough in itself to cause concern to the witnesses at the time. Put together, though, they were sufficient for the police to launch a major enquiry.

Which went nowhere.

I remembered what the old man had told me on the phone. *They haven't found me yet. Never have. Never will.*

In terms of the known facts, that was where Andrew Haggerty's story ended. Despite the efforts of everyone involved, a single car in an otherwise empty car park was the last trace of Lorraine and Kent Haggerty that was ever found.

I had no idea whether that would have made it easier for him or not. On the one hand, he never had to face the horror of the bodies themselves but, however painful that would have been in the short-term, at least then there would have been a sense of closure for him. Even now, ten years on, when he must have known in his heart that Lorraine and Kent were dead, I could feel that absence of resolution. It wasn't just his appearance; it was obvious from his behaviour. He had agreed to speak to my father, and he was speaking to me now. The experience had never finished for him. A line had never been drawn.

It made me feel cold inside. Was this how I was going to end up? If Ally remained missing then the police would take it seriously eventually but they'd believed Haggerty too, thrown their weight behind the case, and his wife and son had never been seen again.

*You'll never see this one again.*

*Never get her back.*

That was not going to happen to her. To them. My fist was clenched on my thigh. I relaxed it.

'Did my father say why he was interested in your case?'

'Not exactly. I got the impression he'd read about it at the time, and it had stayed with him. He did mention you and your mother – that he couldn't bear to think of losing you both. I think that's what made it stick in his mind.'

I nodded. Maybe that had been part of it, but there was more. Other connections. Obviously, the location wasn't far away from Whitkirk. There was the old man arguing with Lorraine Haggerty, and a larger, younger man. A rust-coloured van. My father would have recognised many of those things from Wiseman's novel. Perhaps even from whatever *real crimes* lay behind it.

Something else occurred to me.

'Did he ever . . . contact you? The man responsible?'

For a long moment, Haggerty said nothing.

'That was the other thing your father wanted to talk about. I don't know how he knew about it. It was never made public, so I presume he had some inside information from the police.'

I stopped rubbing my hands together.

'About what?' I said.

'About the flower. There were lots of them, of course. We held a service for Lorri and Kent a while afterwards – I can't remember how long – and there were a lot of flowers then. But even before that: flowers and cards and notes from strangers. It surprised me, to be honest. How kind people can be.'

A flower. I felt sick.

'This was different though?'

'Yes.' He frowned. 'It was the strangest thing. As far as I know, nobody ever established it was even connected, but there was obviously something odd about it. I called the police as soon as it arrived. They took it away.'

'What was it?'

'A black flower. It arrived a year or so afterwards. Just in an envelope, no stamp or anything. Just posted through the door.'

'You said the police took it?'

'Yes. Your father said he wasn't sure what it meant, but that was part of what he was looking into. Do you have any idea if it's connected?'

*Yes*, I thought. I didn't know how but yes, it certainly was connected. The little girl in the book had a black flower in an adult woman's handbag. My father had one too – tucked away in his copy of the book.

But I shook my head. 'I don't know.'

Haggerty didn't need to hear any of what I knew. I wasn't in a position to offer him closure right now, or much of anything at all. The only thing I could have told him was that his wife and child were surely dead, and he must have told himself that a hundred times already without it making an impact.

What did the flowers mean? And where had my father's come from?

I was lost in thought, and almost jumped when Haggerty spoke again.

'Do you know what the worst thing is?'

'The worst thing?' I said. 'No. What is it?'

'It's not knowing *why*.'

I looked at him, and Haggerty stared back, right into my eyes.

'Not knowing why it happened,' he said. 'Why *them*.'

I didn't really know what to say.

'Maybe there is no reason. They were just in the wrong place at the wrong time. Maybe that's all there is to it.'

'No. They were targeted. I'm sure of it.'

There was no way he could know that, and I didn't reply.

He said, 'You only remember the things you did wrong. I told Lorri I loved her a million times over the years. I know that happened, but I don't really remember it. What I remember is resenting them both, especially when work got tough. Thinking how complicated they made everything for me. Being angry when Kent cried in the night and I had to get up early. Those sorts of things. I probably only thought them once or twice, but that's what I remember.'

He shook his head and looked away.

I stood up. Maybe a little too suddenly.

'Thank you for your time, Mr Haggerty.'

'Andrew.' He held his hand out and I shook it; his grip was almost lifeless. 'If you find anything out, anything at all . . .'

'I promise.'

I walked away, as quickly as I could manage without looking as though I was running. When I reached the corner, I glanced behind me and saw that Andrew Haggerty had remained sitting on the bench, almost as still as the bronze figures in the middle of the square.

For him, his past would always remain his present. His entire life, defined now by a handful of guilty thoughts. The kind of thing you shouldn't think but do, and then, when the worst happens, can never forgive yourself for.

That would not be me.

It wouldn't.

Surely, you're entitled to make that kind of mistake. You should be entitled to think something awful so long as you're prepared to edit it afterwards. Because you can't help your thoughts, can you? They're all first draft. It's not fair to be condemned by them for ever.

I thought: *No. I'm going to find you, Ally.*

I was determined to.

*Even if it requires a descent into Hell.*

# Chapter Thirteen

The first dead body Hannah encountered, it was generally agreed, had been a tester.

An obese old lady had lain dead in her detached house one summer for over a fortnight before being found. Hannah's partner at the time, a far more seasoned officer, had gone pale at the sight of her: would probably have crossed himself if he'd had a religion. The elderly woman had died on the settee, but a great deal of her had collapsed onto the carpet by the time they arrived, and decay was misty in the air like pollen. And yet Hannah hadn't blinked as she snapped on the gloves at the doorway. She had felt sad for the dead woman, of course, but nobody had seen that, and it wouldn't have impressed them if they had. What they noticed was the way the young constable moved around the room with such quiet authority, apparently no more disturbed by the dead than she was by the living.

So word got round quickly. Hannah Price had a stomach of cast iron. And of course, there had been much worse scenes over the years. Traffic accidents where people were spread over the tarmac in streaks; a motorcycle helmet, apparently discarded, except for the almost comically screwed-shut eyes visible through its open visor. Four homicides, all women, all DV. One woman beaten to death with a kettle; a second stabbed; two more with necks covered in bruised, fluttering fingerprints. A man who hanged himself from a doorknob, his eyes and tongue bulging out of a plum-coloured face. None of these sights had fazed her in the slightest. Viscera, at least of the physical kind, just didn't bother her.

In theory, then, the bodies found this morning should have been easy.

The autopsy suite was in the basement of Whitkirk's mortuary, situated almost directly below the place where Hannah had stood with Neil Dawson while he identified his dead father's clothes. That room upstairs was designed to be sombre and respectful, with everything cushioned and curtained, so there were no visual or emotional sharp edges for the bereaved to cut themselves on. Down here, it was very different, albeit similarly fit for purpose.

The suite housed six aluminium tables, each of them separated from the next by weighing scales, sink units and hoses, all of it illuminated by artificial lights that angled out of the walls on adjustable metal hinges. Swabbed down, sterilised and polished, the fixtures gleamed, bringing out every detail in the bodies that lay here.

The dead always seemed unworldly, unreal to Hannah, and seeing them down here amplified that. The complex shapes, colours and textures were a stark contrast to the bright surfaces and clean angles. Usually, that made things even easier. Today, staring down at the remains that had been pulled from the river below the viaduct, it didn't help at all. These bodies, as old and fragmented as they were, were as real as a clench in her chest.

*Or a mark on a map. Right, Dad?*

'We have the remains of two victims.'

The pathologist, Owen Dale, was walking back and forth between the metal dissection stations in the autopsy suite. His boots squeaked slightly on the white tiles. They were fresh and new, but of the same generic type as the ones he'd been wearing at the riverbank when she'd arrived back there again this morning, after the phone call from the dive team co-ordinator. As dawn broke, Dale had been half waded in, directing both the divers and his assistants, laying out plastic sheeting, supervising the awkward retrieval of two bodies from the water.

Hannah had watched from the bank, staring blankly.

Trying to hold herself together.

The search team was looking for the woman seen with Dawson, in case she had also ended up in the water. But neither of these two bodies belonged to her. They might, she thought, have some relation to a cross drawn on an old map.

Now, she was just trying to hold herself together. Beneath the disinfectant and chemicals, the air in here still stank of that river. It made her think of weeds and mud, and stagnant pools deep in forests.

'This is the first set.' Dale stopped by the nearest table. 'I'll call this Victim A for the time being, as it was the first to be retrieved from the river. It appears to be a complete skeleton, albeit broken into a number of pieces.'

Hannah was rubbing the backs of her fingers against her lips. *Victim*. She tried to put that word – and its necessary opposite: *murderer* – out of her mind, forcing herself to examine the remains instead.

Most people's image of skeletons come from ghost stories and children's cartoons: smooth, bright-white bones and pitch-black eye sockets; a grin that was almost friendly; a cackling pirate's flag. The reality was a world away. The bones Dale was standing beside now looked organic, but barely human. The skull was recognisable, and yet even that reminded Hannah of old, brown pottery unearthed after years spent underground; it was difficult to imagine there had ever been a face stretched over it, or that thoughts and emotions had taken place inside.

The idea that the body became one with the earth after death was common and, of course, it was true. Flesh decays; cells break down; molecules scatter. Eventually, the body is recycled, the physical essence of a person absorbed by the world and transformed into something new. That was why some cultures had myths about trees growing in graveyards. But looking at the remains before her now, Hannah thought the opposite was also true. As the body of Victim A had decayed, it appeared to have taken on characteristics from the landscape around it. Just as the river had absorbed this body, so, it seemed, the body had absorbed the river. The arm and leg bones were brown and weathered as twigs, while the hands and feet were mottled a mossy-green colour. The ribs were uneven – straggly and twisted, like the roots of a fallen tree. On the left-hand side, a number were broken, bent inwards as though clasping for the long-absent heart.

She said, 'What do you mean, "broken into pieces"?'

Dale waved it away.

'It's the wrong word. The body has been in the water for quite some time. I'd say several years at least. Given the environment – the turbulence of the river – it's not surprising to observe this level of detachment at the joints. I mean, we've both seen our fair share of floating feet over the years.'

'But the body wasn't dismembered?'

'There are no tool marks on the bones.'

'Okay.' Maybe that was something. 'So what can you tell me?'

Dale pulled a face. 'Not much beyond the fact that Victim A is a fully grown adult male. I'm trying to get a forensic anthropologist in. He or she will have a better chance at estimating the victim's age and how long he's been in the water. But I can't promise anything. On the plus side, there's a good set of teeth available for identification. Unlike Victim B.'

Hannah couldn't look at B for the moment. Fortunately, Dale nodded at a sodden pile of fabric on the station beside the first victim. 'It might also be possible to identify some of A's clothing, after we've finished unravelling it.'

'Cause of death?' Hannah asked.

'Again, it's impossible to say for certain. But there's a clear injury to the skull, and I'd say that looks like a solid candidate.'

Hannah had already seen what Dale was referring to. A coin-sized piece of bone was missing from the side of Victim A's skull, with tiny fractures cracking out from it. Obvious blunt-object trauma: a lot of force onto a small area.

She gestured towards the broken ribs.

'What about that injury?'

Dale peered at the corpse. 'Impossible to say. Whether it's pre- or post-mortem, I mean. My guess would be it was caused by the weight that was included in the sack with the body.'

Hannah shifted slightly – reluctantly – and turned her attention to the third table along. The bodies had been found in two separate hessian sacks, both resting five metres below the surface in the silt of the riverbed. Each bag had also been given its own dissection station. Both were vile, sodden slumps of material, which had originally been tied at the top with rope. Dale and his team had cut them open at the side to remove the bones, allowing the pans beneath the tables to catch any remnants of river water and decay that ran off the plastic sheets. Aside from the bones, the mulch, and whatever tatters of clothing had survived, each sack had also contained a large, heavy rock.

Dale rolled his hands around each other.

'Tumble, tumble, tumble. Bang.'

She could easily picture what he was implying: the bag falling down through the air, then striking the water; the boulder breaking the dead man's ribs as the sack smashed through the surface of the river. True to Hannah's reputation, that picture didn't trouble her. What she found much harder to imagine was the face of the man on the viaduct above: the one who'd tipped the body over the edge and watched it fall. For now, he was just a silhouette against the sky, leaning over, watching as his victim sank away out of sight. She didn't want to give that man a face, but she couldn't get away from the question:

*Is this it, then, Dad?*

*Is that you?*

'And so to Victim B,' Dale said. 'What's left of him, anyway.'

The second set of remains – *the second so far*, she reminded herself – had clearly been in the water for much longer, and the bones had made an almost full transformation into something from a riverbed. It was much worse than the first. She found it hard to look.

'Male,' he said. 'But, once again, I can't tell you how old he was at the time of death or how long ago he died. Not yet.'

'Do you think it's the same killer?'

As soon as she said it, she regretted the question. For one thing, that was her job to figure out, not his. For another, the answer was obvious. Maybe she was just looking for even the smallest scrap of hope. There was none, of course. Her father had done this – killed not just one, but two people. She knew it deep down.

Dale glanced at her, a curious expression on his face.

'It's not my place to confirm or deny,' he said. 'But even without the method of disposal being identical – the sacks – I'd say you're looking at the same perpetrator. Victim B shares a similar injury to A. Even if he's been a bit more *aggressive* with this fellow.'

Dale made a knocking gesture with his fist.

'As you can see, the front of the skull is entirely missing.'

Hannah nodded.

Yes, she could see that.

It was the obvious aggression she found hardest to deal with. The first body was bad enough; this second one was something else altogether. Even in death, you could see it: that someone had squatted over Victim B and repeatedly brought an object down onto the man's face, literally caving in the front of the skull. And then they had folded him into a sack and dropped him into the river.

*Someone.*

Hannah looked at the empty cup of B's skull, then back to Victim A. At its missing coin of bone.

'The weapon,' she said.

'Blunt object. Small diameter.'

'Consistent with a hammer?'

Dale pursed his lips and nodded to himself.

'Yes,' he said eventually. 'I think you're right.'

Hannah was driving.

*You're going to get yourself in trouble.*

Maybe. Well, she was already in trouble of course. There was a potential murder weapon lying in her father's house right now, and there wasn't a single thing she could do about it that wouldn't lead to even more trouble. Not just for her father, but now for her.

Call it in? That was the sensible thing to do – except, without the map, it was just a hammer. There was no reason to look at it twice. Obviously, with the *map*, it made sense. But if she reported that, she was opening herself up to scrutiny. Hannah had sat on what she knew, made that anonymous call, not told anyone her suspicions. She wasn't confident enough she'd covered all the angles. There was no CCTV on that payphone, for example, but lots elsewhere. If she put herself in the crosshairs, someone would surely be able to find her nearby, close to the time the call had been made. Circumstantial at best but that was only off the top of her head, and who knew what else she might have missed? These little details added up. One thing police work taught you was that however careful someone thought they'd been, there was always something.

So she wasn't going to call it in.

At least the fear – the dread – was diluted slightly now. She'd found out something close to the truth, and it was as bad as she could have expected. But now, she was annoyed as well as scared. With him. With herself.

Why had he done this to her?

*Never mind that*, she thought. *Why are you doing it to yourself?*

Hannah slowed, then indicated and turned into Mulberry

Avenue. The first cross on her father's map – the furthest inland, at any rate – was over this road.

From what the dive team had found, it looked as though the viaduct had been a dump site for bodies. What about the other places he'd marked down? Were they the same, and, if not, what did those other crosses represent?

She'd driven down Mulberry Avenue a number of times before. As far as she'd been able to tell, it was just a quiet residential street, indistinguishable from many others on the outskirts of Huntington. She couldn't see anything different now. It was a reasonably affluent neighbourhood, and the houses were spacious and detached, with neat, crew-cut grass verges outside, and neighbourhood-watch notices on the lamp posts.

No wasteground. No obvious disposal sites. Where the viaduct was secluded and disused, Mulberry Avenue was very conspicuously not a place you'd choose to hide something.

*Unless there* used *to be something here.*

That idea occurred to her as she reached the end of the street and turned right. It was possible, wasn't it? Her father's map was an old one, after all, so back when he'd drawn those crosses perhaps some of the houses behind her hadn't been there. Or maybe one of them had a poisoned secret or two of its own, throbbing beneath a cellar floor. She would need to check the records for that.

*Well, you can do that.*

The thought followed quickly, hollow now:

*After all, you can do anything.*

It took a twenty-minute drive to reach the place marked by the second cross. Whitkirk Park. The entrance was gated: great big iron railings. Across the road, there was an old block of flats, with an estate sprawling away behind. This was no good either; there were too many people around for too much of the time. During the day, the park was full of women strolling with prams, couples meandering, teenagers sitting around in circles on the grass, playing guitar. At night, older kids got drunk here. Men cruised. There was nothing she could hope to find hidden here that someone else wouldn't have uncovered long ago.

A short drive away, Blair Rocks was much the same. It was a small but well-known picnic area on the edge of Huntington Woods. Hannah turned into the car park. At the end, there were wooden benches, and beyond them a large field with a wall of trees on either side. Three other cars were parked up, and the field was speckled with families. Children's laughter echoed across; two kids were chasing each other across the grass. A kite trailed in the sky.

The area took its name from the large boulders that scabbed the far end of the field. There was an embankment there, steep enough in a few places to be scaled by serious climbers, but most of the rocks were small and safe enough for children to play on. As a result, this place was reasonably well attended for most of the year.

Which meant there couldn't be anything here either: once again, logic dictated this wasn't a dump site, because anything disposed of quickly would have been found quickly. And anything hidden more carefully would have been hidden far more easily somewhere else.

*What did these places mean to you, Dad?*

The fourth cross.

Hannah reversed the car, and headed away.

A few minutes later, she was parking up on the old patch of scattered gravel that faced into the remains of Wetherby Cottage. It was halfway along one of the small roads linking Whitkirk to Huntington. Not a quiet road, perhaps – but not a busy one either. Like the Rocks, it also ran along the edge of Huntington Woods. In fact, it was only about a mile north of here that the river cut through below the viaduct, where her father had marked his fifth and final cross.

*This place is more promising, isn't it?*

The front of the main structure appeared to be still standing:

a wide, low building that, in life, had probably been painted as white as the flesh of a fish. In death, it was grey: sodden and worn. The windows were just empty holes, with the undergrowth wrapping itself in and out of them. Around the corner, the side wall had collapsed inwards. The roof was clearly long gone.

Derelict for years. But . . .

*What's here?*

*Or what* was *here when you made that cross?*

Hannah's phone vibrated against her hip. She took it out.

Barnes.

Without even answering, she could play the call in her head. As much of an arsehole as he could be, once again he would be right in what he said.

*Sorry, sir*, she thought. *I didn't hear it ring.*

But even so, there were places she should be right now, and things she should be doing. Inconsequential things, maybe, in the face of what she'd uncovered, but not in terms of her everyday life, of what was expected of her. And that was the issue, wasn't it: the question that had occurred to her on the way to Mulberry Avenue. Why was she doing this to herself – risking everything and getting herself deeper and deeper in trouble?

Because she had no choice. If she lost her father – not just physically, but her good memories of him – then she lost everything she'd ever taken for granted about herself. And it was too late to forget about it or pretend. Now, she needed to know.

But she also needed to start looking after herself a bit more. She should get back to the department and see if Neil Dawson had returned the message she'd left. If not, try to chase him up. In the meantime, there were a hundred other things she should be doing in terms of the two bodies found.

Keeping up appearances, all of them.

But appearances were important.

Hannah indicated, waited and then pulled out. The road

wasn't too busy, but there was traffic. If she was going to investigate here, it would be better to wait. As she drove away, starting back to the department, she watched the broken farmhouse recede away behind her.

*Later*, she thought.

*Maybe later we'll have a proper look at you.*

# Chapter Fourteen

I arrived in Whitkirk along the coastal road. It ran down from the cliff-edge to the north, and I had to drive through the smaller villages first, with their little green squares and holiday cottages and closed-up craft shops. The sky was dull but clear, the clouds like half-hearted smears of paint over the sea. Inland, the hazy sun was already settling down in the distance, already beginning to drape itself in the steam of evening mist rising off the land at the horizon.

The town of Whitkirk had gathered itself together slowly over the years, on a gentle slope that curled around a bay, a jaw-bone shape of mismatched buildings. Before the road descended properly to the seafront, I could see the whole village: an intricate, terracotta spread of houses, uneven, angled rooftops, and cobbled streets. On the opposite cliff, the spire of the abbey was coal-black against the sky.

So here it was. From what I'd read, this was the town on which Robert Wiseman had based parts of the *The Black Flower*, and driving into it now felt like entering a place that was half real, half fiction: somewhere I'd been before, but only in my mind's eye. In the real world, of course, it was the former home of the Carnegie Crime Festival, and the place where both Wiseman and my father had ended up. Two writers, both staying at The Southerton, both researching the same material. Both dead.

I wasn't a writer in the same way, but now I was going there too.

The quickest way to the hotel was along the seafront itself. There was a wooden promenade on the left, and, having read the description in *The Black Flower*, I made the association. But I guessed that, without the book, Whitkirk would have just seemed like any other seaside town. I passed cafés, bars and hotels, painted pale pink and yellow, all vaguely reminiscent of summer holidays in entirely different places. There were the usual dark amusement arcades, with their gangs of kids inside, shadowy as ghosts, leaning into the machines. The sounds drifted across: the occasional chatter of money, the forlorn whoop-whoop noise of failure. Along the pavement, there were toy aeroplanes and trains, blaring and lurching, for younger children to sit in.

The Southerton was obvious when I reached it. It was an old-fashioned, five-storey building made of enormous red-stone blocks, and markedly different from the smaller Neapolitan-coloured bed and breakfasts I'd already passed – much grander and far more ornate. Out front, wide steps led up under a glass-domed entrance, with disabled ramps curling up to either side. The name of the hotel was painted on the dome, in a curling script that reminded me of the Paris Metro system. It made me think of inscrutable black cats and *Amelie*.

The turning for the car park was just after the building. I drove into a stretch of tarmac behind the hotel. Mostly empty, which was good, as I was going to need two parking spaces.

I pulled up and checked my phone. Nothing from Barbara Phillips. I slipped it back into my pocket.

There was no entrance to the hotel from the car park, so I walked back round the front. The doors at the top of the steps slipped sideways automatically, releasing the gentle sound of classical music.

I stepped inside.

In contrast to the old-fashioned exterior, the reception was glamorous and modern, filled with plasma screens and plush settees. The floor was black marble, polished so clean that my reflection hung down below my feet. The whole area was built on slightly different levels, giving it the feel of a lavish bathing room that had been drained of water. There were plants everywhere – great elaborate fronds fanning up from large earthen pots – and plump, black, leather sofas around glass coffee tables. All but one were occupied by groups of suited businessmen, communicating over laptops, tethered to mobile phones, drinking tiny foam-tipped cups of coffee with handles the size of rings. In one corner, a fountain was tinkling and trickling.

*Very posh, Dad.*

The reception desk was to the side, fashioned seamlessly from the same black marble as the floor, with large round clocks on the wall behind giving the times in London, Paris, Sydney, Tokyo and New York. The man and woman on duty were both dressed in smart grey suits, the man on the phone, writing something down as I approached. The woman smiled at me, but the smile faltered slightly as she took in my cheap jeans, shirt and trainers, all of it slept in. To be fair to her, she hid any disapproval quickly. I couldn't entirely blame her anyway. The cheapest room here cost two hundred pounds a night, and I didn't look like I could afford that because I couldn't.

'Good afternoon, sir. How may I help?'

'I have a reservation. Neil Dawson?'

'Okay. Let me check for you.'

But worrying about the cost of a hotel room was an everyday thought. I was past that now. Money no longer mattered. I'd spend what I needed to. I'd sleep on the fucking beach if it came to it, or in the car, or not at all.

'One adult for three nights?' she said.

'Yes.'

'Can I take a swipe of your credit card, Mr Dawson?'

I slipped it out of my wallet. As she dealt with the paperwork, I glanced around the lobby. *Very posh, indeed.* The cost was something, wasn't it? Because I didn't imagine my father could afford this place either. If he was simply researching a book, there must have been cheaper places to stay that would have done just as well – and yet he'd come here. Why? Just because the Carnegie Crime Festival had been held here? To be closer to Wiseman, in some way?

What?

The woman tore some paper off a strip, folded it, and slipped a keycard into it. 'Would you like the porter to show you to your room, Mr Dawson?'

'No, thank you.' I took the card. 'I'll bring my bag in later.'

'Okay. Is there anything else we can help you with today?'

'Yes,' I said. 'You could book me a taxi please.'

'Certainly, sir. Where are you going?'

I did my best to smile.

'Huntington Police Station, please.'

Although my father's body had been found closer to Whitkirk, the vehicle forensic unit was based at Huntington, and so his car had been waiting there for me to collect: parked up amongst the corpses of vehicles that were more obviously crashed and ruined, but not more sad. There were also his belongings, retrieved from The Southerton. I'd received a phone call mid-week to advise me they were available for collection. At the time, it hadn't seemed like a priority, but it felt more urgent now. If the old man on the phone was telling the truth, and my father really had found his grown-up daughter, maybe there would be some clue in his belongings as to how he'd done it.

But that evening, standing at the reception desk of Huntington police department, I learned it wasn't going to be that simple.

'I don't have permission to release the car,' the desk sergeant told me.

I shook my head. 'I was told it would be okay.'

'Well, it seems it's not any more.' He rattled his fingers over a few more keys. 'There's a block on the system. That normally means the release has been held back for some reason.'

'Some reason like what?'

'Let's see. I probably won't be able to tell you precisely.'

Except I didn't really need him to. *Some reason like reopening the investigation*. That was the only explanation I could think of, and it meant something had changed. Recently too, as I was pretty sure Hannah Price would have tried to get in touch with me. She didn't have my mobile, and I hadn't been home in the last twenty-four hours to take the call.

The desk sergeant nodded to himself.

'Yeah, as I suspected. You'll need to talk to DS Price's team at Whitkirk. She's the lead on this one. There's no notes on the system as to why.'

'Okay.'

It was frustrating; I wasn't sure what to do next. An avenue of investigation had just been closed to me, and I wasn't sure what others remained open. Barbara Phillips still hadn't called me. There wasn't much else I could think of left to follow up.

'Thanks anyway,' I said.

I turned to leave, still uncertain about what I was going to do, beyond finding a taxi and getting back to Whitkirk, when he said:

'Don't you want them, then?'

I turned back. 'Sorry?'

'Your father's belongings?' he replied. 'There's no block on them. It's only the vehicle.'

*It's only the vehicle*. What the fuck was going on here?

Regardless, the possessions were something.

'Yes.' I walked back. 'Sorry. I'll take them please.'

By the time I'd signed for everything and found another taxi, night had fallen. The driver took us on a different route back to Whitkirk, through the countryside. The car bumped and rattled, and my body moved absently with each motion. I felt too tired –

worn out both physically and emotionally – to fight it, and the driver didn't make any real attempt at conversation. He must have sensed the mood I was in.

Because it had turned out that my father's scant possessions weren't actually *something* after all.

They were beside me on the back seat now: bagged up unceremoniously in rubbish sacks. When he'd brought them out to me, even the desk sergeant had seemed a little embarrassed by the sight of them; the way the police had dealt with them, it was as though not simply throwing them away altogether had been an afterthought. There was one bag of bundled clothes, gathered from his room at The Southerton, and a second containing toiletries and the usual, bog-standard items that had been left in the car itself: a battered, ring-bound road atlas; a can of de-icer, rusted around the rim; a cloth. There was also a small selection of random CDs, some of which I recognised and imagined I'd never be able to listen to again. And that was everything he'd brought with him, except for the clothes he'd been found in and the missing laptop. All of it was itemised on a printout. I'd scanned down, stared blankly at it for a while, and then signed.

There was nothing there.

No clue as to how he'd found the woman I was supposed to be looking for. Slumped there beside me, the bags contained the bare minimum of everyday items, ones he'd never use again, and which just seemed terribly small.

*Keep it together, Neil.*

It was hard. There was nothing there but sad memories of my father; it felt like I could even smell the clothes slightly, reminding me of him, and making my chest ache from the loss. So for most of the journey, I forced myself not to look at them, not think about him. I just stared out of the taxi's windows. There was little to see there either. The fields to the left were entirely dark except for occasional farmhouse lights dotted here and there, while, to the right, the woods were dense and black: a wall of constantly shifting static, flashing past.

Until, up ahead, there was a sudden bright glint of yellow.

On a subconscious level, I recognised it immediately: a policeman's jacket, catching the headlights. And as we got closer, I made out more details – grey shapes parked up along the side of the road. The taxi driver didn't slow down, and so I turned in my seat, watching out of the side window. There was one officer standing there, hands clasped in front of him, and two vehicles just past him. One was a standard police van, while the other was much longer, more like a caravan. *Some kind of incident vehicle?* I caught a flicker of blue and white tape. But then we were past, and it was all receding away behind. I craned my neck round and stared out of the back window. A few seconds later, the road curled, and the scene swung away out of view.

The viaduct.

I'd been too distracted to think about the route we'd taken, but that had to be it: the dirt track that led through the woods to where my father had been found. Not only were the police keeping hold of his car, they were still investigating the scene itself.

So what else had they found there? What were they looking for?

*Maybe they know he wasn't alone there that day.*

I turned forward again, staring at the back of the passenger seat. Trying to think. Up until yesterday, when I'd been convinced his death wasn't suicide without knowing it for certain, I'd probably have welcomed a new investigation. But now it complicated things. The old man on the phone had warned me not to tell the police anything about him or his daughter, or about what had happened to Ally. He didn't want them to know. But what if Hannah Price had discovered the woman had been with my father? If she was actively looking for her, there was a real danger our paths would collide, and I'd have to talk to her whether I liked it or not.

And I didn't know what that would mean for Ally.

Ally . . .

I felt a sudden stab of frustration – of absolute powerlessness. Anything could be happening to Ally right now, and I just didn't know what to do any more. Go to the police? Maybe they'd believe me more easily if they did know about the woman – except it might put Ally at even greater risk than I already had. I just didn't know. My heart was tight in my throat, and as the panic hit me properly, it was almost impossible to fight it down. What was I supposed to do? What was I—

Everything blurred.

*Come on,* I told myself. My fists were clenched so hard that my knuckles had gone white in the gloom of the car. *Come on.*

Hold it together.

But I couldn't. To his credit, I guess, the taxi driver maintained the same careful silence as before, although he seemed to drive the car a little faster.

Back at The Southerton, every surface in the lift was either sleek black metal or scrupulously polished mirror, aside from the small video screen of an animated goldfish built in above the control panel.

I pressed the button for the third floor. It outlined in red, probably matching my eyes, and the lift began to glide gently upwards. On all sides, I could see reflections of myself stretching back to infinity. A man with a rucksack over one shoulder, and bin bags of clothes resting at his feet. A man with swollen eyes, head tilted back to stare upwards, avoiding catching his own gaze so he didn't have to face head-on just how fucking lost he was.

After what seemed like for ever, the lift *tinged* and the doors slid open, and I stepped out into a corridor that smelled sickly sweet, like old flowers.

My bedroom was plush. Of course, for two hundred pounds a night, it should have been. I dumped all the bags on the bed, then stood in silence for a moment.

*Come on, Neil.*

My father's stuff was of little interest to me right now; nothing in the bags would help me. So instead of looking at that, I opened my rucksack. I'd bought my laptop and the notes I'd printed in the office last night, and also my father's copy of *The Black Flower*. There had to be something I'd missed. There had to be.

For some reason, it was the book I turned to first.

## Extract from *The Black Flower* by Robert Wiseman

When the call eventually comes, it is Sullivan who takes it, and that is not by coincidence. The man on the other end of the line asks for him specifically.

In some ways, that makes sense, because his name has been attached to the appeal for two weeks now. But most of the callers, seeking attention, have been happy to relate their lies to the first person prepared to listen. According to the switchboard operator who puts him through, this man is different. Far more insistent. *And creepy as hell*, she says, before giving a nervous, slightly embarrassed laugh that he lacks the patience to indulge.

'Put him through.'

As he waits, Sullivan listens to the silence on the line. There is no way of knowing for sure this is their man, of course, but a part of him already does. A shiver runs down his back, as though an ice-cold fingertip is slowly, slowly tracing a snake there.

The sound on the line changes. The connection is made.

'This is Detective Sergeant Sullivan. What can I do for you?'

In the background, he can hear the rush of the breeze, the crash of the sea. He checks his watch and the window. Outside, rain is stinging the glass. It is high tide; the weather is wild. The call is probably coming from somewhere nearby.

*A phone box on the seafront?*

And then the man speaks.

'I'm phoning about the girl.'

It is a dirty, gravelly voice, as though the man's throat is full of rocks that chip the edges off his words. The way he says 'the girl': there is a dirtiness to that, as well, but of a different kind.

'Okay,' Sullivan says. 'Can I ask how you know her, please?'

'I'm her father.'

He looks around the office. He already has Pearson's attention, but he mimes clicking his fingers and captures the eye of a few others, then gestures with his head toward Gray's office.

'And what's your name, sir?'

For a moment, there is no answer on the phone line beyond the crash of the sea in the background. Then the man sighs wistfully.

'I was so annoyed to lose her. She's never run away before. My little Annie.'

The chill Sullivan feels increases. Is that the girl's real name, he wonders? It is a popular one, of course, but it is also impossible for him not to feel it as more than a coincidence. Anna Hanson and 'Charlotte', now Annie: two little girls echoing each other; the universe making a rhyme.

'She ran away?' Sullivan asks.

'I'm afraid so. We were all together in that café, and when I looked up she was gone.'

The café on the other side of the promenade, directly opposite where Sullivan had crouched down in front of the little girl. The man must have been right there the whole time.

'Your name, sir?'

'It was very bad of her to run away. Very bad. She's always causing problems for people, my little Annie.'

Around him, the office is buzzing with activity. Gray has emerged from his office and is leaning against his doorframe, arms folded. Sullivan decides to abandon his previous question.

'Not at all, sir. We just want to see her home safe and sound, the same as you do.'

The man says, 'I'd like to come and pick her up.'

'That would be very helpful.'

'When and where?'

Sullivan pauses at that. It's an odd way of phrasing things: the sort of words a kidnapper might use, or someone arranging to exchange illicit goods. *Where can we meet, so that nobody will see?* Even though the girl is safe, and will remain safe, he feels a thrum of danger in the air and wonders, momentarily, if there is something he might be missing.

He forces himself to breathe slowly, calmly. The obvious answer, the one he would normally give, is that the father must come to the police station. But he knows the man will never agree to that.

'Where would suit you, sir?'

Immediately, the man says, 'How about that same little café?'

The implication within the words is clear: *I'll take her back as though it never even happened.* There is a sense of symmetry to it, Sullivan thinks. The little girl disappearing again – stitched back into whatever crease of the world's fabric she had escaped from.

He will not allow that to happen.

The man says, 'In an hour.'

Sullivan only checked his watch a moment ago, but he does so again now. It is one o'clock in the afternoon. It is, of course, unlikely that the man will turn up, but they need to act as though he will. What can he organise by two? Obviously, the café will need to be watched. But there are other things to consider. Sullivan looks around the office, wondering who he can send to the Fitzgerald foster home to make sure the girl remains safe. There are so many things to plan out; so many approaches to consider. An hour isn't enough.

'Let's make it three o'clock,' he says.

'No.'

Another odd response. And again, Sullivan bites down on the obvious reply. This is not a normal parent who has lost a normal child; in fact, the man isn't even making a pretence of it. So what are his intentions? He doesn't want to give Sullivan enough time to . . . do what?

What is he missing?

'Okay,' Sullivan says. Across the room, Gray raises his eyebrows. Privy to only one end of the conversation he is clearly concerned. He is right to be, but Sullivan says, 'Two o'clock it is.'

Other than the breeze and the sea, there is silence.

Then the man says, 'Fine.'

And he hangs up.


'He's not coming,' Pearson says.

It is five past two, and they are standing in the same spot where Sullivan first kneeled down in front of the little girl. He pulls his scarf around him, wincing against the swipe of the sea breeze.

137

'Maybe he's already here.'

Despite the severity of the weather – cold rain whipping across; the sea, an angry foaming surge beyond the wall – the promenade is busy. It is a harsh day, but the sun keeps breaking intermittently through, and people are braving the elements, determined to enjoy it. Some of them are actually eating ice creams bought from the van further back along the promenade, when even the van itself is shuddering in the wind. It is hard to spot stragglers amongst them. The café across the street has its share of customers, but nobody there is obviously waiting. Nobody is watching them. Certainly, no men on their own.

And yet how could he be sure? Perhaps the man would bring his wife, or his little boy with him – or both. They have no real physical description of the family to work with.

Sullivan turns his wrist and checks the time again.

Seven minutes past two.

With Gray's reluctant agreement, he has officers stationed along both approaches here, watching for single men, suspicious men, men. Miles from here, two officers are outside the Fitzgerald address. They have reported in already. Nobody has followed them and the street is empty. And whether she is Charlotte or Annie, the little girl is playing happily inside the foster home right now, entirely oblivious to the activity whirling quietly around her.

Pearson says, 'Mike.'

'What?'

Sullivan's attention has been focused on the café, but he glances at Pearson now and sees the other officer is looking off to one side, caught by something further along the shop-side of the promenade.

A moment later, Sullivan sees it too.

'Shit.'

A fractured chain of children is slowly approaching their position. The little girls are all wearing the navy-blue dresses of the local school; the little boys, the grey-trousered, blue-jumpered equivalent. There are fifteen, twenty of them. A couple of the girls are skipping; one of the boys is holding the hand of a teacher. In all, there are four adults accompanying them, two bookending the chain and the others forming larger links within, corralling and ushering. 'Come on, come on. It's raining.'

'Coincidence?' Pearson says.

Sullivan says nothing. He isn't sure. Instead, he simply watches the children and the teachers. They don't come as far down as the café. Instead, they stop at the RNLI station a few units further up: an open garage where the flat, white nose of the lifeboat pokes out onto the pavement. The walls inside are festooned with inflated lifebelts and old photographs. Bolted to the wall outside, there are plaques and a collection bin. The children begin to go inside.

A school outing.

Can that be a coincidence? Sullivan doesn't know what to think, or what the connection is, but the sight of the children has set a sense of unease humming inside him. The man on the telephone was adamant about the time, and here is a trail of school children, going about their day. That can't be a coincidence. Perhaps it is some kind of threat. But, for the life of him, he can't understand what the man is trying to say.

And then he sees something else.

The wind, still present, still biting, seems to fall away, and all he can hear now is the pounding of blood in his ears.

'No,' he says. 'It's not a coincidence.'

From the front of the lifeboat station, metal ridges run straight across the street, crossing the tramlines in the middle, all the way to a break in the coastal wall, where a stone ramp leads down into the sea. Just past that break, Clark Poole is leaning awkwardly against the metal railings on top of the wall. He is wrapped in his familiar raincoat, stiff with grease, and watching the entrance to the lifeboat station. Watching the children going inside, an ice cream in his hand.

Pearson follows his gaze and sees him too.

It is his turn to swear. 'Shit.'

Sullivan nods to himself, understanding now. His name, attached to the appeal. His name, lodged in Clark Poole's head as a figure of mockery, a figure of hatred, a figure to taunt at every opportunity. And the unidentified caller. The insistence on this time, this place. The name of the dead girl.

He watches as Poole waves his fingers delicately at the children in the lifeboat station. The children don't notice it, but Sullivan does. From the way he feels Pearson's body tense up beside him, he knows his partner does too.

Poole turns to look at them.

Smiles.

And – just like that – the wind starts up again. The noise. The activity on the promenade. Except that Pearson now has a palm flat on Sullivan's chest, pressing him backwards, holding him in place. He can see a bulb clenching in the corner of his partner's jaw as he is wrestled backwards against the sea wall.

'Stop it, Mike. Stop it.'

Gulls are reeling overhead. The sea is crashing.

Sullivan takes a deep breath and stares upwards at the swirling grey of the sky, trying to calm himself down. But he can't. Even without seeing him, he knows that, further along the promenade, Clark Poole is still watching him and still smiling happily to himself, pleased with the work he's done here today.

# Chapter Fifteen

I was making love with Ally.

It was a couple of months ago, on the only holiday we'd ever taken together. Just one night away, to celebrate the anniversary of us getting together. It was worth marking, we'd figured, and so had splashed out on a hotel in a spa town in the Dales where we booked our own cabin. It had three rooms, all of them opulent, and there was even a log-burning stove in the front room. There was a sun-drenched swimming pool outside the cabin, and a fine restaurant in the main building. It was, without doubt, the single most luxurious place I'd ever stayed.

The weather had been bright and warm. We'd lounged by the pool, sitting on the edge with our feet dangling in the cool water. We'd drunk too much wine, eaten great food. And now it was the evening, and we were having sex in subdued light in the cabin's large bedroom. The fan, whirring overhead, was the only sound apart from the two of us. It whispered round: blew soft, cool air down on my naked back, and then hers. And then, finally, the tops of our heads as she sat astride me, her heels in the pillows, one hand pushing down behind on the inside of my thigh, the other clutching the back of my neck, refusing to slow down, forcing me to stare right into her eyes as I came.

And then, afterwards, we laughed about it.

*That was stupid, wasn't it?*

*Well, it won't happen to us.*

Ally's head was thrown back – not in passion now, but the tortured, blood-flecked centre of a black flower.

I bolted awake.

My mobile was ringing on the bedside table.

I snatched for it too quickly, nearly knocking it to the floor. The number was unknown, and that set my heart going even faster. Was it him? Telling me I hadn't found her quickly enough and so . . .

I felt my pulse in my head as I held the phone up to my ear.

'Hello?'

'Is that Neil Dawson?'

It was a woman's voice.

'Yes.' I wiped my face with my other hand. 'Yes, that's me.'

'This is Barbara Phillips.'

The hotel room curtains were black with night, but the time was visible across the room: bright-green numbers glowing under the television screen. I peered across. Nearly midnight. As though reading my mind, she said:

'I'm sorry for calling this late. I only just checked my messages. I've been very busy recently – my husband is ill.'

'No,' I said, 'that's fine. Thanks for getting back to me.'

'Not at all. Whereabouts are you?'

I hesitated.

'I'm in Whitkirk.'

'Are you? I suppose that's even easier then. But it's late now, and I'm very tired. Could we meet tomorrow? Say at twelve?'

'Can we meet any earlier?'

'I'm sorry. I have other commitments.' She didn't wait for me to protest. 'Let's see. There's a café on the seafront. The Fisherman's Catch? It's quite good. We should meet there.'

*The Fisherman's Catch.* There was no pen nearby; I was trying to remember it.

'On the seafront,' I said. 'Okay.'

'You should be able to find it. Where are you staying?'

Again, I paused.

'I'm at The Southerton.'

'Ah yes,' she said. 'Of course you are. Well, it's just a little way along from there. It's not far.'

*Of course you are.* Because somehow The Southerton was central to everything that was happening. And, from her tone of voice, Barbara knew that.

'Twelve it is,' I said.

'Good. I'll look forward to it. And Neil? You mentioned you wanted to talk about your father, so I'll just give you some friendly advice in the meantime. Don't talk to anyone else before we have a chance to speak.'

I didn't reply.

She added, 'Especially the police.'

And then she hung up.

# Chapter Sixteen

Hannah stood in her father's kitchen, sipping from a mug of coffee. The sash on the window was up, revealing a black square of night, overlaid by a ghostly amber reflection of herself and the room around her. Through that, somewhere at the back of the garden, she could just make out a texture of midnight leaves.

She was looking through the photograph album again, which was open on the kitchen counter. In her head, she justified it by thinking she was looking for some clue within its pages: some sign that her father had never been the man she thought, but the killer she now suspected. A flash in his eyes, maybe, or a stain on a shirt cuff. That was ridiculous, of course – but then, it felt equally ridiculous to believe there had been no sign at all, and that the two sides of Colin Price had been as distinct and separate as the faces on a coin.

That was the justification. In reality, she knew she was still searching desperately for that old feeling of safety and reassurance. Trying to reclaim the father she remembered, and wanted to remember, and herself along with him. Oddly, now that she'd discovered at least some of the truth, it was more comforting to look through the album than it had been over the last few days. Because in a way it helped to know. However monstrous something is, it always feels worse when it's lurking out of sight behind you.

Hannah cupped the remains of the coffee in her hands.

One thing hadn't changed: out of all the photographs, it was still the second that she kept returning to, the one that showed her cradled in her father's arms just after she'd been born. The place and time it had been taken were lost in the past; it recorded a moment in which she had been present but could never remember. And yet the fact remained that an invisible line cut jaggedly across the world and the years, connecting the baby in the photo to all the other Hannahs in the album, and finally to her, standing here right now.

That was something, she thought. *That line is important. There is comfort in being able to follow your life backwards like a rope, hand over hand, and know there's some coherence to who you are.*

More than that, the photo before her now was clear evidence of how much she had meant to her father. A few pages further on in the album, he would let go of her bicycle so she could pedal herself alone. It was those things she had to remember: that he had always loved her enough to push her out into the world, to tell her not to be afraid, to tell her that she could do anything. Which meant he *had* been a good man, whatever else he'd done – whatever the bodies in the water meant, and whatever she found out tonight or afterwards – and that knowledge was tight like a fist. Mentally, she clasped it fiercely against her now.

*You were a good man.*

The cup in her hands was only lukewarm. She half considered making a fresh one, but it was nearly midnight, and another would just be putting this off out of fear. *You wouldn't approve of that, would you Dad?* So she splashed the dregs into the sink, set the cup on the side, and made her way through to the lounge.

It was warm in here tonight. Earlier on, she'd brought logs in from the storehouse in the back garden, brushing away the spiders that tickled across, then laid them carefully on top of the old ashes in the grate. Now, the fire burned brightly behind the grille, flicking and cracking, casting checked light across the hearth and shadows on her father's empty chair. Standing in front of the fireplace, the heat was a gentle, comforting pressure on her face.

Deep in the grate, the map had already burned away to nothing. When it caught, the evidence bag around the hammer had *puffed* briefly with green flame then melted, folding into itself. The hammer inside was now scorched down to bare, blackened metal. Whatever evidence might have been clinging to it had fizzed and curled and vanished.

*There you go, Dad.*

He had almost certainly done something criminal – maybe even something genuinely evil – but after deliberating all afternoon, she had decided there was no reason anyone else needed to know that. Not unless they absolutely had to. If the official investigation into the two bodies turned up a connection to Colin Price, she would deal with it as it happened, but she wasn't going to volunteer that connection. As of now, there was nothing physical that linked him to the viaduct, and, beyond some ashes in a grate, the world was no different from how it was before, back when it had felt safe and secure, and she'd known who she was.

Nothing *physical* – but of course, she still knew. The question now was whether she would be able to live with that knowledge, given time, or whether the memories she cherished of her father were ruined forever. She could tell herself over and over he was a good man, but would she ever really believe it again? It was a question that couldn't be answered until she found out the full truth of what he'd done.

Hannah warmed her hands against the fire and looked down at the items she'd assembled. It was impossible to know for sure what she was going to need, because she had no idea what she was going to find, or what she was willing to do in search of it. So she'd prepared for insanity. In addition to the rubber bulk of her father's heavy-duty torch, she'd scoured the garden, garage and pantry, coming out with a large bucket, lengths of tow rope, rubbish bags. Several coat hangers, simply for their strong, metal hooks.

The spade was already in the back seat of her car. In addition to the black jeans and sweatshirt she was already wearing, there were dark gloves and a pair of wellington boots waiting to be put on when she'd reached her destination.

An extendable baton hanging from her belt.

Anything else?

There was nothing she could think of. But still, she stared down at the flames. In the furnace of the hearth, a log split, and a dusting of fire ribboned up into the chimney breast.

*Now or never.*

One by one, Hannah began piling things into the bucket.

Half an hour later, she reversed into the gravel passing place opposite the derelict Wetherby Cottage.

Behind her, an expanse of night-black fields criss-crossed their way to the horizon. The stars prickling the sky above were blurred in the rear-view mirror. In front, half revealed by the headlights, the ruin of the old cottage was visible between the trees. In the surrounding darkness, the walls seemed more brightly fish-white than before. Looking at it, the car engine still idling, Hannah could feel the atmosphere of the place. It reminded her of the house at the end of that Blair Witch film: the broken down, abandoned one, deep in the woods. She thought of motes of dust illuminated by torchlight and cracked-plaster walls covered with children's handprints.

She killed the engine. The world fell silent and the remains of the structure blinked out of view.

Hannah got out of the car, went round to the boot, and removed what she needed. Just the torch and the gloves. She didn't bother with the boots, tools or rope for the moment, partly because she didn't know what she might be faced with, but also because she'd convinced herself she would be faced with nothing at all. Just another variation on the park or Mulberry Avenue, where the mark would remain a mystery.

She clicked the torch on. The beam was anaemic after the headlights, as though half the light was missing, but it would be good enough.

A few insects drifted lazily through.

*Let's see what's here then.*

There would be nothing.

Hannah began tramping through the overgrown grass and brambles in front of the farmhouse. She approached the ruined building at an angle, and the black windows seemed to follow her, the vines and grass wrapped over the broken sills like streaming tears. Aside from the soft *cracking* beneath her shoes, it was profoundly quiet, and yet she could still feel a presence. The air felt tinged with sadness and regret, as though something awful had happened here and the place could never forget it.

*Just your imagination*, she told herself.

*Nothing happened here.*

She peered through the nearest window, shining the torch around slowly. The internal walls were all gone, but she could tell where they'd been: jawbones of stone half buried in the forest floor. Everything else had been taken. The back of the farmhouse had tumbled down entirely. Beyond a mosaic of tiles and timber in the undergrowth, there was little behind the front wall. No inside left. It was a face without a skull.

Hannah shone the torch as far as she could, moving the beam slowly, searching. What she was looking for, she had no idea.

The cool breeze kissed the side of her neck, blew softly into her ear. She remained intent.

Nothing obvious.

But there wouldn't be, would there? It wasn't enough. So she made her way down what remained of the side wall, turning the torch on the undergrowth instead. It was so thick here, so tangled, that she had to lift her knees high in order to traipse through it; every step felt like putting her foot down through coils of barbed wire onto nests of twigs. *Click. Crack.*

She stopped at a molar of rock in the ground, where the building would have finished, and the abandoned farm fell silent.

That was when she saw it.

A moment later, her ears began ringing gently.

Behind the building, the brambles thinned out. The torch's beam was hazy, making the world appear full of pale mist, but it revealed a clearing of sorts before the woods began: a wall of trees and shadows that defeated the light. And just before they started, in the corner of the clearing, there was a well.

The silence continued to ring.

Then broke softly as Hannah began walking slowly through the long grass. Leaving the missing skull of the farmhouse behind. Moving closer towards the edge of the forest.

The well was at least as old as the building, and it was almost lost now: a cylinder of brick wrapped in the grass. The remains of three wooden struts poked up from the undergrowth around its circumference, the wood broken off at knee height. The lip of the well itself had crumbled away in places and, if there had ever been a cover, it had eroded long ago. The whole thing was only a metre across.

Hannah leaned carefully on the edge, pointed the torch in and peered down its mossy throat. Far below, a semicircle of water reflected the torchlight back at her: a shimmering moon, as small and distant as the one in the sky above. She moved the beam a little and found a thatch of something. She couldn't tell what. It was like the flotsam that collected on the sea by the wharf: a dirty froth of splinters.

She knocked a stone loose. It rattled and ticked off the inside of the well, then hit the water with a sound that made her think of tumbling coins. The moon down there shimmered and swam, settling gradually.

*Okay.*

*Now what?*

She leaned back. It might be possible to do something with the bucket, she thought – attach a rope to the handle and lower it down, see what, if anything, she could scoop out. That didn't seem like the most efficient method of accomplishing anything, but what else was there? Tie the rope round her waist and belay down?

*Whoever's daughter you are, you're not doing that.*

She wasn't really considering it as a viable option, but still, she turned the torch in the direction of the wood anyway, wondering if there was anything to secure the rope to. The beam passed across the man standing beside her.

There was a sudden flash of light. Hannah stumbled backwards in shock, the beam zagging down over the man's legs but then the back of her calf got tangled in the grass, and she felt herself falling. It happened almost in slow motion; she couldn't stop it. *Fuck.* She landed on her elbow. The grass cushioned her from any real injury, but the impact jolted her heart.

*Baton baton baton baton.*

She fumbled at the clasp on her belt, at the same time angling the torch back towards the wood, sweeping the beam from tree to tree. Nothing.

Gone.

Immediately, she stopped moving. Listened. In-between the quick, heavy thuds of her heartbeats, she heard it: a distant cracking and trampling sound. Someone moving quickly away through the forest.

*Well. Don't just fucking lie there, DS Price.*

She heaved herself forward, up onto her feet. The baton extended with a click. And then she went straight between the trees after him, slashing the torch sideways, back and forth, trying to catch a glimpse. She caught flashes of the trees, snatches of undergrowth. Shadows that hung like bats, unfolding their wings as the light moved away.

A moment later, she stopped and listened.

This time, there was no sound at all.

*Okay.*

*Let's not be stupid.*

She took a quick glance around, judging the terrain as best she could, then thumbed the button on the torch. Everything went dark – almost pitch-black – but Hannah moved quietly to one side. Just a short distance from where she'd been, but enough so that if he'd been watching the light he wouldn't know where she was now. Then she crouched right down, opened her mouth slightly, and listened again.

Again, nothing.

Not human noises, anyway. But beyond the galloping thud of her heart, she became aware of the sound of the forest. The little cricks and buzzes; the whisper of the breeze in the branches high above.

But he *was* here somewhere. He had to be.

So Hannah remained crouching, as still as her thigh muscles would allow, and tried to remember exactly what she'd seen. There hadn't been time to take in much: she'd seen black jeans and boots, a dark jacket. It wasn't a rough-sleeper. No, it was someone who was out here for a particular reason. Maybe even the same reason as her. He'd caught the torchlight and the sound of her trampling down the side of the farmhouse, and just taken a step back between the trees. To watch her. Or else . . .

*Or maybe the activity drew him* out *from the woods.*

Hannah shivered at the idea and took a better grip on the baton. The woman who'd gone to the viaduct with Dawson was still missing. So was she sure the person she'd just seen was a man? Hannah thought so. She scanned the night-black wood-land for any sign of movement and couldn't see a thing. Who-ever it was, they had to have a torch, didn't they? You couldn't move in this mess without one. But there was no light. And the forest remained quiet, sounding only of itself.

She considered her options. Even with the baton and the

torch, she didn't fancy going much further forward in the dark. The alternative was to wait it out: see which of them had the most patience. Or she could get the hell out of here instead, but she wasn't going to do that.

*So you go forward.*

All right, then. She stood up, intending to do just that, when red lights flickered between the trees a short distance ahead of her. And then she heard the noise. A car engine.

A crackling of pebbles.

*Shit.* She flicked the torch on and moved quickly through the undergrowth, not frightened any more. Determined now. But it was no good. She stepped out onto a wide dirt trail cutting through the forest. Dark and empty in both directions now, although the smell of petrol still hung in the air.

*The flash*, she thought.

When she'd first seen him, there had been a flash of light. Had that come from a torch he was holding? Her imagination?

Or had it been something else?

Hannah stood there for a few moments, her heart thudding, as an awful possibility occurred to her.

Had that flash come from a camera?

# Chapter Seventeen

For the first time ever, Cartwright was woken up by the pain.

He had been dreaming about a tree. It was old and gnarled, growing twisted out of the ground like a thick length of silver rope. His father had planted it, or his grandfather, or possibly even his grandfather's grandfather. The tree was thick and strong at the base, so that you could imagine its roots spreading away metres underground, tonguing through the soil and hooking the tree solidly into the earth. Further up, though, it dwindled, the trunk thinning as it rose. The branches stretched out without buds. Leaves flickered here and there, but the bunches were tiny and weak. At the top, where the main trunk resembled a broken bone, a few hopeless branches reached higher, tapering to vicious points.

In the dream, Cartwright looked at the tree and thought it resembled a malformed skeleton, stretching up to the gods for acknowledgement that had never arrived. It stood motionless, backdropped by a blue sky filled with swift, stop-motion white clouds.

He was woken, abruptly, by the fresh life the tree lacked.

The main tumour was pulsing against his ribs, so hard it threatened to slip between them and sprout suddenly, pushed out through his side like a fanned deck of cards.

This pain was too much to ignore. He sat up, and clutched at his chest and then his abdomen. Clawing like he couldn't find the source. But at least he managed not to cry out, not to disturb the room full of silently slumbering bodies. As he fought for his breath, he breathed in the stink of disease. It filled the room. He was sweating it out. The rank, old duvet below him on the floor was wet with his dew.

He was dissolving.

Cartwright waited for the pain to subside. It took a lot longer than it normally did. By the time he finally turned his body, his heels knocking, stuttering, on the bare floorboards, dawn was lightening the shuttered window on the face of the house. He heaved himself upright. His limbs felt heavy, even though he was little more than skin and bones now. He rubbed the greasy sweat from his face, and then his body trembled as he stepped falteringly over the sleeping forms of his family, and out into the corridor.

Downstairs, moving more easily now, he opened the front door and stepped out into the misty darkness on the porch, then stood listening for a moment. The world was numb, and the farm was mostly silent. Even the chickens were quiet. But shortly, ahead of him, a shadow loomed amongst the shadows.

His eldest was stalking through the treeline, returning to the house with a log over his shoulder. He often patrolled the compound at night. Sometimes he went out into the fields to hunt. But never far, not by himself. For the most part, his entire existence was circumscribed by the fence around the farm, while the outside world was hazy and difficult: a place to hunt different prey, and to be hunted in return.

*What will become of him? All of them?*

When Cartwright pictured the future, he felt an ache of a different kind in his body. He saw this place sealed tight, surrounded by armed police. He saw his family hunted down from a wide circle to a tiny dot: one that, finally, blinked out of existence altogether. In teaching his family about the reality of the world, he had failed to prepare them for the illusion everyone else believed. Those that believed it would discover this place when he was gone, and they would overcome it.

His eldest approached him across the dusty front yard, and grunted as he dropped the log at Cartwright's feet in the dust.

'For the fire,' he said.

Cartwright nodded, but his thoughts were elsewhere. Now that he was near the end, the other thing he couldn't stop thinking about was his daughter. It was a question of the past, rather than the future. *What has become of you?* he wondered. At least he had an image of her now – her startled face at the viaduct, before she had turned and ran, leaving Dawson to stand in their way – but that wasn't enough. He wanted to know more. Did she have children of her own? Had a seed from this life blown away on the wind and started a patch of its own elsewhere?

*You belong here.*

'Are you all right?'

Cartwright blinked. His son was looking at him, frowning slightly. None of the family knew about his illness, but he would have been disappointed if they hadn't picked up something, especially his eldest, who had always seemed attuned to his teachings. The illness was seeping out through his pores and whirling around him like dust in the air. It would have been strange for his son not to notice the change taking place, more and more quickly.

'I'm fine,' he said.

His eldest wasn't convinced.

'Tell me?' he asked.

'I'm just thinking about her.' That would be enough. Cartwright knew the boy missed a sister as much as he missed a daughter, that time had not dulled her absence for either of them. Brother and sister had been very close at the time she ran away, even if, he imagined, they had grown into very different people since.

Cartwright rested a hand on his son's shoulder.

'Do you know? I think she's coming home today. Can you feel it on the breeze? I can sense her.'

His eldest paused, then cocked his head as though sniffing the air, but his expression remained blank. No, he couldn't sense it. For a moment, Cartwright wondered whether he'd even meant it himself, or if he'd just said it to distract the boy. Sometimes it felt like their whole existence here, the philosophy behind it, was hand-to-mouth, a story being made up as it went along, passed down through the generations, with sections filled in as needed. On that level, it didn't really matter what Cartwright said, so long as they all listened and believed.

*No,* he thought. *That's not the case.*

*There are patterns.*

'Well, I can sense her.' He tried to sound more decisive. 'I can sense the pattern. Try harder.'

The eldest looked around for a few more seconds. He closed his eyes and breathed in the world. Then said, 'Maybe.'

'*Maybe.*' Cartwright repeated it derisively, as though the boy wasn't trying hard enough. He believed it himself now; if he repeated something enough, it always seemed more solid, more likely to be true. He said, 'It will happen. It has to.'

His eldest nodded, and Cartwright was pleased. So pleased that he wasn't thinking about patterns any more, and didn't consider the grand scheme of things as he said:

'I'm going out this morning to the hardware shop. We need some things. The charity shop too. Some clothes for our new arrival.'

The boy nodded again, but looked miserable.

'What is it?' Cartwright said. 'Tell me.'

'What if she doesn't come home?'

He was doubting him again, which should have annoyed Cartwright. But as the pain slowly throbbed, beginning to bloom in his side, he was too distracted to be angry.

'I'll call the man finding her,' he said. 'I'll tell him his time is up.'

'Yes.'

'And if he can't find her . . .' Cartwright began. But the words afterwards failed him. His insides had come to life again. He thought of unpeopled jungles, sunlight streaming through the trees, stained green. He thought of leaves clicking open, undergrowth stretching, flicking quickly then slowly into slightly different shapes. All of that, taking place within the barrel of his torso. He was becoming overgrown, and his forehead was suddenly dappled damp with hot-house sweat.

'If he fails,' he said, 'then she'll be yours.'

His eldest glanced off towards the back of the farm. That promise was enough for him, as Cartwright had known it would be. Because yes, the world was numb, the farm was mostly silent, and even the chickens were quiet. But not the woman behind the house.

She was still screaming for help.

# Chapter Eighteen

The next morning, I was far more hungry than I would have thought possible. It seemed such a mundane thing in the circumstances, but then, my body didn't know anything was wrong, and I'd been running on vapours, most of them coffee, for longer than I could remember. I couldn't run much longer without collapsing. So while I showered, I boiled the small, wobbling travel kettle in my room, consumed another dose of caffeine, and then took my key card and went down for something to eat.

The breakfast room was decked out entirely in white; the tables caught the early morning sunlight from the high windows. The crumbs, grease stains and leftover jam packets from earlier diners stood out against the cloth. I heaped a plate with everything hot from the buffet, then carried my tray over to the closest single table I could find. Fuel up, head out. That was my plan, as much as I had one.

The table happened to be next to the wall, which is the only reason I noticed the complementary newspapers. Even then, I didn't think to check straightaway. But halfway through eating, I remembered what I'd seen from the taxi – the fact the police were still at the viaduct – and cursed myself. Maybe whatever was going on had made the news. I stood up, licking butter off my finger.

There was the usual selection of dailies in the rack, but I

scanned down and found a copy of the local paper, the Whitkirk and Huntington Times, then sat back at the table and held it awkwardly over the remains of my breakfast.

Shit. It was right there – front-page news.

## MORE REMAINS FOUND AT SUICIDE SPOT

Further remains have been discovered at a remote spot between Huntington and Whitkirk, a police spokesman confirmed yesterday evening.

The site, known locally as the Horley Viaduct, was in the news last week when the body of author Christopher Dawson was discovered there. At this stage, police stressed, there is no reason to suggest the new remains are linked to his suicide.

'They appear to have been in the water for a long time,' the spokesman said. 'Investigations are ongoing as we attempt to identify the deceased and establish a cause of death. At this point, we are not connecting this discovery to that of Mr Dawson, although we are pursuing several lines of enquiry.'

It is believed the grim discovery was made by divers searching the river. The area is now sealed off, and police forensic teams remain on-site. Anybody with any information is encouraged to call the incident number below.

Until I'd got to the bit about the remains being in the water for a long time, I'd gone cold inside, thinking it might be *her*: the woman I was supposed to be looking for. But it couldn't be. So what the fuck was going on?

The telephone number listed looked like the same one Hannah Price had left on my father's answerphone. For a moment, I half considered just fucking ringing it – demanding to know outright what was happening. I had a right to know, didn't I? I might have to explain why I was here in Whitkirk, but I could probably come up with something, or just dodge the question. I'd pretty much run out of other options. What made me hesitate now, though, was what Barbara Phillips had said on the phone last night.

*Don't talk to anyone else before we have a chance to speak.*
*Especially the police.*

What was going on here?

I scanned the article again, trying to tease out additional detail. It was phrased carefully, leaving it unclear whether there was one body or more. Instead, it was just 'further remains'. But how had they been found in the first place? Why were police divers dredging the river at all? *They appear to have been in the water for a long time.* And yet a person who had been in the water for a long time wouldn't just lie there, would they – their body would have been swept downstream, the way my father's laptop was supposed to have. Which meant the remains must have been weighted down somehow to keep them hidden. Not suicide, then.

*Christ*, I thought. *Could it be Wiseman?*

'Are you finished with this?'

'What? Oh yeah – sorry.'

I folded the newspaper out of the way, so the young waitress could clear the table. Then I moved the chair back.

'Actually, I'm done,' I said. 'Let me get out of your way.'


It was too early to meet Barbara Phillips, so I walked for a while, trying to fight back the feeling that time was running out.

Many of the cobbled streets here were little more than alleyways and it was difficult to tell them apart. The pavements were blocked by racks of postcards, and wicker bins full of plastic, primary-coloured spades, and windmills on sticks that spun in the breeze, rattling like playing cards in bicycle wheels. The shops were mostly indistinguishable: every other one seemed to be a newsagent of some kind, their windows full of blown-glass miniatures of ducks and whales, or tiny porcelain ashtrays and ships. There were second-hand bookshops. There were God knew what shops, with smudged glass displays containing curved lock-knives, pipes and lighters, and air guns resting in old, weathered card cases.

The whole time as I walked, I kept half-recognising things from *The Black Flower*. It wasn't anything specific: more the atmosphere of the place. Maybe Wiseman had imagined he'd just been describing a generic seaside town, but it *felt* the same. It was obvious to me that Faverton was Whitkirk. Wiseman hadn't just stolen real crimes for his novel, he'd stolen the entire setting.

Wiseman.

If it was his remains the police had found at the viaduct, how had they ended up there?

The man who'd taken Ally had heard of Wiseman. *He knew me*, he'd told me on the phone. *He wrote about me*. Presumably he'd read *The Black Flower* at some point and recognised himself in it. Would that have been reason enough to kill Wiseman? Maybe. With this man, there was no telling what he'd do. But then, why hide Wiseman's body at the viaduct? And what had led my father there?

There was obviously some other significance to the place. One I didn't understand yet.

I came back down to the promenade, then turned and made my way further along the front, past The Southerton. There were boats moored up beyond the stone sea wall, bobbing on the laps of the tide. I crossed over and looked out to sea for a bit. The wall itself was thick with moss, while the sea below was thick and rich, its surface covered with fractured thatches of leaves and twigs. Out of the corner of my eye, I could see the abbey on the clifftop, poking up like a broken tooth. I looked up at it.

That was where Wiseman's car had been found abandoned. The cliff fell down steeply. From this distance it was impossible to judge how high it was, but it was certainly high enough. At its base, the sea was nobbled with rocks, the sea frothing in tiny white curls amongst them. Anyone jumping would probably be killed immediately by the fall; depending on the time of day, it was also possible the currents would take their bodies out into the sea. And not everyone washed out to sea is washed back again.

But that was only *if* someone jumped.

It was assumed Wiseman had thrown himself off the cliff solely because of his car being there. But maybe it hadn't happened like that. Perhaps he'd left the vehicle there for some reason – met someone and then driven away in *their* car. Or else someone could have taken his car to the clifftop to make it look as though he'd killed himself when, in reality, something else had happened to him. All of this for some reason I couldn't fathom right now.

I stared up at the abbey for a moment longer, then shook my head and started walking again. A little further ahead, past the boats, there was a break in the sea wall and a long stone slope, the water rolling lazily halfway up, green and meaty. To the right, on the far side of the road, was the café.

*The Fisherman's Catch.*

From the outside, it looked like most of the cafés I'd spotted already, albeit noticeably older – and also much emptier, as though there was something about the place that put people off. The sign above the glass front was faded and chipped. Inside, I could see one lone waitress. She was young, early twenties at the most, and she was leaning down and swabbing a table roughly and hurriedly, like a hospital cleaner in a room you weren't intended to see.

The place didn't look anything special, and I wondered what had made Barbara Phillips suggest it. Until, glancing a little further along the promenade, I got my answer. There was an open garage front, with the nose of a boat poking out onto the pavement. Traffic lights marked a section of street where it could be wheeled out, directly towards the stone slope, and then down into the sea.

Whitkirk Lifeboat Station.

For a moment, I was frozen on the spot, just looking at it.

And then I wasn't quite sure where I was any more. It felt like a place that was a mixture not just of fact and fiction, but also of past and present, the boundaries between those things suddenly too blurry to see.

I heard children laughing – and there really *were* children here, a little way ahead of me along the promenade, but my mind linked the sound to a chain of imaginary boys and girls instead, coming in clusters down the other side of the street, on their trip to see the lifeboat, as a paedophile stood across the road, waving his fingers delicately at them. I could feel the pulse of *The Black Flower*, and of the past it had been drawn from. It was sealed away inside the surface of the world, but at this spot, at this moment, it was pressed so tightly against its skin I could sense the outlines.

I looked along the promenade again.

She wasn't really there, of course, but in some strange way she was: the memory of a little girl, standing motionless amongst the couples and families trailing obliviously around her. This would be the place where Charlotte Webb had appeared. Where the police had held the stakeout.

In the book, and in reality. Because it was all real, I thought. Standing here now, I no longer believed Wiseman's novel was fiction at all.

I waited for a break in the traffic and jogged across the street to The Fisherman's Catch. A bell tinkled as I pushed the door open and walked inside. The waitress looked up.

'Hi there,' she said. 'Be with you in a moment.'

'No worries.'

As she finished mopping the table – so hard that it looked as though she was trying to push it through the floor – I glanced around. There were photographs hanging on the wall, most of them sepia prints of Whitkirk 'back in the day'. Some captured fishermen standing by boats, their beards almost supernaturally bright against the beige backgrounds. Others showed the streets themselves: the familiar cobbles, overhung here by antique signs like wooden shields. Distinguished couples stood proudly outside shops, faces serious, eyes staring into the camera. I glanced around the walls until I found one that interested me, then walked over to peer at it more closely.

It was a colour photograph of the seafront. A tram was parked up close to the camera. Beyond it, wires and poles extended down the road. It wasn't as old as the other photographs, but time had drained it, giving it the look of a black and white picture that someone had daubed watery paint on.

'Do you remember the trams?' I said.

'Sorry?'

The waitress had just blown a strand of hair out of her face and was standing facing me, hands on her hips.

I nodded at the print. 'The tramline in the picture. I noticed it's not there any more. Do you know when they got rid of it?'

'Ummm.' She thought about it. 'Can't tell you to be honest. Ten years ago? Maybe more. There was a big thing about it between the residents and the council. I can check if you want?'

'No, it's all right. It doesn't really matter.'

'What can I get you?'

'Just a coffee for now.'

She gave a mock salute. 'Coming up.'

I took a seat at the nearest table. It was superficially clean, but her efforts couldn't hide the older stains, the ones dyed into the surface. There were salt and vinegar dispensers, a bottle of ketchup and a menu with large photos of battered fish on it. The place reminded me of a chip shop I'd gone to as a child: one my parents had taken me to. It was a memory of comfort rather than anything else: warmth and sizzle and smell.

The waitress disappeared through a flapping door into the kitchen. A coffee machine began rasping and hacking. I opened *The Black Flower* and scanned through the first few pages until I found the passage I wanted.

As if the world shifted in its sleep, then woke with an idea so important, which needed to be told so desperately, that the idea became real. And now that idea is standing there, waiting to be discovered.

Waiting for someone to claim it.

In the book, it was Sullivan who'd discovered the little girl.

Years later, Wiseman had been photographed in a hotel just up the road with a grown woman – ethereal and eerie and beautiful. A photograph in which he seemed guilty but excited, while my father looked uncomfortable, nervous even. Wiseman: a man who didn't care where ideas came from, only what he made of them as an artist. My father: a man who believed a person's stories were all but sacred, belonging to them and nobody else.

It *was* her. I was sure of it now: just as 'Sullivan' had found her as a child, Wiseman and my father had encountered her as an adult. They had listened to her story, and Wiseman had claimed it for himself.

Based his whole fucking book on it.

I checked my watch: there was still half an hour before Barbara Phillips was due to meet me here. I flicked through the book to the point I'd reached and began to read on, treating the story as simple truth now.

And so I knew exactly whose remains had been found at the viaduct.

### Extract from *The Black Flower* by Robert Wiseman

Sullivan has been reading about flowers.

He has learned this: as a plant grows, each leaf on its stem appears
first as a bud, and then, as the stem grows taller, further buds appear
below. But there is a problem to overcome, because leaves require
sunlight. A leaf that grew directly below another would not survive in its
shade. The plant as a whole would suffer.

And yet, if you stare down at the face of a flower, you realise how
cleverly its structure has been refined over millennia. Imagine that as
the flower pushes its way out of the ground, it begins turning slowly.
Whenever it has completed exactly 138 degrees, a new bud will
sprout. It is a perfect angle, a golden ratio found throughout nature,
which guarantees that each leaf gains the maximum exposure to the
sky, the minimum shade from its older brothers and sisters above.

It could not be designed to be more efficient – although, of course, it
is only the illusion of design. In reality, the trial and error of natural
selection has withered millions of badly angled leaves, prevented the
genetic pollen of those designs being spread. Flowers are the way they
are because they have to be. Because their other possible structures
have been tried and have failed.

It is nearly midnight, and Sullivan thinks about all of this as he waits
in his car. The engine is silent; the interior is dark. The road before him
curls quietly into the distance. On the left-hand side, is the litter-strewn
sprawl of Faverton Park. On the right, a little further up from where he
has pulled in, is the grey face of a block of flats.

It is as wide as it is tall – five properties over five stories – and like a
flower, this place has also been built for efficiency, but of a different
kind, and certainly not to maximise the occupants' exposure to sunlight. When it was modernised, ten years ago, the architect, faced with
an old monstrosity of partially conjoined council flats, had simply
crammed as many separate properties in with the minimum of renova-
tion. And so the eight houses in this soulless block are a maze of
random shapes and sizes, built simply where damage to the earlier

block allowed. One person's living room might rest above another resident's kitchen, but below the bedroom or bathroom of a third. There is no guarantee, heading upwards, to which corner of the building each door will take you. Many of the windows on its front lead not into rooms, but into small, bricked-up spaces.

Clark Poole's home is directly in the centre and, by accident rather than design, it takes the form of a flower. The stem is a concrete staircase running up the middle, with three basic rooms twisting off it at angles as it goes. The bathroom is at the bottom. Lost inside the block, it has no window. Poole's bedroom is on the second floor; it provides a sideways glance onto the flat expanse of the estate behind. Finally, the kitchen is one turn away again, on the third floor, with a window that overlooks the street and the park.

Sullivan has been inside before, when Anna Hanson was murdered. He has watched officers strip every surface, lift every carpet, crack away the skirting boards, all to no avail. Because Clark Poole is too careful: he always has been and he always will be. And he has made his intentions known. If he can take another little girl, this time a Charlotte, then he will.

Sullivan watches now, as the pale-yellow square of Poole's kitchen light goes off, as he prepares for his evening walk.

As he starts the engine, he thinks again about flowers. How they have become what they are not through any design or desire of their own, but because of that one simple truth. That all other possibilities have been tried, and all other possibilities have failed.

As Poole emerges into the cold night air, he glances left and right along the street. There is nothing there – no cars parked up. After his recent activities, he had been expecting to see the policeman, stationed once again at his laughable vigil. Over the past year, his presence has been intermittent. Surely tonight?

And yet, not.

Poole is disappointed. He has even come out without his cane, especially for the occasion. Such a waste.

It is his only joy, really – or his principal one, these days – to torment

DS Michael Sullivan. Poole is not as young as he used to be, and he has to be far more careful. Chances, real ones, are scarce. After the business in his hometown and his subsequent incarceration, he was relocated here to his small hovel of twirling squalor, a place in which he feels both constantly observed and yet somehow small and dismissed. To the authorities, he is an aberration; they have pressed him into the most convenient hole, and patted down on his life. And so, with real pleasures restricted, he has mostly had to occupy himself in different ways. Tormenting the policeman has become his favourite.

He crosses the street slowly, a little awkwardly.

He thinks about the little girl he saw on the promenade, and how helpless and lost she looked. The truth is that he saw her first, before any of them, because, while his activities might have been dulled, his instincts have remained sharp. Still possessing the insights and experiences of a predator, Clark Poole was quick to recognise a baby bird that had fallen from its nest. In a sane world, they would simply have given her to him. He would have taken good care of her, just as he took good care of Anna Hanson.

In this one, however, he was forced to watch as she was taken away.

Poole is forced in so many ways. Taunting the policeman, *forcing* him back, is almost enough to satisfy the dark emotions inside him – but he has physical needs. Unable to express himself as he would like, he is forced, on lonely nights such as this one, to take what comfort he can from wherever he can find it.

As he reaches the far side of the road, Poole glances around again. It is very still. The only sound is the cold hush of the night air. For a moment, the streetlight above creates a swirling yellow sheen over his partially hunched back, like a moon reflected in shimmering water, and then he passes through the old gates of the park and disappears into its green-black depths.

Faverton Park is quiet and small, and it causes the police a correspondingly quiet and small amount of trouble. There is a bandstand in the centre, where teenagers congregate to drink. On a night, they are all but invisible – just black shapes in the shadows – but you can often hear their voices, and the sound of breaking bottles, echoing quietly across the park. You will not hear the sounds of the other shadowy figures, though: the men, sometimes with dogs, sometimes alone, who follow the tarmac path around the edge, skirting the area of trees, bushes and undergrowth that covers one corner of the park, like a patch of rust encroaching onto a metal panel.

Neither group causes serious problems, especially at this time of night, close only to the run-down estate, so the police only make occasional sweeps through the park. They respond to public concerns that things are getting out of hand, or, more rarely, following a spate of attacks. Otherwise, they leave the area be. Everyone knows there are far more important crimes to deal with.

Sullivan organised the team that swept the park an hour earlier: gently but firmly moving the men and the teenagers on. A police van has remained pulled up in the car park at the far end to dissuade others entering from that side. This time, however, the sweep was done for reasons of public service. It was arranged so that now, as Clark Poole begins his walk along the path at the edge of the park, the entire area is as close to empty as it can be.

Dressed in black, Sullivan follows Poole from a distance, keeping far enough behind and holding close enough to the treeline that he won't be spotted. Occasionally, the old man pauses and turns, scanning the open grass to the left, curiously silent tonight, and then glances behind him. Sullivan holds very still and waits.

Poole soon begins walking again.

Gradually, Sullivan closes the gap between them.

*You're doing this for her*, he thinks.

But he's not sure who that refers to any more. Is he doing it for Charlotte, whom he has now failed to visit for the first evening in a fortnight, or is it really for Anna, who is long past being protected? Perhaps it doesn't matter. In his head, there is little difference between the two any more, beyond the fact that one of them is in a position to be saved and the other should have been.

He draws closer.

They are about halfway across the park now. Here, the path curves to the left, as the wooded area begins to spread further in from the boundary wall. The trees and bushes to that side form a pitch-black maze: easy to lose yourself in, or to hide and wait for company. If they are going to be observed, if anyone has been missed, it will be here.

Poole stops again, peering between the trees.

Sullivan is metres away now. With a burst of fear in his chest, he understands that this is going to happen. It is actually going to happen. His heart is beating very quickly.

Then Poole puts his hand to one side of his mouth.

He whispers, 'Hey?'

And a man steps forward out of the treeline.

Sullivan holds still.

The man is dressed entirely in black, and is much younger than Poole. Not tall, but good-looking. From here, Sullivan can only see the side of Poole's face, but he sees the old man smile. It makes him shiver, because it isn't entirely from lust; it is an oddly human expression, childlike and awkward, almost shy. And Sullivan realises that, as well as being evil and wicked and all the other things he is, Clark Poole is also a profoundly sad and lonely man.

The man from the wood swings what looks like a handkerchief into the side of Poole's head. Immediately, the old man falls sideways and rolls onto his back.

'*Nnng.*'

Poole falls silent for a moment – but then begins *cawing* like a bird. It is a hideous sound, and it echoes across the empty park. Pearson stands over him, hesitating. Sullivan's hands flutter by his sides, and his partner looks over at him, slightly helplessly. Now that it has come to it, neither of them know quite what to do.

In his hands, Pearson is holding a hammer wrapped in a white plastic bag. He clenches his jaw, then steps astride Poole and hits him four times square in the face. *Thud thud thud thud.* The bag whips through the air, making a noise like an angel's wings flapping.

Poole is silent.

Sullivan moves closer. As he reaches them, Poole's arm lifts up and falls lazily across the remains of his face.

'Oh God,' Pearson says. He wipes his nose with the back of his coat sleeve. 'Oh God. Oh, all right then.'

He uses the hammer to move Poole's arm out of the way. It is a tentative, arms-length gesture: the way someone might use a stick to uncover a wasps' nest. Sullivan sees that Poole has no nose or teeth any more.

'All right then, you old cunt.'

Pearson grits his teeth and hits him solidly three more times on the side of the head. And then again, harder. Even before the last, Sullivan can tell Poole is gone: the old man is suddenly as limp and loose as rags. But Pearson hits him again just to make sure, or perhaps out of some odd kind of fear.

*He will never hurt anyone again*, Sullivan thinks.

But the violence is settling in the air, and a part of him understands the world doesn't work like that. He knows only too well that the dead can hurt people just as sharply and for just as long as the living. In the sudden stillness of the park, Sullivan senses something. It is a little like seeds. Seeds that have been knocked furiously into the air and which are now billowing away on the slight breeze. Who knows, really, what structures they will form when they take root and grow?

And yet he tells himself this anyway, because he has to.

*He will never hurt anyone again.*


It is the early hours of the morning as they turn right, and start driving down the long, bumpy, dirt track that leads to the viaduct. The forest around them is black. To Sullivan, it feels haunted. Sometimes he is prepared to believe in the supernatural, and, if ghosts exist, then this is surely a place they might congregate.

It is, most likely, the spot where Anna Hanson's poor body was thrown over the side and lost in the frothing storm of the river below. From this spot up ahead, she was washed out to sea, before being pummelled backwards by the currents and coming to rest on the hard rocks at one end of Faverton beach.

The van judders and rolls with the undulations of the land. The tyres, tracking through the sticky mud, make a sound like tape coming slowly, slowly unstuck from a parcel.

Unlike the little girl he murdered last year, Clark Poole, wrapped in his weighted sack, will not escape into the ocean; he will neither be washed back to shore nor lost at sea. Instead, he will sink to the bottom of the river and rest there until it washes his bones as clean and smooth as the rocks of its bed. That feels appropriate to Sullivan. It is a kind of cleansing. A sacrifice to this slighted land.

They are nearly there. Sullivan imagines that he can hear the water raging up ahead, although, in reality, he knows it is just the blood rushing in his head. Beside him, Pearson is gaunt and determined. His face is set; his hand grips the steering wheel.

This is when the police radio crackles into life.

Sullivan picks up the handset, stretching out the spiralling black cord that attaches it to the console.

'Sullivan.'

'We've got an oh-eight-two,' the dispatcher says. 'At one-eighteen Bracken Road. That's a safe house. Got your name tagged on it, guys.'

A panic button.

The address is Mrs Fitzgerald's.

# Chapter Nineteen

'Thanks,' Hannah said. 'I'll be in as soon as I can. In the meantime, call down and have them start getting the files together.'

She hung up.

*Shit.*

Hannah stepped out through the back door of her father's kitchen onto the small flagstone patio. From somewhere beyond the trees, she could hear the sound of a neighbour strimming. Overhead, the sky was clear and bright.

She took a deep breath.

Well, it had been stupid to think the whole thing could be put off. After arriving back in the early hours, she'd ended up calling in sick this morning, not from physical tiredness, so much as mental and emotional. She decided she'd be in no state to deal with the intricacies of the case. But one of her sergeants had just phoned her mobile anyway. She was going to have to go in.

They now had a list of missing persons in the Huntington area since 1950, filtered for adult males. There were over five hundred names on the list. While they were still awaiting a dental exam on Victim A, they had managed to salvage some of his clothing, which was a start. Officers could now begin cross-checking those against the missing person reports in the hope of finding a match. Victim B was harder, but he would be there too. The pathology reports on both bodies were due in later that day and, hopefully, the forensic anthropologist had been able to narrow down the age ranges they needed to look at. All of which meant that, before long, they were going to have at least one name, and possibly both.

*And then?*

That was the question – or rather, the last hurdle. Until they had the IDs, she wouldn't know for sure what the implications were. It might turn out that neither of them had any obvious connection to her father at all. She didn't think that was entirely wishful thinking, either, because what *could* there be? Especially now the evidence he'd kept here was gone. In a worst-case scenario, one she couldn't picture right now, she'd just have to play it by ear. Given she was in charge of the investigation, perhaps certain details could be made to disappear. But she couldn't plan for any of that until the names came in and she had a handle on what they were dealing with.

Either way, it was nearly over.

Apart from the stranger at Wetherby Cottage, last night.

In the cold light of day, it was easier to believe that it could have been anyone, and there were any number of reasons for them being out there like that. None of them were *good* reasons, exactly, but at least they were reasons that weren't connected to her. It was harder to believe the flash had come from a torch, rather than a camera, but she kept telling herself she was just imagining the worst. Even so, she was still kicking herself for being so stupid.

*You shouldn't have gone.*

*You should have left it alone.*

Hannah shook those thoughts away, and looked at the garden that lay in front of her. The grass itself was in dire need of cutting. Her father had always been scrupulous in his care for it, but in his absence it had been allowed to grow wild. Around the edges, it was lined by a privacy wall of conifers. In one corner, there was the ramshackle shed where he'd kept logs for the fireplace; in the other, a patch of earth that was more bare.

That was what caught her eye. It was his flowerbed – or had been once. As a little girl, Hannah had always loved it. She remembered the intense reds and blues and yellows; the flowers nodding, bright and pretty, in the summer sun. None there now, of course, and the weeds were already creeping in.

She wanted them back.

She wanted those memories back so badly.

Hannah stepped into the kitchen. But just as she was about to close the back door, a ringing noise filled the air.

The doorbell at the front of the house.

It cut off after a second, and in the silence that followed, the house felt like it was slowly untensing. Hannah stood very still, holding her breath. Someone at the door. Her thoughts turned back to the man in the woods last night. But he had *run away*. And besides, how would he know where to find her? In fact, nobody had any reason to come looking for her here. Nobody had any reason to come here at all.

But the doorbell rang again.

A cold caller, maybe. She hesitated for a moment, then made her way quietly into the hall. The baton was on the end of the kitchen counter; she picked it up as she went. In the hall, the grandfather clock's *tocking* was heavy and insistent. It took her a few seconds to fumble with the chain she'd attached to the front door, and then she opened it.

Nobody there.

Hannah stepped outside, holding the baton out of sight behind her leg. The spread of tarmac in front of the house was dappled with sunlight, and, at the far end, the gate was closed. Nobody in sight. But surely nobody could have got off the property that quickly either? She remembered the scrape the gate made. No, she'd have heard that. Which meant they must have gone round the back of the house.

Where she'd left the door open.

Hannah stepped back in and closed the door, but left the chain off this time, wanting an easy escape route if it came to it.

Then she edged down the hall towards the kitchen. Nervous, even though there was no reason to think—

'Hello, Hannah.'

She faltered in the kitchen doorway. DCI Graham Barnes was standing on the patio, just outside the back door. For a moment, she was almost relieved to see it was him, but then the incongruity hit her. Barnes himself was not a shock. But Barnes standing here: something about that was not right.

'Sir,' she said.

'May I come in?'

That was wrong, as well: too mannered and polite. And he looked so prim and proper standing there, dressed in his neat, dark-blue uniform. It was an old-fashioned copper suit: fabric ironed tight and straight; buttons and boots polished. Just like her father in the album. And while Barnes's face remained as pointed and hawkish as ever, there was something else she wasn't used to seeing there now. Deference, almost. He looked humble, like an officer who'd come to deliver bad news to an unsuspecting family.

'Hannah?' he said.

'Sir – yes. Of course.'

Barnes nodded a gracious thank you, then took one careful step over the threshold. She forced herself not to take a corresponding step backwards. He was still far enough away. And Barnes was not, in himself, a threatening man. He was much smaller than she was, and much older. Physically, she should be able to overpower him if it came to it, even without the baton, which Barnes had either not noticed or chosen to ignore.

'Thank you,' he said.

As he spoke, the smell wafted across, rich and strong. Whiskey. So he'd been drinking this morning – another piece of information to add to the list. The DCI had turned up at her father's house, acting strangely, and most likely drunk.

Hannah leaned her hip against the counter.

Barnes had lost interest in her for the moment. He had seen

the photo album, still open on the counter where she had left it last night. He rested his hands on either side of it and peered down intently.

'Lovely.'

He was looking at the picture of her father holding her in the hospital.

She said, 'Yes.'

'I was there you know.'

'You were—?'

'Well, not *there*. But your father and I were friends back then. I was one of the first people to visit you all in hospital after the birth. He and I went out afterwards. We had cigars and champagne. You could smoke inside back then.'

He smiled sadly to himself.

'Yes, I remember that day very well indeed. Waiting for the phone call. Colin was so very proud. May I?' He glanced up suddenly. 'Look through?'

She nodded.

'Thank you.'

And Barnes began thumbing through the pages of the album, one by one. There was a reverence to his touch.

'It must be nice to have this to look back on,' he said. 'To have everything laid out like this, I mean. The story of your life.'

She felt herself tensing.

'Yes.'

'Colin was thoughtful that way. He was a very clever man.'

'Yes,' she said. 'He was.'

Barnes had reached the photograph where she was on the bicycle without stabilisers, her father grinning in the background.

'This is probably it,' he said.

'Sir?'

'This is about the time it happened.'

'Sir, are you . . . are you all right?'

It was a ridiculous question given the circumstances, but what else was there? This man in front of her – even though she knew him, he might as well have been a stranger. She needed to pull the situation back towards some kind of normality, or else press the strangeness right out into the open where it could be dealt with.

'I'm afraid not.' Barnes, still looking down at the album, gave that sad smile again. 'You were outside my house again yesterday.'

'Outside your house?'

'On Mulberry Avenue.'

Just a quiet residential street, she thought. Nothing out of the ordinary to see; reasonably affluent; no waste ground. Anyone might live there.

He said, 'And I saw you at the old farmhouse last night.'

Hannah realised she was holding her breath. She forced herself to let it go, and said:

'That was you then, sir?'

'Yes.'

'What were you doing there?'

'I might ask you the same question, Hannah. The same as I might ask why you called the Dawson crime scene in anonymously. Or what you were doing out at the viaduct in the first place.'

She started to deny all knowledge of that, but Barnes read it in her face and shook his head. *There are only two of us here*, the gesture seemed to say, *and we both know that's not true*.

For a long moment, she just looked at him.

'I wanted to know the truth,' she said.

'Ah – the truth.' He nodded. 'I understand that; it's a good answer. Some things are more important than the law, aren't they? The truth is one of them.'

'Maybe.'

'No, I know you, Hannah. You found Colin's map, didn't

you? I know what you must have been thinking. You loved your father very much; he meant everything to you. So you wanted to find out what he'd done. You *needed* to. And the law didn't come into it.'

It bothered her how right he was.

'Why were you there, sir?'

'I was paying penance.' He said it simply, decisively. 'Visiting a ghost, I suppose. That place is haunted, isn't it? I don't normally believe in spirits, or things of that nature, but you can certainly feel one there.'

'Paying penance?'

'You found your father's map.'

Again, there didn't seem any point in denying it. 'Yes. And a hammer, as well. Paying penance for what?'

At the mention of the hammer, Barnes closed his eyes. He seemed to be swaying slightly – from the drink, she guessed – and his face was suddenly pained, as though he was remembering something he could hardly bear to think about.

'I burned them,' she added quickly. 'The map and the hammer. Nobody ever needs—'

'Too late.'

Hannah extended the baton down by her side. *Click.*

'Okay,' she said. 'I think you should stay where you are.'

Barnes opened his eyes.

'I should have had this with me last night,' he said. 'I just wasn't sure.'

She looked down, noticed the gun-shaped object in his hand and blinked. It took a second – an unbelievable second – for her to realise what she was seeing. He was holding a taser. Her mind started to object. The devices were recorded, traceable. If he fired it in here, the kitchen would be filled with punches of paper that would lead back to him. He couldn't expect . . . This was madness.

'Sir—'

Barnes gave her that sad smile again. 'It's much too late, I'm afraid.'

And she could tell that he meant it.

# Chapter Twenty

'Neil.'

I looked up to see a woman turning away from me, closing the door to the café. I'd been so lost in Wiseman's book that I hadn't heard the bell tinkle.

'Ms Phillips?' I said.

'Barbara.'

I put the book on the table and stood up. If I'd been nervous about meeting her, then I needn't have been: it was immediately obvious that she wasn't going to be throwing me off anything in the near future – not without help, anyway. At the same time, she didn't look quite as old as I'd been expecting. Her white hair was shot through with dark streaks, and she was wearing a neat black suit and scarf, and small circular glasses that made her eyes look tiny. Beneath the suit, she still looked slim and young. Something about her made me think of country houses, yoga and middle-class allotments. In fact, she reminded me more of an academic than whatever image I'd had of a journalist in a small seaside town.

She shook my hand, then nodded at *The Black Flower*.

'I thought you'd have finished that by now?'

I sat back down. 'I've been distracted.'

'Yes, of course.' She looped off the scarf. 'My condolences.'

She slid a little awkwardly into the seat opposite me, her age more apparent now through the obvious flare in her joints. And

181

her hands, resting on the table, looked far older than the rest of her; the skin there was shrink-wrapped over the thin bones. I noticed the large wedding and engagement rings and remembered what she'd said on the phone last night.

'I hope your husband is okay.'

'Unfortunately not.' She reached up and brushed her hair back behind her shoulder. 'He has Alzheimer's. Has had for a long time now. He's not really very well at all, although it's rare for him to know about it any more. That or anything else.'

'I'm sorry to hear that.'

'Thank you.'

There was a note of finality in her voice. It said, *I don't want to talk about it*. I remembered not saying much the same thing myself a number of times while my mother was dying.

Barbara craned her neck and peered over my shoulder at the waitress. Her neck was as thin as a wrist.

'Coffee, please.' Then she looked back at me. 'What are you doing here in Whitkirk, Neil? What do you hope to accomplish?'

How much was I going to tell her? I'd been wondering. Certainly not the truth about Ally; not yet, anyway. And so I started to give her the same answer I'd given Andrew Haggerty, but then the fresh pot of coffee arrived, fast as magic.

'I'm psychic,' the waitress said.

Barbara smiled, her eyes wrinkling at the corners.

When the waitress had retreated again, I said, 'After my father died, I suppose I felt guilty.'

'Everyone feels guilty when someone close to them dies.'

'Probably. But it was true: I hadn't seen enough of him over the past few weeks. At first, I wanted to know if there was something I could have done – something I'd missed. Given who he was, I thought the best way of doing that was to look at what he'd been working on. The whole time, I'd just been presuming he was writing about my mother's death.'

Barbara poured herself a cup of coffee. 'Maybe he was.'

'What do you mean?'

'Not *about* that specifically.' She put the pot down, then gave the end of her thumb a delicate lick. 'But you know, stories can be dangerous, can't they? Telling them can have repercussions.'

I nodded.

'And sometimes,' she said, 'stories are so dangerous that you have to *wait* to tell them – wait until you can't hurt anyone else with them.'

'What are you saying?'

She shrugged. 'Perhaps your mother's death freed Christopher to pursue something that had been on his mind for a long time.'

'Robert Wiseman?' I said. 'Or the book anyway.'

'Or both.' She tore open a sachet of sugar. It hissed as she poured it into her coffee. 'Anyway, you learned what he was working on. And I presume you're here, wanting to talk to me, because of the message I left on his answerphone?'

'Yes. Because you wanted to meet him.'

She looked aghast. 'God, no. *He* wanted to meet *me.*'

'All right. Did you meet him?'

'No. There was nothing set in stone: we'd only exchanged a few emails and phone calls. I was *reluctant* to talk about the subject, shall we say, but eventually agreed to meet up with him in person. And then I never heard back from him. He seemed like a nice man, for what it's worth. That was the impression I got from our brief correspondence. So if we had met I would have told him exactly the same thing I'll tell you now.'

'Which is?'

'To leave this alone.'

I said nothing. It was easy for her to say that, and easy for her to talk of stories being dangerous. She didn't have my current first-hand experience of just how fucking dangerous that was. She didn't know about Ally, or that 'leaving it' wasn't an option for me.

183

Barbara looked at me, her eyes like tiny beads behind her glasses, and emphasised the point.

'Leave it alone, Neil. Let the past be the past.'

'What if I can't?'

'Can't or won't?'

'Or both.' I leaned back and folded my arms. 'But to be honest, I think a part of you doesn't want to leave it either. I mean, if you were so reluctant, you wouldn't have chased up my father, would you. And why meet me? Why suggest here of all places? This *particular* café, I mean.'

Barbara sipped her coffee and smiled. It was a bittersweet expression, which, for some reason, made me remember what she'd said about her husband. *He has Alzheimer's. He has had for a while now.* Yes, I thought. Sometimes stories are so dangerous that you need to wait to tell them until you can't hurt anyone else.

'Perhaps you have a point,' she said. 'And I suppose it's true that what your father did changed things. I take it you've seen the news today?'

'About the remains they've found.'

'Yes. So on one level, it does seem that things are beginning to unravel. Maybe the truth is finally going to come out regardless. Because if the remains belong to who I think they do, I'm not sure it can be covered up much longer.'

I tapped the cover of *The Black Flower*.

'The child-killer, I'm guessing? Clarke Poole.'

She nodded. 'That would be my guess too.'

'What was his name in real life?'

'Charles Dennison. His identity hasn't been confirmed yet, of course. But that's only part of the story. My understanding from colleagues is that police divers have found remains from *two* victims.'

'Two more?'

'So far.'

'And presumably the other one is Wiseman?'

184

'Most likely. I don't know for sure, but both are male, both appear to have been in the water for quite some time and both are suspicious deaths. Unlike your father, these two are certainly *not* suicides.'

I let the implication there go for the moment.

'You think the police killed them both?'

'Keep your voice down, Neil.' She sipped her coffee. 'Years ago, when Charles Dennison vanished, there were a lot of rumours flying around about who might have been responsible. Unofficially, of course. Let's just say that some of the explanations for his disappearance were very similar to what Robert Wiseman ended up writing in his novel.'

I shook my head, thinking of the photograph. I was sure Wiseman had got his information from the woman he and my father met.

'How would he have known about that?'

'Well, he was a writer, Neil. Writers do research. Nobody knew for certain what happened to Charles Dennison, and I don't suppose there was any way Wiseman could have either. He just looked at various facts in the public domain, perhaps a few that weren't, and fashioned what he thought was a good *story*. However.' She gestured down at the book. 'I think it's possible that he hit on the truth – or landed close to it at any rate. Close enough to rattle the wrong people. And then—'

'Disappeared.'

'Yes.' She smiled. 'Until now at least.'

I looked down at the book. *Real crimes*. I'd been a fucking idiot. Ever since reading Barbara's article at my father's house, I'd assumed the reference was to the little girl – to the serial killer and his van. But it was nothing to do with 'Charlotte' and her family at all. She'd been implying that the 'real crime from the 1970s' was the murder of a paedophile; that, by connecting a few pieces of information, Wiseman had fictionalised a real-life killing by the police. As a result of that, she thought they'd silenced him.

'But why would the police bother to kill Wiseman?'

'I didn't say they did.' She tutted at me. 'What did I tell you about being careful?'

I was too frustrated to care. I needed a different story from this one.

I said, 'Wiseman's book was already published. It was a bestseller. Why bother getting rid of him? What would that achieve, apart from risking even more attention?'

Barbara was unfazed. To her the answer was obvious.

'Because of his wife.'

I blinked, then tried to remember the details. Vanessa Wiseman. She died in a car accident, just after meeting her estranged husband here in Whitkirk, a year or so after *The Black Flower* had been published. The day before Barbara Phillips's interview with him had run.

I said, 'You were the last person to interview him before her accident. Is that right?'

'No. I was the last person to interview him *at all*.'

'Due to his breakdown?'

'Yes.'

'Which was caused by her accident.'

'Which was *exacerbated* by it. He was already flaky when I met him. They'd been separated a few months by then. You've probably read that he was an incorrigible womaniser, which is true, but he loved her and needed her. He was like a lot of men in that regard: always seeking what they can't have; never happy with what they do – until it's gone, of course. Wiseman had been given the freedom he'd always hankered after. But it was obvious to me he'd lost something far more important deep down, and was in the middle of realising it.'

I thought about the cover shot for *The Black Flower*: Wiseman looking suave and smug – handsome and knowing it. In the picture with my father, he looked like the kind of man Barbara was describing: someone who enjoyed being caught out, so long as he wasn't *really* caught.

'Pitiful, to be honest,' she said. 'He touched my knee, you know? Even then – when it was quite apparent he was pining for his wife – he couldn't help himself. Some men can't. So sure of themselves on the surface. Needy, lost little children underneath.'

I picked up my coffee.

'He met her afterwards, didn't he? At the abbey.'

'Yes. That afternoon. I think after our interview, he had some kind of crisis and phoned her. Clicked his fingers and she came running. And what happened afterwards . . . happened.'

'An accident.'

'Almost certainly.'

I put my cup back down again.

Barbara said, 'You shouldn't believe *anything* you read online, Neil. There *was* a car accident. But some details about it were strange.'

'Strange, how?'

'No body for a start.'

'*She* disappeared as well?' I stared at her. 'A lot of people seem to disappear in Whitkirk.'

'They do, don't they? As it happens, I'm being slightly melodramatic. The accident was on the coastal road, close to the cliff edge. It was presumed that she wandered, dazed, from the scene and fell. Her body was never found, but there's no reason to doubt the official story.'

'So—'

'No sensible reason anyway. But Wiseman swore blind that he saw a van of some sort, just after she'd driven away. Very much like the one he'd described in his book. The way he told it, it was as though his characters had come alive and were punishing him.'

She snorted. Except it didn't sound funny or stupid to me, because I knew the truth: his characters hadn't come to life; they'd *already* been alive. What exactly had happened though – why would the old man target Vanessa Wiseman? There was no way of knowing for sure, not now, but maybe he suspected Wiseman had to have met his missing daughter at some point. If so, perhaps he'd started following Wiseman, seen him with his estranged wife on the clifftop, and jumped to a conclusion about who the woman really was.

'Regardless of what he really saw,' Barbara said, 'it was obvious he blamed himself. Over the next year, he retreated entirely from the world. By the end, when he finally came to stay at The Southerton, he was very unbalanced. He wanted to interview me – much like your father did – but I refused.'

'He was working on new material when he disappeared.'

'More like obsessively throwing himself into old material. He only told me enough to know he was borderline insane. He was reworking *The Black Flower*, he said – a kind of sequel, but in an odd way. This new book was going to be about a novelist who wrote something that came true and who lost his wife because of it.'

I felt sick. 'An autobiography?'

'His version of one.' Barbara leaned forward. 'You asked me why the police would have bothered getting rid of him, Neil. It's a sensible question. If certain people had read *The Black Flower*, it would have upset them. Worried them even. But you're right – the book was published by then. Nothing could be done. And despite its success, any connection to real events seemed to have passed under the radar. So far anyway . . .'

She left that thought hanging. I finished it for her.

'But with Wiseman unhinged, asking people questions, drawing attention to himself . . .'

'Yes, exactly. Attention that might lead to them. Who knew what he might say, or who he might say it to?'

I rubbed my forehead. I could see how it made sense. It was perfectly possible everything Barbara had just said was true. The problem was that she didn't know as much as I did. She only had half the story, and it wasn't the half I needed.

'What about the little girl?' I said.

She looked blank. 'Sorry?'

'In the book. Charlotte.' I could tell from her expression what the answer was going to be, but I asked it anyway. 'Is she true, as well?'

'Oh God, no. Of course not.'

*No*, I thought, *of course not*. Barbara didn't know that the family were as real as the murder of Charles Dennison, and she wasn't going to be able to help me find Ally, or the real Charlotte, or even back me up if I went to the police. Given what she'd told me, I doubted she'd even speak to the police. It was another dead end. The panic was rising.

*What the fuck are you going to do now, Neil?*

After what she'd just told me, was it even possible to go to the police? Who could I talk to? It wasn't just getting them to believe me any more; it was about who was safe to tell any of this to.

Barbara was frowning. 'Why do you ask about the little girl?'

'I thought . . . maybe that part was true as well.'

'A serial killer kidnapping people to take back to his farm?'

I forced myself to smile. 'It's just that so much of the book seems to be based on reality. I was starting to wonder if Wiseman made any of it up at all.'

'He stole a lot of real people and places,' Barbara said. 'In some cases he barely made an effort to conceal them. But as far as I know, nothing like that ever happened.'

My coffee was nearly finished. I needed to get out of here. I wasn't going to get anything else that was useful out of Barbara Phillips, and felt an urgency to get moving, do *something*. I didn't know what though, and that made me feel even more sick.

'Where have you got to by the way?' Barbara said. 'In the book?'

She reached out for it but I picked it up before she could. I didn't want her seeing the flower. I just wanted to leave.

'I've got to the attack on the foster home,' I said.

'Ah yes. I know that section. That's where the tone of the story changes, if I remember rightly. Let me set your mind at rest, Neil, and save you some reading time. Whatever the truth about Dennison, everything from that point in the book is totally made up. It didn't happen.'

'Right,' I said. *As far as you know.*

She continued, 'The foster home was never attacked. The little girl, if she ever existed, wasn't abducted. And the policeman didn't end up being tortured to death on a farm. That whole storyline was just Wiseman's invention.'

I did my best to smile again as I stood up.

'You've just spoiled the ending for me.'

'No.' She smiled. 'I really haven't.'

# Chapter Twenty-One

Up close, Whitkirk Abbey looked even more ancient and weathered than it did from the seafront. As Barnes drove them towards it, Hannah watched the bare arches forming odd shapes and angles against each other. They had been blackened by time, so that the whole structure resembled the scorched ribcage of a giant, set on fire on top of the cliff.

'Where are we going?' she said.

'Here.'

It was the first thing he'd said since they left her father's house. In the confined space of the car, the smell of alcohol was much stronger. He was, she had realised, very drunk. For the whole journey, he'd concentrated hard on the road, but kept the taser in his hand, balanced against the steering wheel. She hadn't wanted to risk a move. If she'd succeeded in grabbing it, the car could still have ended up anywhere. People might have been hurt. Regardless, what on earth would she be able to say in the aftermath?

Barnes pulled into the car park just past the abbey.

'Why here?'

He didn't reply. The tyres crackled over the gravel as he parked up next to an old yellow estate. It was the only other car here. Hannah saw an elderly couple, standing over by the fence at the edge of the cliff, wrapped tightly in raincoats, despite the relative warmth of the day. She presumed they were watching the boats out at sea down below. Other than them, the place was deserted.

*Signal to them?*

No. Barnes still had the taser. As far as she could tell, it was his only weapon, and it would be safer to tackle him now they were no longer moving. However, there was still no guarantee that would end well. And despite the implicit violence of her abduction, he hadn't actually hurt her yet. She'd been prepared to be driven to far more anonymous locations than this, but it seemed he had something on his mind other than harming her.

For a few moments, though, he said and did nothing. Hannah glanced around. The land on the far side of the road was rough – scruffy and unkempt. Huntington Moor. Technically, this was Whitkirk, but the moor curled around, eventually growing into the woodland nearer the larger town. Here, it was just an expanse of rock and heath. You half expected to see goats and sheep scraping their teeth against the dirt, trying to eke out a shivering life, but it was flat and empty, and the only movement came when the wind blasted across, sending quivers rippling through the grass.

Hannah turned back to the windscreen. The remains of the abbey towered overhead, unreal, standing out starkly against the ice-cold white sky.

'Sir?'

The continued formality was absurd now, but it came anyway, out of habit. Beside her, Barnes's expression was dark and troubled. He was staring at the couple by the fence as though he resented their presence for some reason, as though it bothered him.

Eventually, he said, 'I knew your father would have kept those things. The map, especially. That was just him. He found what we did even harder to cope with than I did. It was an awful, awful thing. You really can't imagine.'

*Paying penance.*

'What did you do?' she said.

Barnes thought about it.

'Can I tell you a story?'

She nodded.

'It's a story about a little girl,' he said. 'It doesn't matter what her name is any more. What matters is that, a long time ago, when your father and I were much younger, this little girl came to your father and told him a man had been following her. But your father didn't believe her.'

Hannah started to interrupt. Barnes shook his head. *Don't.*

'Colin had his reasons. This little girl was quite well known at that point for making up stories to get attention, and your father was very busy, so he didn't take what she said seriously. He should have done, but he . . . well, he wasn't to know.'

*Oh God.* Hannah could see where this was going.

'At the time, this little girl was friends with my own daughter. There was a birthday party, and I was supposed to be looking after everyone. We went out for a picnic at Blair Rocks, my ex-wife and I, along with eight children. And the thing is, Hannah, I wasn't paying close enough attention. You've seen the area.' He smiled ruefully. 'I *know* you've seen the area. It touches the woods.'

'Yes.'

'At one point, I looked up and realised she'd disappeared.'

Hannah didn't reply, just watched him. His hands were trembling slightly. *You could take the taser away from him now and he'd hardly even notice.*

But she didn't move.

'Of course, we combed the woods and we managed to find a few traces of her, but not the good kind. We found her underwear dumped in that well behind the old cottage. A little way north from there, we found more traces of her blood on a bridge over the river. Not her body, though. He'd thrown that over the viaduct into the water. It washed up on the beach the next evening.'

*I'm familiar with that river, DS Price,* she remembered.

*It's very deep and very fast, and it flows straight into the sea a little way down the coast.*

'The map,' she realised.

'I was there when Colin made those crosses.' Barnes nodded. 'We were plotting various movements on that day. Trying to work out the killer's route. Which way he went. Which way he took her.'

'Looking for patterns.'

'Yes. Although we knew who it was.'

'You knew?'

'Oh yes. Charles Dennison. The block of flats by the park was where he lived. He never made any real secret of what he'd done, but he was very careful and very clever. There was never any proof, but we knew. Dennison had previous experience with children, and he enjoyed taunting your father afterwards. Knowing Colin hadn't stopped him only made him enjoy the whole thing more.'

'Christ,' she said.

'Dennison was the man we killed and dumped in the river. You will have been about five years old when all this happened.' Barnes looked at her. His eyes were bloodshot. 'You couldn't possibly have known how much it affected your father, but it really did. Very much. He felt he had betrayed the little girl, and I blamed myself for letting her down. For letting him down too, I suppose. For failing.'

Hannah tried to reconcile what Barnes was telling her with the memories she had of her father. In some ways, really, what she was hearing was much better than it could have been. Maybe it was as good as she could have hoped for.

'So you both . . . killed this man for revenge.'

'No.' Barnes said it firmly, shook his head. 'For *protection*.'

'What's that supposed to mean?'

'The year after she was killed, Dennison set his sights on another little girl. In her own way, she also came to your father for help. But this time we were ready. There was no way either

194

of us would let Dennison hurt anyone else. That's why we did it.'

'To protect this little girl?'

Barnes nodded, and putting it like that, he made it sound almost noble. But it wasn't the whole story, was it? There was more than one body in that river. Before she could remind Barnes of that inconvenient fact, he carried on.

'It haunts me, Hannah. You have no idea what it was like. And I know it haunted Colin too. Ultimately, it ended both our marriages. It's why your mother left. But despite everything, I've never regretted it. In fact, I only wish we'd done it a year earlier instead.'

Hannah's question fell away for a moment.

*It's why your mother left.*

Some way before the halfway point of the photograph album, her mother did indeed vanish from the pictures, just as she had from their lives. Hannah had only a bare handful of memories of the woman herself, and those were all of disapproval: blank stares and thin, difficult smiles. Eventually, she had moved away and started again with a new man, and Hannah had worked hard over the years to forgive the woman for leaving. She'd succeeded, but never felt any kind of need to seek her out and see what type of new life she'd formed. The base thought was always *my mother just didn't love me enough*. Maybe it had even caused her to cling to her father harder.

Now Barnes was implying there was a different explanation: that her mother simply hadn't been able to live with the ghosts her father carried. The ghost of a dead little girl. The ghost of a man he'd murdered.

'What about the *second* body?'

Barnes laughed, but it was an empty noise.

'Robert Wiseman.'

'What?' She knew the name, of course. Wiseman wasn't exactly famous in Whitkirk, but most people had heard of his suicide. 'What did he have to do with any of this?'

'You've not read his book?'

She shook her head.

'No,' he said, 'of course you haven't. Well, this was years later. Wiseman found out what we'd done – or at least I thought he had at the time. That was what his book was about. It was painfully close to the truth. And he started talking about it. Investigating it more. He was putting all of us at risk.'

'Jesus Christ, Barnes.'

'I know.' He looked at her suddenly. 'It had nothing to do with Colin. It's important you know that, Hannah. He refused to get involved. He told me that if the truth came out, so be it. I did it. All by myself.'

She wanted to believe him. Looking at him, she thought it might be true. But even so. It didn't change what he, at least, had done. It didn't change the overall fucking mess they were in.

'To protect *yourself* this time,' she said. 'Not quite as fucking noble.'

'I did it to protect Colin.'

'Oh yeah, of course you did, Barnes.' She shook her head in disgust. 'Not because you didn't want to go to fucking jail, or anything like that.'

'I'll never go to jail, Hannah.'

'I wouldn't be so sure about that. And abducting me hasn't made that any less likely, has it?'

'Oh, this?' He looked at his hand, and seemed almost surprised to see the taser was still there. 'I just needed to make sure you listened to me. I needed to explain so that you didn't think badly of him. I know how much he meant to you, and he wouldn't have wanted you to—'

'Still protecting him, are you?'

'Is it so hard to believe I did it for Colin? That's why you've done what you have.'

'For God's sake, Barnes. It's not the same thing.'

'Isn't it?'

Hannah didn't reply. Anger was surging up inside her. Rather than getting out, running away, she suddenly wanted to attack him: pummel him. The only reason she didn't was because he already seemed so beaten, as though additional blows would just bounce off him, maybe even be welcomed.

'What about Christopher Dawson?' she said. 'Did you kill him too?'

'No.' He gave another hollow laugh. 'I have no idea what happened there.'

'You don't. Well, forgive me if I find that hard to believe.'

'I forgive you, Hannah. For more than you know.'

'Oh, what the fuck's that supposed to mean?'

'It means it's all going to come out now. The truth. All because of you.'

'I burned the map,' she reminded him. 'I burned the hammer.'

'That doesn't make any difference. Don't you see? Wiseman will be identified, and people will look into his life. They'll read his book again, where two policemen dump the body of a paedophile over a viaduct in a place that's obviously based on Whitkirk. They'll read the file on Charles Dennison and make the connection.' Barnes shook his head. 'Wiseman was a bastard. Don't you understand, Hannah? Even dead, he's going to reveal everything.'

'Shut up. Let me think.'

'I've spent the last two days thinking. There's no way to stop it. The entire file on Dennison is damning. He'd made complaints. Colin and I were actually questioned when he disappeared. It's all there, and more. You don't understand yet, but you will. Christ, I was even investigating officer for Wiseman's suicide. I made sure I was.'

Hannah started to say something but stopped. Because he was right, wasn't he? Certain things could possibly be made to disappear, but not identities, or published books, or entire files. And it was stupid to attempt it: the more you tried to cover up something that extensive, the more obvious it became.

*I was even investigating officer for Wiseman's suicide.*

The media would run with it, and everything would unfold. Hannah ran her fingers through her hair, her mind racing.

'So what are we going to do then?'

'I've been thinking,' Barnes said. 'And there is a way out of this. It won't protect you from the truth, won't protect me . . . but it might at least protect your father's reputation. And that's what we both want, isn't it?'

Hannah frowned. 'What do you mean? What do we need to do?'

'I'm sorry,' he said. 'Your father was a good man, and he always kept you safe. Now it's your turn to repay that – to help me repay it as well. You can keep his good name safe, but none of it is going to be easy for you.'

Hannah looked out through the windscreen. The elderly couple had turned around and were walking back towards their car.

'How?' she said.

Barnes nodded towards the old couple.

'When they're gone, you're going to get out of the car and go to the department. To the archives. You'll find the file for Charles Dennison.' He thought about it. 'And the file for a girl called "Charlotte Webb" as well. Those are the two you'll need.'

Beside them, the doors of the estate slammed shut.

'I can't make those files disappear, Barnes.'

'You're not going to. You're just going to read them.'

She shook her head. 'How is that meant to help anything?'

'You'll see. If you want a more selfish motivation, then there's always the fact that the photo I took of you last night is in Charles Dennison's file.'

'What?'

'I put it there first thing this morning: a photo of you at the scene where Dennison was suspected of murdering a little girl. That's going to be hard to explain, isn't it? And Dennison is registered as a missing person, so I'm guessing that file will be making its way upstairs very soon.'

Hannah didn't reply. *You bastard*.

Barnes smiled ruefully, reading the expression on her face.

Beside them, the engine of the estate rattled into life. There was a scratch of gravel as it pulled out.

'I'm sorry.' Barnes's gaze tracked the vehicle as it passed in front of them. 'I needed to make sure you did what I wanted you to. You'll understand when you read the details. It's not going to be easy though.'

'Barnes—'

'But you'll face up to it.' He stared at her. 'You'll do it for him, and you'll do it for yourself.'

'And what are *you* going to do?'

He took a deep breath. 'There's one last thing that needs to be taken care of. Now get out, Hannah.'

*You bastard*, she thought again. Barnes had dropped her in the shit and was forcing her to make a decision. Attempt to take him in – turn him, her father and herself over to the law – or run. Try to get to that photograph before anyone saw it. Read the two files, whatever that was supposed to achieve. And whichever route she took, there would be no going back.

Barnes gestured with the taser.

'Go on,' he said gently. 'You'd better be quick.'

And after a long moment of silence, in which they did nothing but stare at each other, Hannah made her decision, got out of the car, and began to run.

# Chapter Twenty-Two

At least my father's road map had turned out to be useful.

The small village of Fenton was almost indistinguishable from the other little hamlets dotted along the coast here: places so nondescript they barely warranted a name. Fenton had a neatly mown village green, with houses around three sides, and a few shops along the road by the cliff-edge. A series of stone steps wound down, presumably to the beach. Today, the whole place was almost deathly quiet and still. I parked up by one corner of the central square, outside an unassuming two-storey cottage, and then sat in the car for a few minutes.

What the hell was I going to say to this woman?

After leaving the café in Whitkirk, I hadn't been sure what to do next, but Barbara Phillips's words had stayed with me. *He stole a lot of real people and places. In some cases he barely made an effort to conceal them.* Of course, she thought that applied only to the strand of the story involving Charles Dennison, but I knew better. I'd got to thinking – might there be anything else there, hiding obviously between the lines?

So I'd gone back to the hotel and flicked through the book, looking at individual characters, and eventually something caught my eye in the chapter on the foster home run by Mrs Fitzgerald.

*Out back, the garden ends where the cliff-edge allows it to. One day, erosion will take this house from her.*

I'd stared at those words for a while. That seemed a strange detail to include; it had no obvious bearing on the story. So I'd booted up my laptop and googled various combinations of 'foster home', 'Whitkirk' and 'erosion', wondering just how little effort Wiseman had really gone to, hoping it wasn't much at all.

It turned out he'd barely even changed her name.

A children's home had been run near Whitkirk by a lady called Denise Fitzwilliam in the seventies and eighties. It was long gone now: one of several properties lost from the clifftop as the sea knocked the legs out from below the land. When the home closed, Denise Fitzwilliam had been forced to rely mainly on savings and charity donations, and had moved here, to what, at the time, was a cheap house in a run-down village.

A sad story, especially for the caring and selfless woman presented in the book, but, as it turned out, the intervening years had been kind to her. Fenton had tidied itself up and grown at least slightly more desirable in the time since. These days, the little two-up two-down she owned was probably worth twice what she'd paid for it. It was almost as though, after a lifetime spent looking after others, someone had looked down and decided she probably deserved a little better than what she'd received.

And now I was here to confront her with the past.

*Just play it by ear, Neil.*

*See what happens.*

I got out of the car. In the small, flagged-over area at the front of her house, there was evidence of care still being taken. A row of small trees were growing in pots down one side, and there were two baskets of brightly coloured flowers hanging from struts in the wall. Flat on one window sill, a box was thick with herbs. The flagstones themselves were freshly swept, still bearing giant fingerprint swishes from the wooden broom leaning against the wall by the door.

I knocked and waited.

Silence.

*Come on,* I thought. *Don't be out.*

I was just about to knock again when I heard a shuffle of movement from inside. It sounded awkward, as though whoever was in there was having some trouble, but still determinedly making their way.

When the door opened, it was by a woman in her seventies, with a mass of grey, frizzy hair. She was overweight, her body packed tightly into a threadbare red jumper and old black tracksuit bottoms, and her cheeks were plump and red. Her eyes, almost lost above them, were milky. One hand clung to a rail that had been screwed onto the wall inside; the other clutched the top of a walking stick, enfolding the nub of it almost totally.

I'd never seen her before but I recognised her immediately.

*Mrs Fitzgerald.*

It was the strangest sensation – a fiction come to life in front of me – and, for a moment, all I could do was stare at her. It didn't help that the next thing she did was smile and nod to herself.

Because somehow, she had recognised me too.

'Welcome home, my son,' she said. 'Welcome home.'


Mrs Fitzwilliam ushered me through into the lounge at the back of the house. It was a small room with exposed wooden beams across the ceiling and a cheap carpet on the floor, worn down to a meagre grey thatch along the obvious, shuffling routes she took. The bay window looked out onto a pleasant back garden, full of white afternoon light. There was an old two-seater settee in the alcove there. To the other side, an armchair and a wooden cabinet with glass doors, and . . .

'Here we are,' Mrs Fitzwilliam said.

But I stopped in the doorway for a second, staring around the room in disbelief. Almost every available surface was covered with photographs. The sheer number of them was almost overwhelming. There were several crammed onto the mantel-piece above the electric fire, but it was the ones covering the walls that really caught my eye. Forty, fifty, too many to count at a glance.

From what I could see, they all showed Mrs Fitzwilliam with children. Sometimes in groups; sometimes just the two of them. Children she'd cared for, I guessed – her extended family. All gone now, like the original home, but in her retirement she had surrounded herself with their images and memories. The collection as a whole must have spanned decades.

'You have that.'

She was motioning at the settee. I crossed the room and sat down there, then watched as she eased down carefully into the armchair opposite, chuckling to herself.

'And now you're going to have to excuse me,' she said. 'Who are you, dear?'

'Sorry?'

'Which one are you? You remember my eyes, don't you – how bad they were. Don't you worry, though. I'm still sharp. But it means you'll have to remind me who you are.'

That was when it clicked. *Welcome home, my son.* She hadn't recognised me at the front door at all. Between my reaction and her bad eyesight, she'd just made an assumption. She thought I was a boy she'd once cared for. A child who'd come home, not to the place where he'd grown up, but to the woman who helped raise him.

For a second, I wondered if that was that something I could play on. I needed her to trust me, after all, and given how accurate Wiseman's description of her was, maybe I knew enough from *The Black Flower* to carry off the deception. Wiseman had threaded real details throughout his book. Perhaps it was possible to pull them out again.

Except . . . I wasn't like him. Looking around the room now at all those photographs, I didn't think I'd have the heart to carry it off, even if I did have the knowledge.

'I'm sorry, Mrs Fitzwilliam,' I said. 'We've never met.'

'Oh.'

Her free hand clutched slightly at the arm of the chair, close to where she'd rested her cane.

'I'm sorry,' I said again.

'No, no. It's my mistake. That just tends to be the only people who come to see me now. The boys and the girls. I just thought—'

'I know,' I said. 'I didn't mean to mislead you.'

'No matter. Who are you then, and what can I do for you?'

'My name's Neil Dawson.' I still hadn't really decided what I was going to say, so I just took a deep breath and came out with it. 'I wanted to ask you about a man called Robert Wiseman. Have you ever heard of him?'

She pursed her lips, considering it, and then shook her head.

'I don't remember if I have. When would this have been?'

'He wouldn't have been one of your children,' I said. 'Actually, he was a writer. A novelist. Years ago, he wrote a book called *The Black Flower*.'

I gave her a chance to recognise the title, but she just looked blank.

'You've never heard of it?'

'No, I don't think so. What is it?'

'A crime novel,' I said. 'Well, maybe more horror than crime.'

'Oh no, no.' The shake of the head was much more definite this time, the matter clearly settled by that detail alone. 'Those aren't the kind of books I read. There's *far* too much horror in real life to waste time reading about it in stories as well.'

'I know what you mean.'

And I believed her too. At the same time, though, Wiseman *must* have spoken to her at some point, because his description was simply too vivid to have come about any other way. Which meant that he hadn't told her his name or his real intentions when they'd met.

'What does it have to do with me?' she said.

'In one part of the book, he writes about a children's home. It's very specific. I think he based it on the one you used to run.'

'I see. Well, that feels like a very long time ago now.'

'Yes.' I leaned forward. 'It's not really the home itself I'm interested in. It's actually one of the children who stayed there. A girl you used to look after.'

Mrs Fitzwilliam didn't reply, but I sensed the slightest of hardenings to her. After all this time, she was still protective of her charges.

Maybe I should have tried to bluff it after all.

'It will have been about thirty years ago,' I said. 'I'm not sure exactly. This girl would have been five or six years old. She was found on the promenade in Whitkirk, and all she had with her was a grown-woman's handbag, containing a flower.'

The more I spoke, the harder Mrs Fitzwilliam's expression became. It wasn't just protectiveness either.

*You know*, I thought.

*You know who I'm talking about.*

And so, despite the hardening, I felt a flash of hope. If she knew about this girl and what she'd gone through, she could corroborate her existence. Christ – maybe she even knew how to contact her.

I started to gabble.

'The little girl, she told a story about escaping from a farm, but nobody believed it. I know she was telling the truth though. I think her father was exactly the type of man she said he was.'

'I won't talk about my children.'

'I know you don't want to,' I said. 'And I know you probably shouldn't. But I really need to know about that girl.'

'No.' She shook her head firmly. 'No, you have to leave.'

'More than I can tell you.'

'I'm going to call the police, Mr Dawson.'

I closed my eyes and pictured Ally. Forced myself to continue.

'All right, then,' I said. 'Maybe you should. Because that man is still out there. And if someone doesn't find him in time, he's going to kill someone else.'

'I'm telling you to—'

'Not just a woman. A baby too.'

And at that, something inside me just crumpled. I was so tired, so scared for Ally. There was nothing left to say.

The silence that followed seemed to go on for a long time, and when I finally opened my eyes again Mrs Fitzwilliam was staring at me. Her face was grim. Her jaw working slightly. I couldn't read what she was thinking.

I held my hands out, palms up.

'Please help me. Please.'

After a moment longer, she sighed to herself. Then she eased out of her chair and began to follow one of the worn grey trails to the doorway.

'Wait here,' she said.

# Chapter Twenty-Three

'You were wrong before.'

Mrs Fitzwilliam walked back into the lounge, half bent over, pushing a small trolley. The cups on it rattled against the teapot, letting off small porcelain clinks. She had been in the kitchen for five minutes, and I was now back sitting where she'd left me. In her absence, I'd stood up and walked quietly around the room, checking the photographs. It hadn't helped. There were so many children, and almost any of the girls might have grown into the woman photographed at the Carnegie Crime Festival.

'Wrong about what?' I asked.

'You told me that nobody believed her.' She began pouring my tea. 'The truth is that not many people even got to hear her story. Certainly not the media.'

She passed me the cup.

'Thank you.' I thought about Wiseman again. If the full story had never been reported then he *must* have heard the details from someone else. 'I've spoken to one journalist who had no idea she'd ever existed. Was it not in the press?'

'There was an appeal, an attempt to trace the parents, but the exact details of what she told the police were never circulated.' Mrs Fitzwilliam began pouring her own drink. 'It wouldn't have registered in the brains of most journalists. It's even worse these days. They just want something horrible to sell their newspapers with, which means they're only interested in children who are missing or worse.' She gestured around the walls. 'They're never interested in the ones who are still here and need help.'

'No,' I said. 'You're right.' Mrs Fitzwilliam was shuffling back across to her chair. 'You believed the girl, though? What she said?'

'Oh yes.' She eased herself down, delicately balancing the cup and saucer in her hand. 'It was a horrific story, but I can tell you with absolute certainty that she wasn't lying. You develop a nose for these things over the years. However, that isn't the point.'

'The point?'

'A girl of that age shouldn't have such pictures in her head. A normal little girl from a good home wouldn't be able to tell the story that she did. Even if she was making it up, I ask you: where did those ideas come from?'

'A policeman believed her too.'

'Yes.'

'He came to see her?'

Mrs Fitzwilliam nodded. 'I remember him vaguely. He was a good man, from what I can recall. He seemed to care very deeply about children.'

*Yeah*, I thought. *Very deeply*. So deeply that he'd murdered a child-killer and dumped his body in a river. Wiseman too. And God only knew what else.

'I have no wish to know, by the way.' Mrs Fitzwilliam sipped from her cup. 'What you mentioned before. About her father and someone else being missing. I'll tell you what I can, but I want no more involvement, and that's final. It's better that way.'

'Better?'

'Safer.'

That word kept coming up, didn't it? *Safer*. There was something to it: the more I learned, the more this girl's story did feel dangerous. Of all the people who had come into contact with it, so many had found themselves entangled in it. Threads of real life made into fiction. They seemed to reach back out again and wrap around you. Pull you into it.

Mrs Fitzwilliam balanced the cup and saucer on the arm of the chair, the saucer resting exactly in place.

She said, 'And as much as I looked after her, the same as I would have done for anyone, I was glad when she finally left. It shames me to admit that, but it's true.'

'That's not shameful,' I said. 'I can understand that, given the man who was out there looking for her.'

'It wasn't just about him. We were protected, after all. That old address was private, unlisted. There was no way he could find us, and the police made sure we were safe.'

'So what was it?'

She grimaced. 'It was that she *talked*. She kept telling her story, over and over. It was bad enough hearing it once. The other children didn't need to hear it at all. Do you want to see her?'

'Yes,' I said immediately.

'She's in the middle photo on the mantelpiece.'

I stood up and put my cup and saucer on the trolley, then walked across. I'd already looked at this picture when she was out of the room, and nothing about it had struck me in particular. But as I lifted it up, I felt a jolt. She was obvious now that I knew she was there.

Mrs Fitzwilliam said, 'That's her on the right.'

I nodded; I could tell. In addition to a much younger version of the old lady sitting across from me, there were three children in the picture: two girls and a boy. The girl on the right was small, with slightly straggly hair, and she was staring straight into the camera with a *furious* expression on her face. The sheer intensity in her eyes might as well have knocked the other children out of the shot altogether.

I said, 'How long did she stay with you for?'

'Nearly five months. Longer than most, but the circumstances were unusual. With most children, they're either taken away from their family, or the parents have died. It's rare in this day and age to get an abandoned child. And so obviously, the police wanted to track down the family, regardless of whether she was telling the truth about them or not. Either way, they needed to find them.'

'But nobody came forward?'

'No. Never.'

'And what happened to her?'

'She was adopted,' Mrs Fitzwilliam said. 'They found a permanent home for her.'

'Do you know where?'

She shook her head, and my heart fell slightly.

'No. I never did. It was always better not to, for my sake, and they were especially careful with Charlotte, due to her background.'

*Charlotte.* So Wiseman hadn't even been bothered enough to give her a new name. I guessed he would have been keen to keep the *Charlotte's Web* detail, and maybe he'd thought the case was obscure enough for using the name not to matter. Presumably the adult Charlotte was also called something else now anyway. But still.

I shook my head, almost missing the next thing Mrs Fitzwilliam said.

'And she's never talked about it.'

I put the photo back down. I was going to ask something else when I realised what I'd just heard.

'You've seen her since then?'

'Yes.' Mrs Fitzwilliam grimaced again. 'Every year.'

I took a step towards her. The hope was fluttering again.

'You've seen her *every year*?'

'Yes. My children often come back to see me. And I might be retired now, but that doesn't mean I'll ever turn one of them away.' She shook her head sadly. 'Not even her.'

It felt like my mind had gone blank, the individual thoughts obscured by the sheer number of them competing for attention.

Almost on autopilot, I rummaged in my pocket, searching for the photograph I'd printed from the Carnegie Crime Festival. I was still unfolding it as I passed it to her.

'Is this her? Sitting between the men?'

'Let me see.'

She peered at it, screwing her damaged eyes up so tightly they almost disappeared entirely. And then she nodded.

'Yes. She's older now, but that's her.'

'Are you sure?'

'I'm quite sure. It's one thing not to remember every child. It's another not to recognise a grown woman.' She looked up at me. 'Especially this one.'

Time was slowing down. I took the sheet from her and then it felt like I was backing away across the room. I sat down carefully, trying to think.

'When did you last see her?'

'A week or so ago. Always the same. Every year.'

Always the same. I glanced down at the photograph of the ethereal woman – Charlotte – sitting between my father and Robert Wiseman. Taken at the Carnegie Crime Festival, which had been held every September, up until 2003. This picture was from September 1989. Wiseman had disappeared in September. My father had booked into The Southerton in September.

Finally, I understood.

'She comes home,' I said.

'Yes.' Mrs Fitzwilliam nodded once, then took a sip of her tea. 'She comes home. To mark her birthday. The only one she's ever had.'

I closed my eyes.

All those years ago, the little girl had appeared on the promenade in September. As an adult, she had returned on the anniversary of that date, to mark the moment at which her real life had begun. That was the month she'd encountered Wiseman and my father. That was why Wiseman had come back here in September, researching his follow-up. He'd been looking for her in the only place and at the only time he knew she would appear, as regular as a haunting. And that was how my father had found her too. Not by detective work. Simply by knowing where she would be on one particular date.

Which meant that I had no chance of tracking her down now.

I was about to say something – I don't know what – when I felt a vibration against my hip.

And then another.

My phone was ringing. I scrabbled in my pocket.

Ally Mobile

*I'll give you a couple of days. After that, she's mine for ever.*

I stared at the screen for a moment. My time was up, wasn't it? And it meant the old man hadn't thrown Ally's phone in the water after all; he'd just turned it off. Perhaps I could have . . .

But that chance was gone now.

I closed my eyes for a moment, then pressed accept and held it up to my ear.

'I'm here,' I said.

But it was a woman's voice that answered me.

# Chapter Twenty-Four

Back at the department, Hannah had to go underground. The files from before the early 1980s were all hard copy, and archived in a large room in the basement of the building. It was possible to call up the references and tags from one of the computers upstairs, but she didn't want to risk visiting her office and encountering any of her colleagues. For now, she was off the grid.

Maybe she would be for ever after this.

*Some things are more important than the law, aren't they?*

Barnes had been right. Even if she hadn't openly acknowledged it to herself, Hannah had been moving away from her profession at a tangent ever since finding the map and the hammer, and the events of the past few days had taken her fully into the area of misconduct. She'd lied, she'd withheld evidence then destroyed it, and none of it had really troubled her, because the truth about her father had been far more important. This extra step right now probably couldn't be taken back, but it was an entirely natural one along a route she'd already begun.

*There is a way out of this. It won't protect you from the truth, won't protect me . . . but it might at least protect your father's reputation.*

She had no idea how that was supposed to happen, but Barnes had seemed sure. For now, she had no choice but to trust him. And to find that photograph, assuming he was telling the truth about it.

The desk sergeant raised an eyebrow when she started talking: he was more used to being handed reference numbers and conducting his business in relative silence, and he seemed to resent having to use his own computer system for searching.

As he keyed in the details Hannah gave him, she looked around. It was the world's most dismal library down here: row after row of grey shelving units stretching away backwards into the gloom, all of them bristling with documents, and all of those cataloguing crimes. Some large, some small, and almost all of them forgotten now. At night, she imagined the room made a rustling noise like beetles. For now, the only sounds were the squeak of a trolley, echoing back from somewhere between the aisles, and the clattering of the desk sergeant's key strokes.

'Charles Dennison is ticked,' he said. 'So's Robert Wiseman. Either they're in the pile or they're due to be in the pile.'

He nodded at the stacks of files gradually accumulating on the desk beside him: the missing person reports being prepared for transit upstairs.

At least she'd got here in time.

'They're going to my office,' Hannah said. 'Can you either search through them for me, or else prioritise the names I've given you and make sure they get pulled out next?'

The desk sergeant pulled a face, but nodded.

'Good,' she said. 'In the meantime, see if there's a file for Charlotte Webb.'

'As in the book?'

'What book?' She thought of Wiseman for a moment, but then realised what he was referring to. 'Oh. I don't know. Double "b", I'm guessing.'

As his fingers clittered over the keys, Hannah remembered what else Barnes had said: *it's not going to be easy for you.*

*Why?* she thought.

After everything else he'd told her, what could be worse?

'Charlotte Webb,' the desk sergeant said. 'Double "b".'

'You've found her.'

'Indeed I have.' He tinged the bell on his desk, then shouted off into the aisles. 'Come on, Igor. Break off for a minute. Got a rescue mission for you.'

Five minutes later, Hannah was sitting at a battered old workbench that ran down one wall of the entire basement. It looked like something you'd see in the science lab of a poor secondary school: gnarled and dark, more tree still than furniture. There were plug sockets dotted along, with an angle-poised lamp positioned between each. She flicked hers on, and tried to ignore the echoing clatter of the trolley somewhere behind her.

WEBB, CHARLOTTE.

Hannah's fingers seemed to tingle slightly as she opened the file. The first sheet inside was a record of the interview data.

**Date of Interview:**
7 September 1977

**Location:**
Whitkirk Police Department

**Attending Officers:**
DS Graham Barnes
DS Colin Price

**Others:**
Helen Daniels, Duty Child Care Supervision Officer

**Interviewee:**
Name not given [*Charlotte Webb*]

Beneath this, there were dotted lines where, under normal circumstances, the address, phone number and birth-date of the interviewee would have been filled in, along with any reference numbers and details of associated cases. On this form, however, someone had drawn a diagonal line through those, crossing them out. Her father, she assumed, as it was his handwriting that had been added in to the side.

The subject of this interview is an unknown female, approximately five or six years of age. She was found, wandering alone, on the date of 07/09/77, by DS Colin Price, after he was alerted by a concerned member of the public. DS Price located the subject on the promenade of Main Street, opposite Lot-82, currently occupied by the Fisherman's Drift cafeteria.

Subject is four-feet-two-inches tall and has blue eyes [see attached]. At time of finding, subject had unkempt blonde-coloured hair and was dressed in old-fashioned clothes, and was carrying an adult handbag containing a pressed flower [see attached].

When DS Price approached her, subject was uncommunicative. She was unable to give her own name, those of her parents, an address, or details of how she arrived at said location. Upon mention of parents, subject became distressed.

Interview takes place in Room 3.8. In accordance with section 4 (1967), interview attended by Dr Helen Daniels.

Note: Interview 'informal' in structure: gentle non-specific questioning; toys; breaks; etc. Summary follows. Audiotape included. Statement [see attached] agreed by attending officers and Dr Daniels as accurate, and signed accordingly.

Hannah put that sheet to one side and turned to the next.

And shivered a little. This was actually a blank page with two photographs paperclipped to the side. They were in colour, but noticeably aged. She was used to digital prints these days, and these seemed archaic and quaint, like old holiday snaps. But it was the way they were laid out that disturbed her – just like the photographs in her father's album.

*But then, he probably did this too.*

The top one was a relatively informal shot, taken shortly after the then-unnamed Charlotte Webb's arrival at the police station. She was wearing a dirty, blue-and-white checked dress, and her hair was straggly and wild, half knotted into dread-locks. Hannah's first impression was that the girl must have been sleeping rough – and possibly for a long time – but on closer inspection, her appearance wasn't quite that of a run-away or a homeless child. It was more like a little girl who'd not been taken care of, and who'd been dressed thoughtlessly in whatever clothes could be scavenged. Her father's introductory comments – *old-fashioned clothes* – didn't go far enough. The dress in particular simply looked odd. It was out of time, like an outfit a child might wear in some Victorian etching.

'Charlotte' had been staring directly into the camera when the photo was taken, and her expression was hard to decipher. It wasn't sullen, exactly, but it was certainly wary and untrusting, like a nervous animal that was ready to dart off if required, or else defend itself with tooth and claw if escape wasn't an option.

*Fierce little thing.*

The bottom photograph was more revealing because it had been actively staged. It was a portrait image of Charlotte's head, taken from the shoulders up. Clearly posed and obviously captured a few days later. By the time this picture had been taken, her face had been cleaned and her hair washed, the tangles straightened out. However, the biggest difference was in her expression, where that initial wariness had visibly softened. It wasn't gone entirely; the camera captured a flash of it in her eyes. But this fist of a girl had already begun to unclench slightly.

Hannah had a thought. Could this be the woman from the CCTV footage with Dawson? There was still no obvious con-nection between the cases, but, calculating it in her head, the age seemed approximately right.

Hannah squinted at the photo. There was no way of telling, though. Despite the ferocity – the wildness to her – the girl was very young, still growing into her features. If Hannah passed her now, as an adult on the street, she wouldn't be confident of recognising her. And the woman in the footage with Christopher Dawson had been so far away and indistinct that the same could well be true of her.

Hannah turned the page. Another two photographs were clipped to the side of this sheet. The top one showed the handbag. The one below showed a pressed flower.

A black flower.

Something in Hannah's chest tightened.

That wasn't right. That couldn't be right.

A *coincidence*. It had to be. The human brain looks for patterns, and that was all this was. Just sheer coincidence.

It didn't have anything to do with the story her father used to read to her. The one she'd been looking for on the day she'd felt afraid and ended up searching in the attic, finding not that book but a map and a hammer instead.

And yet, as she stared at the photograph, it felt like the shelves behind her were slowly receding into the distance, the noise of the trolley disappearing, until there was only her and the flower and the throb of her pulse. She just sat there, unsure what to do. Unsure whether she was capable of doing anything at all, never mind turning the page.

*Do it, Hannah. Find out.*

*You can do anything.*

The thought came with an urgency that shocked her back into the real world. She recognised her father's voice, and with it the determination and resolve she'd inherited from him, just as surely as her looks, her blood. So she turned the page, found the interview transcript and started to read.

And it wasn't a coincidence.

Even if it had to be, it wasn't.

Q: Can you tell us how you got to the place we talked about? Outside the café on Main Street?

A: I ran away from my daddy and my brother. We were having an argument on the tram and I stood up and ran away and jumped off.

Q: What was the argument about?

A: I don't know. I was just unhappy. I've been unhappy for ever. My daddy and brother do lots of things I don't like. They hurt me. My daddy hurts me, and he makes my brother hurt me too.

Q: Hurt you in what way?

A: Not like they hurt the others. But we sleep in the barn, and they hit me, and sometimes I don't have any food.

Q: When does that happen?

A: When I break the eggs or spill the milk. Or if I don't clean up the stalls properly, because you have to sweep them just right or else the patterns end up wrong. If I don't do things properly my daddy gets angry.

Q: Do they hurt you in other ways?
   [No answer given]

Q: What about your mother?

A: She's sad all the time because she's unhappy too but I still like being with her. My daddy brings lots of books home, and she reads the stories to me and tells me everything will be okay.

Q: Was she there on the tram when you had the argument?

A: Yes. She was proud of me because I did what she wanted to.

Q: She wanted to jump off the tram too?

A: [Emphatic nodding] Yes. I saw her through the window as it pulled away and she looked scared but I think she was very proud of me.

Q: I'm sure she was. She should be. You're a very brave little girl, aren't you?
[No answer given]

Q: Can you tell me about your home? It's a farm. Is that right?
A: [More animated] Yes. There is a house and lots and lots of fields. We have cows and sheep and people and chickens. And pigs too.

Q: You have people?
A: Yes.

Q: You look after them all?
A: Sort of. I do the milking, the washing and the cleaning. But I'm not allowed to do the killing and the changing. Daddy does that, and my brother will when he's older.

Q: 'The changing'? What do you mean by that?
A: [She has trouble explaining this] It's like I have all my eggs already. Everything goes on and on, and nothing dies really. Things just change from one thing to another. That's what my daddy's experiments are to do with, but I don't like them. Like with Jane. I don't like what happened to her.

Q: What happened to her? Can you tell us?
A: Daddy put her under the house.

Q: And you didn't like that?
A: No. He says it makes no difference, but it *does*. Because they stop talking and playing. I don't notice it so much with the cows or the pigs, but the people are different, because the change seems to take things away that I like. Jane doesn't talk to me any more and I miss her.

Q: You said that the flower you had with you was Jane.
A: It's Jane after she changed. After she stopped talking to me.

Q: Can you describe Jane?

A: She was like her. [Motions to Dr Daniels; this seems to indicate 'grown-up' rather than an exact physical description].

Q: What did you talk about?

A: We talked about . . . she told me it was okay. She used to say she would get out of there and make me safe. A lot of the time when I wasn't under the house she screamed and cried, and it made the floor hum. But when I was down there she told me she loved me and that I should . . . I don't know.

Q: Do you think Jane was proud when you jumped off the tram?

A: Yes. [Emphatic nod] I think she still is, even though she can't say so any more. She's still alive, but in a different form now. But I liked Jane better before.

Q: Before?

A: Before daddy turned her into a flower.

'Here you go.'

Hannah jumped as a file landed next to her with a *whap* on the desk.

'What?'

The desk sergeant was already walking away.

'First one,' he said. 'Dennison.'

Hannah glanced at the brown file and saw the name written down the side in black marker. DENNISON, CHARLES. But she was too distracted to give it her attention right now. She kept looking at the WEBB file instead. Staring down at it, staring through it. As though an explosion had gone off in a world skewed just centimetres from this one.

She remembered her favourite story as a child. It was about a girl growing up on a terrible farm, treated as little more than a slave by her cruel father and brother. The farm was drab and colourless, and all the flowers that grew there were black. One day the starving girl stole an apple from the tree, and her father was so angry that he buried her alive in the woods and left her there. But a kind stranger found her. He saw black flowers growing in the shape of a little girl and rescued her from the grave, then took her away to a place where the flowers were all brightly coloured, and where she would always be safe.

*Not a coincidence.*

But – what was it then?

Either this 'Charlotte' had read the same book and concocted a story based on it, or else . . .

Or else it had never been a real book at all.

Hannah closed her eyes and tried to picture it, the solid object in her hands – or even in her father's, him reading it to her. Tried desperately. But she couldn't. If somebody had asked her before now, she would have been adamant it was illustrated, because she had images in her head to go along with the words. Now she wondered. Were they images she'd seen on a page, or had she conjured them up in her mind, listening to the words?

There was no way of knowing.

Hannah leaned her elbows on the desk and rubbed her fingertips over her forehead, trying to clear her head, trying to *think*.

What if there had never been a real book at all? It meant that Charlotte's account was true, and the story had only ever been a creation of her father's. It meant he'd taken the horrors of this interview, fashioned them into a comforting narrative and recounted it to his daughter, over and over again. Why would he have done that?

Rather than rubbing, she realised the fingertips were now *jabbing* at her forehead: pecking like birds. She opened her eyes and made them stop.

Then turned the folder back a few pages, to the two photographs of Charlotte: the fierce little girl and the one who was relaxing slightly. Looking down at them, Hannah felt something crawling inside her. An idea.

If it was possible her father had taken the truth in this file and turned it into a story, one he'd repeated so many times she'd believed it was fiction . . . was it possible he'd also done the opposite? Taken a fiction and repeated it to her, made her repeat it to herself, so many times that she'd come to believe it was actually true?

*You are Hannah Price, daughter of DS Colin Price.*

That couldn't be the case, though.

It didn't make sense.

DENNISON, CHARLES.

Hands trembling, Hannah slid the Webb documents to one side and opened the other file. The photograph of her was on top – Barnes really had done that, after all. She slipped it out and folded it into her pocket.

The first bundle of sheets was a summary of the investigation into Charles Dennison's disappearance: a list of people interviewed; statements gathered. Scanning down, Hannah saw her father's name. Barnes's too. They were both mentioned numerous times, and the next stapled section revealed why: complaints from Dennison himself, written in large and childish handwriting. Accusations of harassment against DS Colin Price. There were several, each with a report of action taken stapled to the back. Her father had been officially reprimanded. *Christ.* Reading through, it looked like he'd stalked the man incessantly, obsessively hounding him. Barnes had been right. If anyone read these, the connection would be obvious.

What she still didn't understand was how that could be stopped.

She put those reports to one side, coming to the last main bundle in the file. This was much thicker than all the others combined, so she knew this must be it: the investigation in connection to the girl Dennison was suspected of murdering. In fact, the reference number was right there at the bottom of the page . . .

Hannah stopped.

*It's a story about a little girl*, she remembered.

*This little girl told your father a man had been following her.*

She didn't move at all. Just stared down at the sheet of paper in front of her.

*Your father was very busy, so he didn't take what she said seriously.*

Inside her head, though, everything had begun whirling around – a storm of words and memories – as the explosion landed, finally, in this world now.

*I was supposed to be looking after everyone. I wasn't paying close enough attention. We found her underwear dumped in that well. Not her body. It washed up on the beach the next evening.*

'Oh God,' Hannah said. Except the words didn't come out.

*Your father and I were friends back then. I was one of the first people to visit you all in hospital after the birth. Is it so hard to believe I did it for Colin?*

*Is it so hard to believe?*

Hannah stared at the reference number.

[PRI-1976a: homicide – Anna Price (aged 5)]

# Extract from *The Black Flower* by **Robert Wiseman**

Up close, Whitkirk Abbey looks even more ancient and weathered than it does from the seafront. As Pearson drives up towards it, the bare arches form odd shapes and angles against each other. They have been blackened by time, so that the whole structure resembles the scorched ribcage of a giant, set on fire on top of the cliff.

There is a car park just past the abbey. Pearson pulls in and parks up next to a battered old Ford. An elderly couple is standing over by the fence at the edge of the cliff, wrapped tightly in raincoats, watching the boats out at sea down below. The old man is mostly bald, with just a monk's crest of white hair round the back of his head, and has his hands clasped at the base of his spine, holding a pair of binoculars, the cord dangling to the backs of his knees. His wife, beside him, is visibly pear-shaped even in the coat. Her hair is grey-white and tousled into a damp whirl by the rain and wind, like a storm on a weather map. Standing side by side, they seem content in their silence.

The sight of them makes Pearson feel unbearably sad.

He will never have that now. Gloria left yesterday. She told him he had changed; that he had become a stranger to her. The truth is that he was never a good enough husband, and they had been growing apart for a long time, but he knows she's right, and that these last three months have been different.

Ever since what happened to Poole.

He thinks of it like that: *what happened to Poole*. As though it is something horrific that occurred by accident, which he was only a witness to. But even looking at it from such an oblique angle, the sight in his head is too much to cope with – yet he can't look away. He thought it would be easy to kill a man. In every sense, it was not.

These past weeks, he has become haunted. He is haunted by Poole's cawing mouth, and the bloody face that was no longer a face any more. Most of all, though, it is the old man's final gesture that bothers him: the fact that when he should have been dead he was not. Poole had no features left to speak of, but he still raised his arm in a futile gesture to protect the remains of his face. His body knew it was dead, but it continued to cling to life.

Sometimes, Pearson imagines him down there at the bottom of the river, still moving inside his sack like a foetus. Alive in a different sense now; inert, perhaps, but not without influence. In Pearson's nightmares, the old man poisons the water like a dead sheep in a mountain stream. Poole's essence spills down the river into the sea, and washes back with the current, crashing onto the rocks directly below him now. At the viaduct, the trees and flowers all grow twisted, and the next generation of birds caw more obscenely than the last, their cries more and more like those of a dying man.

It reminds him of Charlotte's story, about the dead becoming flowers.

The story that was not a story after all.

Pearson has a hip flask of spirits in the compartment of the car door. He unscrews the tight silver cap and swigs from it. The taste is strong and hot, and amplifies what he has already consumed. The back of his throat is clogged with alcohol.

He watches the ruins of the abbey through the rain pattering on the windscreen, gradually blurring the view. It isn't tourist weather; the elderly couple are the only ones braving the clifftop today. He hopes they will leave soon, so he can be alone.

Thoughts of Poole and the little girl lead inexorably to thoughts of Sullivan, who Pearson knows is far more haunted than he will ever be. Sullivan is different from him though, in that he seems to have an almost otherworldly ability to bear ghosts. Perhaps with the death of Anna Hanson on his conscience for over a year, he has simply had more practice at coping with guilt. But then Sullivan remains convinced Charlotte is still alive somewhere, and won't allow himself to fall down until he has found her and made her safe again.

Pearson believes she is dead. If she is alive, he imagines she is suffering so terribly it hardly bears thinking about. But he suspects she died not long after Poole, and is now having the same awful effect from her own shallow grave as his nightmares grant an old man in a river.

Pearson takes another swig, then screws the top back on.

The couple have finished staring out to sea. They turn and walk back across the car park, their boots crunching in the gravel, steps tentative with old age. The man gives Pearson a glance, but they are not unduly interested in him. The rain has picked up, and they are no doubt eager to leave.

He stares ahead, but hears the car door slam, and then the engine choking into life. Stones scatter beneath the tyres as the old Ford pulls out and away. And then Pearson is alone, except for the tap and patter of the rain and the ghosts in his head.

As he gets out of the car, the drizzle hits his face, and a cold wind blasts across his skin. The world is echoing slightly. Perhaps it's the alcohol, but his pulse seems to be racing around his body: thumping in his throat, then his temples, then the centre of his chest. The remains of the abbey tower overhead. It looks unreal there, standing starkly against the ice-cold grey sky.

He walks across to the barrier. The sea compresses and shrinks as it reaches the horizon in the distance. Directly below it is wild and ridged, throwing itself against the rocks and shattering into pieces, then trying again a moment later. It seems so far down that, like the horizon, his eyes can't focus on it.

Pearson takes a deep breath.

Yes, he is very different from Sullivan. He can't bear it any more. Killing a man really is something. It seems to him that the world knows everything that man would have done, had he lived, and mourns the spiderweb of cause and effect that has been yanked from it. And so the world takes some of you back to replace the parts it is missing.

There is one similarity between him and Sullivan, though: they have both been under scrutiny since Poole's disappearance. There are rumours and speculation. Naturally, given his obsessions with the man, Sullivan has borne the brunt of that.

So at least one good thing may come of this.

Pearson has written a note and left it folded neatly on the passenger seat of the car. It is a confession, but one that gives no clue as to where Poole's body might be found, and makes it clear that he acted alone that night. Without mentioning him directly, it is the best Pearson can do to absolve Sullivan from blame.

He leans on the barrier.

It is cold and wet beneath his hands. Rain stings his eyes.

So that is something, because he knows Sullivan will never give up looking for Charlotte if there is a chance she is still alive, and Pearson wishes him good luck with that. The least he can do is give his friend the time and space to be haunted.

His foot slips on the barrier as he clambers over. It is all slightly less graceful than he would have liked. He has time to think that, and then to feel suddenly cold and see the cliff-top silhouetted against the sky, receding upwards to a new horizon.

He has time for it to feel like flying.

# Part Three

# Chapter Twenty-Five

It was early evening, and the day was beginning to dim and die as I reached the hospital a few miles from Thornton.

The car park at Accident and Emergency was constructed in a circle, the parking spaces surrounding a central flower bed, and stemming off from it like petals. I pulled my car into the first empty bay I saw, then ran across through the shock of the cold evening air, through the sliding doors into the hospital's reception. The area had been transformed into a construction site: boxed off in the middle, with plastic chairs crammed in down the walls to either side. Vending machines were humming softly. The main reception desk was at the far end: a brightly lit cube of Perspex with a middle-aged woman reclining behind a desk.

'Excuse me,' I said. 'Which way is Ward fifty-seven?'

'That way.' She leaned forward, pointing with a biro down a hallway to the right. 'There's a passenger lift a few doors along. It's floor five, then follow the signs.'

'Thanks.'

The lift was easy enough to find, but I kept pressing the button, over and over, as it seemed to take an age to arrive. *Come on, come on.* Eventually the doors opened. Inside, the lift was little more than a small, steel box. The doors clanked shut, and the whole thing rattled alarmingly as it clambered slowly up to the fifth floor.

*Don't die*, I thought.

*Don't you dare fucking die.*

The lift doors opened and I stepped out. The ward was signposted to the left, and I found it a little way along, but had to ring the intercom and wait – again, for what felt like an age.

*Don't die, you bastard.*

When I'd answered the call from Ally's mobile, I'd found myself talking to a woman named Doctor Matheson. A few hours earlier, she explained, an ambulance had been called to attend to an old man on a bridge in the city centre of Thornton. Passers-by had seen him, obviously in severe distress, doubled over and clutching at his chest, and alerted emergency services. According to witnesses, the old man had been determinedly throwing things into the river below: fumbling in his pockets for wallets and keys. A couple of people intervened to stop him – to help him – and the old man had fought back, apparently confused, before finally collapsing and being rushed here. A major heart attack, Matheson told me. He was still alive, but in a critical condition.

They had no idea who he was. The one thing the old man hadn't had time to get rid of was a mobile phone buried deep in one of his coat pockets. Doctor Matheson had turned it on, checked the last number, and redialed it in the hope of making contact with a relative.

*Got you, you fucker.*

The door to Ward 57 buzzed for a few seconds, and then the lock disengaged. I pulled it open and walked down a corridor, round into an area divided up by blue curtains. There was a new reception desk here, and the women behind it were deep in conversation.

'Excuse me,' I said.

'Sorry.' One of them rotated on her chair. 'Can I help you there?'

'Doctor Matheson's expecting me. I'm here to see a patient that's been admitted.'

'Name?'

'I don't know. It's a heart attack, but the patient had no ID. He was found on a bridge in Thornton centre.'

'Oh yeah.'

The nurse craned her neck – *you're in my way* – and stared at the wall behind me. I glanced back to see a white board divided up in straight lines by permanent black marker pen. Names and notes were scrawled on the grid in green. Most of the cells were full, while the empty ones still had ghostly, half-wiped smears detailing the bed's previous residents.

'Room A3.' She pointed back the way I'd come. 'Round that corner there.'

'What, I just go in?'

'Yeah, it should be fine. Just be very quiet, as I think he's sleeping. I'll tell Doctor Matheson you're here.'

'Okay. Thanks.'

*You've got your own room then.*

I approached the door, feeling my pulse tapping in my temples. Was this really going to be him? Even after everything I'd read, everything I'd discovered, it was still hard to believe that such a person existed in real life.

But he did. And it had to be him because he had Ally's phone.

I opened the door and stepped into the room.

It was small and amber-lit. The main overhead light was turned off, but a wall-mounted block shone softly down on the bed and its occupant. With all the clutter of machinery, and the pastel blues and yellows of the wallpaper, it reminded me of a child's room. But the man lying asleep in the bed was far from that.

I paused for a moment, unsure what to do now I was here, with the old man in front of me. Then I closed the door quietly behind me and stepped across to the edge of the bed and looked down at him.

He was stick-thin beneath the covers, and almost bald aside from wisps of greasy grey hair at his temples. His eyes were closed but horribly prominent, as though a thin layer of skin had been draped over marbles, while the lower half of his face was obscured by a soft plastic mask, a tube connecting it to a cylinder that was bolted on the wall. His head was tilted back slightly on the pillow, so that his neck was exposed; the skin there was baggy and lined. His Adam's apple was solid as a knuckle; the tendons around it taut as cables.

He wasn't dead – that was obvious from the steady, pulsing lines of light tracing his heartbeat on the display beside the bed – but he looked closer to a corpse than a living man. Lying very still, his skin waxen and yellow.

He was also much smaller and more emaciated than I'd been imagining. Because of the book, I'd pictured someone strong and fearsome, but this man seemed feeble. Of course, anybody would look feeble in these circumstances, with their life supported solely by bags of solutions and tubes punched into their veins, but even so. It was hard to believe he was the monster I'd been reading about. He looked like . . . nothing.

*But that is what monsters look like*, I thought.

The same as everyone else.

My fists kept bunching: fingers stretching then clenching.

'Where is she?' I whispered.

One of his eyelids flickered. Just a little.

I took a step closer, about to repeat my question, and the door opened behind me. I stepped back, then turned to see a middle-aged woman dressed in pale-blue scrubs.

'Hello there.' She smiled and extended a hand.

I reached out and shook it.

'Doctor Matheson?'

'Yes. Thanks for coming – for getting here so quickly.'

'I didn't know how long he'd have.'

'Oh. Well, he's stable for the moment.' Matheson closed the door then stepped around me to look down at her patient. 'We won't be sure of the damage to his heart until we get the results of the blood tests, but in the meantime we've got him on painkillers and anti-clotting agents, and we're keeping him hydrated. Keeping an eye on him. Aren't we, fella?'

The last comment was directed almost affectionately at the old man. *Fella.* Matheson, of course, knew nothing about the kind of man her patient really was.

'You know him, I presume?'

I'd been thinking about this, how to handle it. I couldn't give him a false name, as I assumed the records were computerised, but given that he had hold of Ally's phone it was going to raise questions if I claimed not to know him at all. I was going to have to call the police now – obviously I was – but I didn't think Doctor Matheson was the first person to confide in and explain all this to.

'Sort of,' I said. 'He's my girlfriend's uncle. His first name's John, but I don't know his surname. The family's all split up. I've been trying to get hold of her, but she's not at home right now. And obviously, he had her mobile for some reason.'

'Does he have a history of dementia?'

I shook my head. 'Not that I'm aware of.'

'The reason I'm asking is because of his behaviour before the ambulance arrived. Throwing his things away. By all accounts, he seemed very confused and disorientated.'

Yes, I thought, that was how it would have looked to people: an old man acting strangely, not knowing what he was doing. But that wasn't what had really been happening, was it? No, caught out away from his home, and thinking he might be dying, he'd been trying to remove anything that might lead authorities to his door. So they wouldn't find his home and discover what was kept there.

Keeping his *family* safe.

'I don't know,' I said.

'Do you know what he was doing in Thornton?'

'No. Have you not been able to ask him anything?'

'He's only been semi-conscious. And not often.' She looked

235

back down at him. 'At the moment, I'm happier letting him rest and settle. I was just curious.'

I nodded: I was curious too. Not so much about *what* he'd been doing. The real question was *where* he'd come from to get to that bridge in the centre of Thornton. Did he live just a few miles away? Was it hundreds? It was frustrating to think the farm might be nearby, perhaps just minutes from where I was standing, and yet there was no way of discovering it. I might be so close to where Ally was being kept right now and never know. Or not know in time.

*Where did you come from?*

Something occurred to me.

'You said he threw everything in the river?'

'That's what I was told, yes.'

'Car keys?'

She thought about it.

'I don't know. Somebody mentioned keys. They might have been house keys. Why?'

'Just planning ahead.' I did my best to smile. 'Working out what we're going to have to do when he's back on his feet again.'

'Oh, of course. I get you.'

What I was actually thinking was whether there might be a vehicle parked up somewhere: a rusty, crimson van he'd been forced to abandon. Because if that could be found, maybe the police could trace the license plate. Get an address from it.

'Listen,' Matheson said. 'I need to do the rounds. It's fine for you to sit with him for a short time, if you like? Not for long though please.'

I nodded.

'Maybe I will, just for a little while. I'll chase up the surname too.'

She closed the door very gently behind her, and I was left alone with the old man.

Silence.

The only movement in the room was the display on the monitor, the beep as it registered his vital signs faltering on-wards. I watched the bony cage of his chest rise and fall under the blanket for a minute. Then I leaned down until my mouth was close to his ear and spoke quietly.

'Can you hear me?'

There was no response. Just the same steady breathing. The same undulating trails of light beside the bed.

'Where is she?' I said. 'Where did you come from?'

Again, no response. I stepped away.

Then took a deep breath and went downstairs to phone the police.

Outside, back in the car, I dialed the number I had for Hannah Price: the number for the investigation into the bodies found at the viaduct.

If I was going to talk to the police, it had to be her. For one thing, she was in charge of the investigation at the viaduct. If the murders of Dennison and Wiseman were coming to light, then it meant she *couldn't* have been involved in them originally – or else she'd surely have been trying to cover them up right now. She was also the easiest person to talk to, because she already knew at least some of what I was going to try to explain. How much, I'd find out shortly.

A woman answered.

'Whitkirk Police Department. How may I help?'

'I need to talk to DS Hannah Price please.'

'One moment.' There were ten seconds of silence on the line, and then: 'I'm sorry. DS Price isn't available at the moment.'

*Fuck.*

'Can you ask her to phone Neil Dawson back as soon as possible?'

'What's it regarding? It's possible that another officer can assist you.'

'No, I have to talk to her specifically.' I thought about it. I needed to get her attention, and there was one obvious way to do that. 'You can tell her it's in connection with the bodies of Charles Dennison and Robert Wiseman.'

'With Charles—?'

'Dennison,' I said. 'And Robert Wiseman. I'm driving back to Whitkirk now. Tell her to call me as soon as she can – on this number, my mobile. It's very important. Urgent. Have you got all that down?'

'Umm . . . yes, sir. I have. Can I just—'

I hung up.

Then picked up my father's road atlas from the passenger seat. *I'm driving back to Whitkirk now.* That was exactly what I was going to do, but the centre of Thornton was only a few miles from here, and it was more or less in the same direction as Whitkirk. Only the slightest of detours.

It would help my story a lot if I could find that fucking van.

My fingertip traced the roads, searching out the route I'd have to take – even though I knew, realistically, I had no chance of locating the vehicle once I got there. The old man might not have driven to Thornton at all, or he might not have used the van. Even if it was there, how the hell was I supposed to find it? He could have parked it anywhere in a town I'd never been to before.

Hopeless. But what else was I going to—

I saw something else, and my finger stopped moving.

Halfway between here and Thornton, where the map showed little but space and thin, empty lines for roads, my father had drawn a tiny cross on the page in black biro. It was almost impossible to see, which must have been how I'd missed it on the drive over, but it was there. Just beside a tiny village called Ellis.

*Ellis F??*

I stared down at the map, feeling cold, my heart tingling. Dad's calendar – the itinerary he'd marked on it. The first note had been 'Haggerty A', and then, on the day he was to travel to Whitkirk, he'd written 'Ellis F' – with two question marks afterwards, as though he wasn't sure whether it was worth going or not.

I'd presumed it was another appointment to see a person, the same as Haggerty, but as I looked down at the cross he'd drawn, right there in the open countryside, another idea began humming inside me. One that didn't necessarily make sense, but which wouldn't go away.

Ellis Farm?

# Chapter Twenty-Six

*Patterns*, Hannah thought.

It was so easy to be fooled into seeing them. A long time ago, her father had taught her some of the constellations in the night sky, and then told her the truth about them: that in reality the stars people grouped together were light years apart and had no actual relationship to each other. But our ancestors found patterns in the sky and named them after gods and animals and heroes. They named them after stories, or else made-up stories about them. And yet, even now, when we look up we see constellations, and believe they're real, because that's what we've been taught to see.

She'd made a mistake with her father's map. From what was found at the viaduct, she'd imagined it showed the location of bodies, but all she'd been doing was forming her own pattern from those crosses. In reality, it marked the distressing, final path a little girl – Anna Price – had taken one afternoon a long time ago. It was a record of her father's grief and anger and self-recrimination.

Hannah stood in his kitchen again now, slowly turning the pages of her treasured photograph album. She started at the beginning, with what she now knew was a picture of another girl entirely, cradled in Colin Price's arms, and worked her way through to the page that Barnes had stopped at earlier.

*You would have been five years old when all this happened.*

The little girl, riding her bicycle unaided for the first time, with her knitted red jumper and a face creased up with a huge smile. Her father in the background, equally delighted. The last photograph of Anna Price.

Feeling blank, Hannah turned the page.

The girl in the next photograph was older, but not by much: not enough to arouse suspicion. This girl had been caught sideways on, kneeling down in the lounge by the fireplace, dressed in jeans and a pale blue T-shirt. Her hair was the same colour. Her face – it was impossible to tell.

Hannah flicked through a few more pages, searching for a shot of herself facing the camera head-on. Page after page, there were none. Not until she reached her early teens, by which time it was pointless to compare faces and evaluate their likeness.

*He was a very clever man.*

Yes, Hannah realised now, he was. He'd been very careful in his construction of this album. Again, patterns. It looked like a straight line from the beginning to the end, one whole childhood, bookended by creaking leather covers, and there had never been any reason to question that because the lie inside was so well concealed. The edges of the ground where it was hidden had been smoothed over, so it was almost impossible to see the join.

She rubbed her face.

*I don't know who I am.*

The album showed an amalgam of two girls – and perhaps that was right, that she was a mixture of both. In some ways, she really was the little girl her father had loved so dearly in that first photograph, or at least she might as well have been. But she was also the grown woman who could look at death and violence and see it as matter of fact, just a progression, one thing transforming into another. Born as "Charlotte", then raised as Anna in all but name, and nearly even in that as well. Her father had told her stories as truths and truths as stories, and now she was an unweavable tapestry of both.

He had done so with good intentions. She kept telling herself that – that as well as healing himself, he had done it to heal her. He had taken the horrors of her childhood and hidden them away; kept her safe and changed her from a hurt and scared little girl into a woman who could do anything.

*You are DS Hannah Price. Daughter of DS Colin Price.*

Except she wasn't.

It wouldn't matter how many times she told herself that any more. Her father's words had been designed to make her feel safe and untouchable, but they were lies. She couldn't remember her early years on the farm right now: all that came to mind was the story he'd told her, and the familiar, now growing, feeling of dread and fear. But the story was a lie, and it wouldn't last. There was nothing to stop the dread taking over. Hannah Price's life was built on the foundations her father had laid, and those foundations had been destroyed.

She closed the album, leaned down on either side of it and rested her face in her hands.

And she began to collapse.


A little time later, her mobile rang. She ignored it. Shortly afterwards, it beeped to let her know she had voicemail, and this time she took it out and listened to the message.

'DS Price? This is Simon at the office. I've got the files up now, and . . . I don't know, maybe you're on your way in like you said, but if not can you give me a ring? It's about DCI Barnes. I really need a word.'

Beep.

Simon was one of her sergeants. She stared blankly at the phone for a few moments, unsure what to do. She didn't feel up to having a conversation about the case right now, but if it was about Barnes she should take the call. His words came back to her. *There's one last thing that needs to be taken care of.*

What had he done?

She hesitated for a moment longer, then called the office.

'Simon,' she said. 'It's me.'

'Hi there. Thanks for calling me back so quickly. This is . . . it's a bit of a weird one actually. Have you seen DCI Barnes today?'

'No.' The lie came easy. She had no idea if it would come back to haunt her. 'Why? What's "a weird one", Simon? Spare me the fuzzy talk.'

'Sorry, boss. It's just that a witness reported seeing someone fall from the clifftop earlier on. A possible jumper.'

Hannah went cold inside.

*There is a way out of this. It won't protect you from the truth, but it might at least protect your father's reputation.* Barnes's name was all over the file on Dennison too. He'd been questioned. He'd be a suspect.

*I'll never go to jail, Hannah.*

She forced herself to ask the natural question.

'What's that got to do with Barnes?'

'Well, his car is in the car park at the top.' The sergeant gave a nervous laugh, as though he couldn't quite believe the implications of what he was saying. 'It's locked up and everything, but it's just abandoned there. I've tried various numbers and he's not answering.'

*I needed to make sure you did what I wanted you to.*

Hannah closed her eyes. Barnes was going to take the responsibility, she realised. *Paying penance.* He'd told her everything he could bring himself to, and planted the photograph in the file to make sure she read the rest before anyone else did. He'd made sure she was prepared for what was to come. And then he'd done this.

*You'll understand when you read the details. It's not going to be easy though.*

*I'm sorry.*

She said, 'You've got the coastguard out?'

Simon had, but Hannah barely listened to his answer.

Where did this leave her, if Barnes really had done what she thought? Was it possible to save her father's reputation? Once the bodies were identified as Dennison and Wiseman, questions would get asked, and in the light of his suicide the answers would now point towards DCI Graham Barnes.

Hannah's real identity – or, at least, the murder of her father's real daughter – might be revealed when people put the details in the files together, but technically that was a separate issue. She hadn't committed a crime by being adopted, presuming that was what had happened, or by forgetting where she'd come from. Nobody had broken the law. Regardless, she could certainly lobby hard to keep it out of press announcements, and the force would close ranks to protect their own.

*Your father was a good man, and he always kept you safe.*

*Now it's your turn to repay that.*

Yes, she thought. Whatever he'd done, and whoever she had been once, Hannah Price probably owed him that much. There was the slightest of possibilities that she could weather all this. On the outside, at least.

'All right.' She opened her eyes. 'Let's try not to worry too much in the meantime. I'll be in shortly.'

'Okay. Oh, there's one other thing. I've had a message passed through from Neil Dawson.'

'Finally. And?'

'He's on his way back to Whitkirk and wants you to call him. Says it's urgent, apparently. About . . . Charles Dennison and Robert Wiseman? Those names mean anything to you?'

Hannah shook her head and didn't reply. *There it is.* Barnes had claimed he'd no idea if Christopher Dawson and the mysterious woman were connected to the older case. Obviously, somehow they were, and Neil Dawson had independently discovered the identities of the bodies at the viaduct. So she wasn't in the clear after all. So there it was: the unknown you didn't expect and never saw coming; the thing that trips you up and sends you sprawling on the ground.

'Boss?'

'Maybe,' she replied. 'I've heard of Wiseman. You don't recognise the name?'

'Nope.'

'Never mind then.'

Hannah took a deep breath.

*You can do this*, she told herself. *You're going to have to do this.*

'Did Dawson leave his mobile number?'

### Extract from *The Black Flower* by Robert Wiseman

There is the steady sound of a shovel crunching into the earth.

Sullivan is staring across a field of unkempt grass. There is a pale concrete bunker to the side on the right, while, ahead of him, he sees a row of apple trees at the edge of a wood. Before them, a fat, bald man is working at the ground. He is sunned-pink and sweating, cumbersome as a pig in his denim overalls, digging at the soil beneath the trees. He finishes and leans the spade against a tree. Sullivan watches as the man pitches something white and flopping into the hole at the roots, then begins to shovel dirt back on top.

He understands what he is seeing.

Beneath the house behind him, Jane Taylor was buried up to her neck and left to die. All around her in that dark crawl space were the black flowers that had grown there, feeding on her life as it ebbed into the soil. Now this man is seeding another victim, only this time in different soil. This body will be drawn up into the trees above it, recycled into bark and leaves and fruit.

When he is finished, the fat man reaches up and clips an apple from the lower branches. Then he bites into it, and the noise is like bone snapping.

Sullivan wakes up with a start.

His small bedroom has an atmosphere of shock in the air, as though someone has just cried out, startling it. But he is the only person here, and he doesn't want to think of himself as the sort of man who screams in his sleep.

He lies there for a while, his body hot and slick with sweat, his heart thudding in his chest.

*You didn't scream.*

But he knows that he might have done.

It has been seven months since Charlotte disappeared. Four since Pearson's suicide. And two months since he separated from his wife and moved into this small terraced house. On the outside, the red brick façade is dulled almost to black in places; the inside is even more dour. All the furniture came with the property, and he spends most of his evenings sitting on the dusty settee, drinking, and then most of his nights dreaming of awful things.

He is no longer a DS. He is no longer much of anything.

Except, in that time, he knows he has become exactly the sort of man who screams in his sleep. His behaviour has grown erratic and strange to the outside world. Hygiene tends to be an afterthought; he washes every three days at best, and never deliberately in time with his occasional trips from the house. When he goes out walking, he wanders aimlessly along country roads, or sometimes through the streets of Thornley. Trying to think. But his thoughts are so random and dislocated that making sense of them is like staring down at a milling crowd and willing it into a straight line.

Today, he showers – or as close as he can get to it in the house. There isn't a shower: just a stethoscope of white plastic tubing, two ends of which go on the taps in the bath, the other a rudimentary sprinkler he holds overhead while sitting in the tub. The water is always too cold; bathing is a feat of endurance. As he sits there, head bowed and shoulder aching, shivering below an ice-cold trickle, he tells himself this is the reason he often doesn't bother washing any more: too much effort; too much indignity. But the truth is that he doesn't bother because he isn't bothered.

Sullivan turns the taps off, one by one, and receives a burst of colder water on his toes. As he towels himself dry in front of the small cabinet mirror, he can see his body is deteriorating in tandem with his mind. The months seem more like years. He is gaunt and drinking too much. The effects are clearly reflected in the mirror. The alcohol is reducing him, so that he is almost painfully aware of his internal organs. It is as though his body is thinning out in preparation for a period of hibernation, or perhaps something worse. As though it is purifying itself in advance of an ordeal.

Downstairs in the front room, the carpet is gritty under his toes, and dust hangs in the air – the whole house is stagnant. Increasingly, he can imagine it eating itself: gnawing away at its insides, the way his own body is beginning to do. The walls seem to be closing in a little more every night, attempting to squeeze him out of existence without anybody noticing.

He makes himself a coffee, then sits at a table by the front-room window, peering cautiously out through the curtains. The gap is the smallest he can make without drawing attention from the street outside.

This is how he spends much of his time. He keeps an eye on the people out there, and watches the vehicles. He always expects to see a rusted red van parked outside, or drawing away slowly down the road, but it is never there. It is only never there because he doesn't look out at the right moment to catch it.

Sullivan thinks constantly of Charlotte.

He remembers how frightened she was when he found her that day on the promenade, and how he tried to show her kindness in the days afterwards and promised to look after her and keep her safe. How he gave her a glimmer of hope and then failed her utterly. She should never have trusted him. Some things, perhaps, it is better not to have had.

And there is something worse even than that. The foster home of Mrs Fitzgerald was never officially listed, and so there is only one possible way Charlotte's family can have located it. However careful he thought he was being, they must have followed him on one of his evening visits. He led them to her. And while he was otherwise occupied, they had taken her away.

That is all he can think of. The only saving grace is the corresponding knowledge that if they were following him back then, perhaps they are still following him now. Perhaps they are a little like Clark Poole in that way. Which is why he keeps looking.

Which is why he opens the curtains a fraction wider now.

The van is not there.


Later, he drives to Thornley.

It is a smaller town than Faverton, and further away, but Sullivan prefers to do his shopping here. There are no familiar faces, and less chance of an awkward encounter with someone he no longer has any interest in talking to. Nobody knows him here. On the ladder of social respectability, nobody he encounters is ever surprised to find him so low down.

It is an ordinary day with no hint of magic to it. Rain speckles the tarmac and the air smells of the sea. He loads heaving bags of groceries and bottles into the boot of his car; the weight makes the handles twist awkwardly, cutting off the circulation in his fingers. Behind him, he hears the rattle and clatter of trolleys being rolled across the stone ground. Sullivan looks around. The car park serves the whole of Thornley's shopping area. There is the small supermarket, a garage, a DIY store.

Sullivan pauses, one bag half supported by the boot, half supported by his hand.

The van is old, rusted and crimson: the colour and texture of dried blood. It is parked with its nose up to the DIY store, practically pushing into the shelves and buckets lined up outside. From here, he can just make out that the cabin is empty.

Without taking his eyes off the van, Sullivan finishes lowering the bag. It rests down awkwardly, the contents slumping. Red vans are commonplace, he thinks; it means nothing. And yet, after he's finished loading his shopping, he sits in his car and continues to watch the vehicle.

Rain builds up on the windscreen.

A few minutes later, the door to the DIY store opens and a man emerges. Almost unconsciously, Sullivan leans forward on the steering wheel. The man is weathered and rough-looking, as though he spends much of his time outdoors. He has no coat, and the sleeves of his shirt are rolled up, his forearms like thick lengths of rope. His hair is dark but greying, medium length and ruffled immediately by the wind. The face it frames is tanned and impassive. He is carrying a large, brown paper bag; Sullivan can't see what's inside.

Behind him, a little boy trails out of the store.

Sullivan watches, heart alive.

But a moment later, the shop door closes. It is only the two of them:

father and son. As they get into the van, Sullivan leans back again. He wants to tell himself it is nothing; he *does* tell himself that. The man he's just seen is very different from the pig-man of his nightmares.

But then, why wouldn't he be?

As the van reverses out of its parking spot and swings around towards the exit, Sullivan makes a decision. What is worse? Following for the sake of it and wasting his time? Ultimately, that is no different from how he's lived these last few months.

He starts the engine and the wipers squeak the rain from the glass.

No, what would be worse is *not knowing*. Sitting at his table, peering through his curtains at an empty street and thinking, endlessly, *what if?*

He follows the van cautiously, maintaining the kind of careful distance that, if this is the man, he himself must have kept seven months ago while following Sullivan. They pass through a small, rural village: little more than a row of old, conjoined cottages, a post office, pub and grocery shop. The road curls through the middle. He drives past an old black church sitting in a yard dotted with gravestones, then he is out the other side.

As the vehicle rumbles ahead of him down the endless country lanes, Sullivan feels a thrill inside him. A glimmer of hope. It does not occur to him that the world does not work this way – that it never gives, only takes – or that he no longer has any real idea where he is.

He allows himself to believe that he is following rather than being led.

He has forgotten that it does not happen like this.

# Chapter Twenty-Seven

I drove along the road my father had marked on the map.

Fields stretched out to the left: grey and gloomy in the dying light. To the right, there was a wood of sorts, where the trees were tall and bare and the ground below was carpeted black with broken twigs and branches. Glancing down at the map on the passenger seat, the cross was about halfway along this stretch of road. Not far now.

Now it was just a matter of keeping an eye out.

*And keeping calm*, I told myself.

*Not getting your hopes up.*

The excitement I'd felt back at the hospital had faded slightly now. My father had drawn a cross on a map, but that didn't mean there was anything conclusive there in real life, regardless of whether it turned out to be a farm. He'd been researching a book, after all, not setting out to solve a crime. And, more than anything else, my father had been a careful, sensible man. If he knew the farm in *The Black Flower* really existed, and if he'd somehow discovered its location, he'd have gone straight to the police and done his best to make them believe in it too. He certainly wouldn't have just pencilled a trip there into his itinerary as though it was no big deal.

So it *couldn't* be that. It had to be something else entirely.

And yet . . . from the calendar, he had probably come here before going to Whitkirk, where he'd found Charlotte on the promenade and gone to the viaduct with her. The old man at the hospital had never figured out how to find her for himself, but he'd killed my father in the woods. How had he ended up there? All I could think was that he must have been following Dad, so he had to have started following him for a reason – their paths needed to have crossed. My father must have turned up at the wrong place and attracted the old bastard's attention somehow.

*Why here, Dad?*

*What brought you here?*

The question was preoccupying me so much that I drove straight past the entrance. Without warning, the trees to the right were suddenly replaced by a drystone wall and open fields. Glancing in the rear-view mirror, I could see a gap between the woods and the wall. I slowed down. The road behind was empty. The car whined angrily back up the road until I drew level with the end of the trees.

It was an entrance, all right, an opening onto a dirt track, only just wide enough for a vehicle to fit through. The track cut down the edge of the field, holding tight to the treeline. A constant tread of tyres had worn the grass away, leaving two strips of bare land separated by a raised, tatty ridge of turf.

An old sign was nailed on a post behind the wall. Red letters, painted on white.

PRIVATE PROPERTY
NO ACCESS

No other indication of what was down there.

On the right side of the track, pressing against it, the stripped-down woodland was dark and forbidding. The field on the open side seemed unkempt and unused. About fifty metres further along the road, it was separated from the next field along by another drystone wall running parallel to the track, and there was nothing to see beyond that except a pylon, standing on splayed metal legs a few hundred metres away.

I turned off the engine and was met by the heavy silence of the countryside. A moment later, I began to notice little clicks and rustles of undergrowth, the sigh of the breeze.

I checked the map again. This seemed approximately right, and there was nothing obvious further down the road. So this had to be place, didn't it? I stared down the track. It was difficult to imagine there was anything *bad* down there – it wasn't even gated off. There was just that sign.

### PRIVATE PROPERTY

I listened to that heavy silence – the quiet that wasn't quiet.

Was Ally down there?

Staring down the path, I thought it out to her: *Are you there?*

I felt a tingle of connection that was surely just fear. But there was no way I could leave without finding out, so I started the engine again and drove a little further on, to where the road widened, and parked up.

*Call the police again, Neil.*

I knew that I should. Even if I couldn't get hold of Hannah Price, I should at least let *someone* know where I was. My phone was in my jeans pocket; I got it out now. The conversation wasn't exactly going to be an easy one. Where to start?

But then it started ringing.

*Christ.* It nearly gave me heart failure.

Unknown number

I answered it. 'Hello?'

'Neil Dawson?'

'Yes. Who is this please?'

'This is Hannah Price – DS Hannah Price. You left a message for me.'

I recognised the voice, but she sounded different from when we'd talked before. At the mortuary, as I identified my father's belongings, she'd been kind, warm and sympathetic, as though she really felt for my loss. Now, though, she sounded . . . blank. Far more controlled and professional, anyway.

'Thanks for calling me back.'

She said, 'How did you know about Charles Dennison and Robert Wiseman, Neil? That information's not been confirmed for certain here yet, never mind released to the public. It bothers me how you know that.'

'Well—'

'Especially given that your father died in the same location.'

'I think I can explain all of it.'

'Can you.' She was silent for a moment. Then: 'Where are you? You said you were on your way back to Whitkirk?'

'Change of plan.'

'Then I think you need to change it back again.'

'This might be more important.' I took a deep breath. 'I'm at a farm.'

Hannah Price started to say something but then stopped. Again, silence panned out on the line, but there was something different about it this time. The mention of the farm had done it. She knew about it. She knew something anyway.

'Where?' she said.

'Just outside a little village called Ellis. You know it?'

'Yes.'

I started talking then. It all came out in a stream and didn't make much sense even to me as I was saying it. But I told her that Wiseman had based one of his books on a real little girl, on a real family who had wanted her back, and that my father had known about them too. I told her they'd killed him and taken Ally.

'And I think she's here.' I was babbling. 'Or she might be. She's pregnant, and I wished it away – that's partly why they took her – and, oh God, I've got to find her. You have to believe me.'

'Neil,' Hannah said. '*Neil.*'

'Yes.'

'Calm down.'

'I'm here,' I said. 'I'm okay.'

'Listen to me. This is really important, all right? Don't do anything.'

'But—'

'*Don't do anything*. Sit in your car and wait for me. I'm on my way; I'm walking out of the door right now. Wait where you are. Okay?'

'Yes.'

I glanced back at the break in the dry stone wall, feeling that tingle of connection again.

'Yes,' I said. 'I'll wait right here.'

Outside the car, it seemed even quieter than before. As I walked down the dirt track, though, I began to hear a different sound from the undergrowth and the breeze. It was the hum of the pylon in the distance: an electrical noise, almost a vibration in the air. The kind of sound I imagined you'd feel in your teeth as you entered an empty place where there'd been a radiation spill.

High above me, the cables stretched over the trees. In the other direction, they spread into the distance, finding a brother, and then a second, all the way to the horizon. It only served to emphasise the vast, empty span of the land here. I felt small and isolated: out of sight of the real world, and far away from its safety.

*Which you are*.

Maybe. But I couldn't wait for Hannah Price. Not when Ally might be down here right now. Not when anything could be happening to her, and when that 'anything' would be my fault.

I kept close to the treeline as I walked. After I left the pylon behind, the only real sound was the occasional snap of a twig breaking under my shoes. The trees to the right were tall and straight. Despite the sheer number, they had a dead feeling to them. There were no leaves that I could see, and the few branches were fragile and skeletal, as though someone had come through here, stripping them methodically for firewood, only to abandon it all on the ground. Even in the early evening darkness, I could tell the undergrowth between the tree trunks was thick with them.

Occasionally, out of the corner of my eye, I kept imagining I saw movement, as though someone was keeping pace with me in there. But whenever I stopped and looked, there was nothing.

Just shadows making me nervous.

Up ahead, the track rode over a hump in the land. When I reached it, I glanced behind me. I could see the wall in the distance, but it seemed a hell of a long way back now. The sprawl of field was shivering in the evening breeze, grey and drained of colour. Everywhere I looked, the night seemed to be seeping upwards from the ground, staining the world darker and darker, like black ink creeping slowly up a sheet of tissue paper.

I started walking again, over the rise and then straight on. Ahead, it was just more of the same, and it felt like there was nobody alive for miles in any direction. But that wasn't true; there had to be. This road had to go somewhere.

A little further on, I found out where.

The first thing I noticed was the corner of the fence. In fact, with the darkness settling in now, I almost walked straight into it: a rusted metal pole, about twelve-feet high, poking up from the ground on the edge of the treeline. Chicken wire extended out from it, stretching away down the side of the dirt track, but also at a right angle, straight into the woods.

Someone had cordoned off a section of the trees.

I stepped closer to the corner of the fence, wanting a better look, and something crunched beneath my foot. But this was a different sound and sensation from the branches underfoot. I stepped back again and looked down.

Then stood very still.

A dead bird. Or the remains of one anyway: just a few dirty tufts of feather still clinging to the fractured bones.

Glancing around, I spotted another.

And then a third.

And also something else. At the base of the fence, there was a thin strip of wire running parallel to the ground, a couple of inches up. Carefully, I moved closer. The wire was clamped to the mesh by large metal crocodile clips, placed along it at metre-wide intervals.

An electrified fence.

Why would someone have an electrified fence? I looked around at the birds again. Was it to keep animals out, or maybe to discourage trespassers?

Or was it, just possibly, to keep something inside?

I listened carefully.

From somewhere in the thick of the woods, on the far side of the fence, I could hear a different noise now. It was far away, only just detectable. A gentle *putt-putt* noise. The sound of machinery left idling out by itself. A generator, I guessed.

I scanned the field, more nervous now, but the night was emerging so quickly that it was hard to see anything. But there was no obvious movement out there. No sound beyond the generator and the vacant hush of the breeze.

I walked a little further down the track.

*What is this place?*

I didn't have to go far to find out. A short distance down, the trees thinned out and I came to a wide break in the fence. The trail of tyre marks veered out here before heading inside, as though whatever vehicle used it was large enough to need a turning circle. Beyond it, there was a wide corridor of dusty, light-brown ground. A sort of half-completed, makeshift drive-way.

There were more dead animals at the side of the open gate, but they were rabbits this time, and these hadn't wandered into the fence and been electrocuted. Instead, they were laid out in a neat row. Someone had caught them, or killed them somehow, then brought them here and left their tiny bodies in a line. The one nearest to me looked like a cat stretching. Except its tongue was poking from its mouth, and one black eye was staring everywhere at once. Flies darted around it. A moment later, I realised I could smell them.

It wasn't odd to go hunting, especially out here in the countryside. But still. Something was very wrong here.

I looked at the gate.

Why had it been left open though? If this was the real farm from *The Black Flower* then that didn't make sense. I kept coming back to the other question too. How could my father possibly have known about this?

And yet the air felt electric.

I stepped through the gate into the compound.

A little distance ahead, the driveway looked to open up into a slightly wider area. I could see a building of some kind, obscured by the hang of the trees to the side. I forced myself to walk forward, still keeping close to the trees. The further I walked, the louder the *putt-putt* of the generator became. It was the only sound I could hear now. Even the breeze seemed to have died.

As I reached the structure, I saw that it was an enormous, corrugated iron barn on the right. The driveway didn't widen, so much as curl around to avoid it. The building was two-storeys high, and there was no door: just an arched black space large enough to drive a tractor into. The ground outside the entrance bristled with spilled hay. I crossed to the other side of the driveway to keep away from the darkness there. On this side, there were ridged strips of earth, topped with sprouting leaves. A neatly tended vegetable patch, several metres square.

Around the far end of the barn, I came into a larger clearing, ending in a wall of trees straight ahead of me. In the centre, there was a well. The generator I'd heard was on the right, *putt-putt*ing loudly inside an awkwardly constructed metal shack. To the left, a series of wooden sheds ran down from the allotment, with several gardening tools leaning against the nearest. I hesitated, then walked across. They looked ancient. The prongs of the garden fork were rusted brown and gnarled: like grotesquely long fingerbones that had been burned in a fire. The wooden shaft was mostly worn away.

I picked it up. Hefting it.

*What the hell are you doing, Neil?*

I really had no idea.

*Putt-putt. Putt-putt. Putt—*

Someone was behind me.

I turned quickly, almost bringing the garden fork up – and stopped myself just in time.

A little girl was standing about ten metres away. She was about six or seven years old, with long, dirty-blonde hair pulled into two bunches at either side of her head, and she was wearing an old-fashioned dress, like something a child would put a doll in. She was looking straight at me.

I shivered, convinced I was seeing a ghost.

But when I blinked, she was still there. There was hay all over one side of her dress. *She must have been in the barn,* I realised. She'd seen me – an intruder on her property – and come out. But she didn't look scared by my presence. She was still just staring at me, as though not only did she not know *who* I was, but *what*.

'Hello,' I said.

She didn't react.

'Is your daddy home?'

Again, no response. I risked taking a step closer.

'I was wanting to see your daddy. Is he here?'

This time, she shook her head, a little uncertainly.

'Where is he?' I said. 'Do you know?'

'He went out.' Her voice was shy and quiet.

I said, 'Do you know where he went?'

'I think he went looking for grandpa.'

I realised I was holding the garden fork slightly raised. I rested the prongs on the ground, leaning on it.

'What about your mummy. Is she here?'

'Mummy's always here.'

The words needed a moment to settle as I took in the implications. The old man – *grandpa* – hadn't returned, and so his

259

son had gone out searching for him. But the mother was here because she always was. Because she never left. According to Wiseman's story – Charlotte Webb's story – her mother had been a prisoner. But that would have been the old man's wife. This girl's mother must be younger than that. Which meant that at some point, the son had selected a wife for himself from their victims, and continued the family.

It couldn't be true.

The idea of it made me feel cold, but an even worse one followed. Something else was wrong here too. The gate was open. The son had gone out. Perhaps this little girl didn't know anything different from life in this compound, but if the mother was some kind of prisoner then why hadn't she tried to escape? Why hadn't she walked out of here?

Unless she didn't know anything different either.

Unless maybe she'd grown up here as well.

*Oh God . . .*

'Where is she?' I said. 'Your mummy?'

'In the house.' The little girl swivelled on her heels and pointed further into the farm.

'Can you take me there?'

She swivelled back.

'I'm not supposed to.'

'It'll be okay,' I said.

She thought about it, then, without warning, turned and ran off in the direction of the trees up ahead. It wasn't clear whether she intended me to follow, but I did. Not running, but walking quickly, trying to keep her in sight. As I did, I raised the garden fork a little, holding it horizontal. Got a decent grip on the wooden handle.

*What the hell is this place?*

She led me around the line of trees. There were chickens in wire cages on the left here, squatting down in the corners, the ground covered in spilled feed and dirt. As I passed, one of them fluttered into life, panicking against the mesh, squawking madly.

Just past that, there were empty wooden pens and another line of trees. Something larger was behind these ones.

A house.

It revealed itself as I stepped around. It was a two-storey, wooden farmhouse. On the downstairs level, there was room for one window and a door. Two windows on the first floor. In other circumstances, the building might have looked homely and welcoming, but right here and now, it reminded me of nothing so much as some kind of hideous fairytale cottage in the woods.

The little girl was running towards it and I had an urge to call out, tell her to stop. But then her shoes tap-tapped up the wooden steps onto the decking at the front, and she disappeared inside.

I glanced to either side, then behind. Nothing.

*Come on, Neil.*

On the decking, to one side of the front door, there was a dirty old settee and a pot full of dead, wilted flowers. When I reached the steps, I saw that below the decking – below the whole house – there must have been about a metre's worth of crawl space, obscured by posts.

*Ally.*

My heart thumped, and I crouched down. There was no chance of seeing much under there – it was too dark – but I peered in. From what I *could* see, the ground looked moist and rich – and it stank too. As I listened, I imagined I could hear beetles chittering, busy with their work. I started to whisper her name—

But then the front door creaked open wider, and I stood up quickly. Stepped back. The woman in the doorway was staring down at me in shock and fear.

As I stared back, I felt exactly the same.

*Oh God, no.*

Years might have passed, but I still recognised Lorraine Haggerty from the photo I'd seen online.

# Chapter Twenty-Eight

Hannah was nearly all the way to Ellis by the time night fell properly.

For a while, she'd been driving straight into the dying strands of the day. In front of her, almost as she'd watched, the sun had lowered itself towards the land, then caught fire at the horizon, flaring like a struck match. As fast as she took the car down the motorway, it had felt like she was chasing the light, while the world turned away from her, pulling it steadily further out of reach.

The last threads of it were barely visible now: a slight glow that painted fading shreds of pink on the underside of the clouds. Overhead, the sky was blue-black, speckled with its meaningless constellations, difficult to see through the orange haze of the motorway lights. The route was busy with the tail end of the work-day traffic, but it was moving. Hannah had stuck to the outside lane the whole way, maintaining a fast, steady speed. She pictured the motorway from above: a vein full of white and orange lights, trickling across the land, with her shooting swiftly along one edge.

She had to drive quickly. If she stopped and thought about this for even a moment, she would turn back again. As it was, she was doing her best to ignore the widening spread of fear inside her chest. But she could still sense it there: that familiar dread, more focused now because of where she might be heading.

*What are you doing? What are you doing?*

The voice in her head fluttered like a bird. Her heartbeat mirrored it, keeping pace with the rising panic. She indicated, crossed the lanes, and almost flung the car down the turning towards Ellis.

*What are you doing?*

The exact opposite of what she should be. Dawson had been gabbling on the phone, but she'd understood enough. Whatever investigation he'd been on had run separately from her own, but the two were coming together now, converging at the same place.

At a farm.

That was where she was going – the very place her father had fought so hard to conceal from her over the years; the absolute definition of *not being safe*. The farm that was the basis for the story he'd told her, about a little girl who had been rescued and could now just play happily somewhere the flowers had colours. All of that had been to keep her from remembering the horrors of this place, and yet now that was what she was driving towards.

She tried to tell herself that – surely – there was no way Christopher Dawson could have located the farm she'd grown up on. That didn't make any sense. According to the Webb file, Colin Price, along with other officers, had tried hard to find it but none of them had any idea where to even *begin* looking. So it was absurd to think Dawson had somehow stumbled onto her original family, or that something astonishingly obvious might have been missed.

But then, something obvious was often missed.

*Which means you shouldn't be doing this.*

And yet, as much as the panic fluttered inside her, there was also something else, and it took her a moment to work out what. It surprised her, but there it was: an odd sense of exhilaration as she hit the outskirts of Ellis. *DS Hannah Price. Daughter of DS Colin Price.* Yes, that was a lie: a curtain built around a scared little girl to keep the real world out of sight. But the curtain was gone now and still here she was: driving straight towards the thing that scared her most, the source of that crawling dread. Maybe – just maybe – her father had given her something more than lies and illusions. Maybe he had also given her armour.

*And it's not your farm anyway.*

It couldn't be.

Ellis was exactly as small and rural as it looked on the map: little more than a row of old, conjoined cottages, a post office, pub and grocery shop. The road curled through the middle. Hannah drove past an old black church sitting in a yard dotted with gravestones, then she was out the other side. She glanced down at the map on the passenger seat.

One more turning and she would be on the right road.

*It's not your farm.*

Well, she would find out soon enough. In fact, she would have been there already if, ever since the motorway, she hadn't been stuck behind this old red van.

# Chapter Twenty-Nine

'Where is she?'

I'd rested the old garden fork against the wall beside the front door. Now, I had my hands on either side of Lorraine Haggerty's upper arms. I was holding her gently but firmly, trying to be reassuring, resisting the urge to shake her. Suppressing the urgency I felt. She was a victim here; I had to keep reminding myself of that, despite the fact Ally was here somewhere. I couldn't even comprehend what she must have been through over the last . . . ten years.

Christ.

'Lorraine. *Where is she?*'

But she wouldn't look at me. She kept shaking her head, partly in confusion, partly in terror. It was as though she'd been living in a nightmare for so long that she'd forgotten it wasn't real. As she spoke, she didn't seem able to process what was happening.

'You shouldn't be here.'

'I *am* here. Where is she?'

'No, you shouldn't be here.'

'The police are coming too. It's going to be okay.'

But that was such a stupid, empty thing to say. Of course it wasn't going to be okay. A long time ago, she and her son had been abducted. She'd been here ever since. *If it's a girl we'll keep it,* the old man had said. I had no doubt Kent Haggerty was dead – and that maybe she'd even seen it happen. I couldn't begin to contemplate what she must have been through, but it was obviously not going to be okay ever again.

'Where is she?' I said. 'Where is Ally?'

'You shouldn't be here. You need to leave now.'

I let go of her arms.

'You shouldn't be here.'

It wasn't clear whether she was actually talking to me or just repeating the phrase to herself. Either way, she wasn't in any position to help me, and I needed to leave her alone.

'The police are coming,' I said again. 'It's all over.'

*Please, Hannah,* I thought. *Come down to investigate.*

*And please have a shitload of backup.*

Lorraine was hugging her elbow, one hand to her mouth, but a look of horror passed over her face, as though she'd just remembered something.

'Oh God.'

And then she ran back inside.

I picked up the garden fork and followed her. The front door led straight into a spartan living area. A staircase went up to the left – she was running up that – and an open doorway at the back of the room led into a fog-grey kitchen. I glanced around. In this room, there was another old settee and a circular red carpet lying half crumpled on the wooden floorboards. An old standing lamp in the corner was buzzing softly. Everything the light fell on looked dirty and gnarled and threadbare. I could almost smell the grain of the wood.

I shouted as loud as I could, *'Ally?'*

There was no response. I glanced into the kitchen – empty – then ran up the creaking staircase after Lorraine. Three rooms up here. At the back, above the kitchen, there was a stinking old bathroom, the white ceramic webbed with black cracks. The space directly above the front room was divided in two. The nearest room was full of bare mattresses, criss-crossing the floor. That was where Lorraine was—

I stopped in the doorway and stared.

'Lorraine,' I said.

She was standing in the middle of the room, cradling a baby in her arms. Rocking it. A younger child – a little boy – was squatting naked behind her legs, frightened, coiled like a spider. He was staring at me with eyes as brown and wide as copper coins.

'Lorraine . . .'

'*Get back,*' she said. 'Keep back.'

'Take them somewhere safe. Get out of here. For God's sake.'

'*Get back.*'

I did – stepped back into the hallway. There was only one more door along this side, and it was padlocked. *Ally.* I braced my back against the corridor and kicked the cross-beam on the door as hard as I could. The door *banged* open, loud as a gunshot, leaving a shredded panel caught on the lock, flames of pale wood.

Dark inside. I stepped in, searching for a switch to one side.

'Ally?'

A single bare bulb illuminated the room.

Nobody here. It was an office or a storeroom, maybe. There was a desk at one end, with filing cabinets to either side. To the left of the door, there were piles and piles of battered old paperback books, their covers dotted with charity-shop price stickers, their pages yellowed and curled, stained with damp. The room stank of mould. Everything else appeared to be a random jumble of items. There were sacks of clothes. Old handbags dumped in one corner. Broken pieces of furniture. Discarded mobile phones and cameras and keys.

And the walls . . .

I stepped closer to the nearest side.

Pages. Every visible patch of wall was covered with them. Torn from books and glued to the wood, so that the tiny text on them was rippled and uneven. I read:

Sullivan squats down in front of the little girl. His starched trouser leg forms a sharp contour up from his knee and over his thigh.

. . . and realised what I was seeing.

Not books, at all. Just one book. The entire room was covered with pages torn from copies of *The Black Flower*.

In his hands, Pearson is holding a hammer wrapped in a white plastic bag. He clenches his jaw, then steps astride Poole and hits him four times square in the face.

I shivered at the insanity on display. Robert Wiseman's words all around me, everywhere I looked. The old man had turned the room into a shrine to the novel. Except not a shrine. It felt more like I was literally standing inside it.

Still gripping the garden fork, I stepped between bags of old clothes, moving over to the desk at the far end of the room. Amongst the calendars and box files and loose papers that covered it, something at the front had caught my eye.

An old, silver laptop.

The sheen on the lid was gone in places, as though something corrosive had been spilled on it – but I knew that nothing had. It was age that had done it: years of the same fingers opening it in exactly the same way, and then closing it again hours later. A story of fingerprints had been worn into the cover, just as more elaborate stories had also been worn, out of sight, into its hard drive. My father's computer.

My heart felt like it was on fire.

Right beside the laptop, there was a photograph album. A4 size. It had a white cover, decorated with swirling black tendrils: the outlines of stems and petals and leaves. I held onto the garden fork with one hand. My other was trembling as I reached out, flipped the cover back.

The first page had two photographs glued onto it. They were both landscape shots, and both looked very old indeed: grainy and flecked, like something developed from a cheap camera. The top one showed a naked woman from above. She was lying on her back and she was dead, her skin so pale it was almost blue, her wrists tied so tightly in front of her that the binds forced her hands outwards, as though they were cupping an invisible heart. Her clothes lay beneath and around her – scissored awkwardly from her corpse.

The photograph below that one had been taken closer to its subject. The thin stem of the flower ran sideways across the print, blossoming into a black spread of petals at the left-hand side of the album. It was an ugly, fragile thing: more like the X-ray of a flower than anything you'd expect to see growing. One of the petals was angled off sideways, and some were missing altogether: a black sun with broken rays.

*Don't . . .*

But I turned the page anyway.

It was a man this time, but otherwise the same: dead, naked and bound. The flower in the photograph below was all but indistinguishable from the previous one, except malformed in its own distinct way.

I turned the page. A little boy I couldn't look at.

More.

More and more.

There were no dates or names, but it was obvious what this was. *A catalogue.* As far as I could tell from the quality of the prints, the images were stored chronologically. My hand shook as I flicked through, taking two, three pages at a time now, a fire in my heart burning harder with each fresh photograph – until I couldn't take any more and flicked straight to the last page, the last set of photographs. A middle-aged woman, lying naked on the grass. It looked freshly added, and there was no second photograph below it.

Not Ally.

I glanced randomly at the pages pasted to the wall above the desk.

Through the open door of his cell, Sullivan can see the flowers that grow in the garden out there.

The garden.

I turned around, headed quickly back through the open doorway. My pulse was pounding in my temples, and everything sounded like it was underwater. Back down the corridor. I glanced into the bedroom and Lorraine was still there, still comforting her children.

I headed to the top of the stairs. The man coming up them had nearly reached the top by then, and he saw me first. I had time to register a bedraggled shock of wild, brown hair, a heavy black coat over the bulk of him and then – *crack crack* – the rifle he was holding. He fired it from the hip without aiming. Needles of stinging pain went through my stomach, burning like matches struck on the skin.

The pain and the panic – *a gun, a gun, a gun* – drove me forward, straight down at him, pushing the garden fork out and driving my weight behind it. I saw a face contorted with hate, and heard – *crack ting!* – as the last shot ricocheted off the prongs, and then they struck him and my weight took us both down the stairs, him backwards, me on top. I lost track of the world. Everything tumbled around me. And then, suddenly, the handle of the fork was wrenched from my hands, and there was a noise like a spade turning turf.

The staircase was above my head, and then my shoulder hit, and the small of my back too, and my heel thudded into the wall above me. I was twisted halfway down the stairs. From above me, the man rolled backwards, over on his shoulder, legs swinging up. The prongs of the garden fork were embedded in his stomach, pinning the shattered wooden stock of the rifle against him, but the handle of it swung down in an arc, and landed hard on the banister, bending slightly, propping him in place, one leg straight up against the wall. Blood was pouring out onto the steps above me.

His leg slowly descended.

I scrabbled up and out of the way, clutching my stomach and darting down the last few stairs. He slid after me a moment later, everything clattering, and landed on his side at my feet. A second later, I stepped back as he drew his legs slowly upwards into a foetal position.

*Oh God.*

'Oh God,' I was saying. 'Oh God, oh God.'

Over and over.

It wasn't a man at all. From the body, that hadn't been obvious; the coat was bulky, and he was thick-set and strong for his age. But he had the face of a teenager. Sixteen or seventeen years old at the most. He wasn't the man I'd seen in the van behind my flat. And he wasn't old enough to be the man seen when Lorraine and Kent Haggerty had gone missing. He couldn't have been the father of the little girl I'd seen outside.

A brother? A nephew?

I thought about Lorraine Haggerty and the children upstairs.

*How fucking many of them are there?*

The idea brought a sliver of fear. *The rabbits*, I realised. That was where the rabbits had come from and it must have been one of the reasons why, despite the gate being open, Lorraine hadn't tried to escape. This boy had been out there in the fields, hunting, watching. The older son had gone out looking for his father, and left this boy in charge of the farm in his absence.

The front door was still open. From outside, I could hear something.

A sound approaching.

A car.

*No*, I thought. *A van.*

I glanced down at myself. The needles of pain in my stomach were scorching hot now, and the front of my T-shirt was soaked with blood. I wasn't sure how much was mine. I didn't want to look underneath, didn't want to unpick the fabric from whatever wounds it had been pushed into, didn't dare. *You're all right.* The pain was insistent and sharp, but not incapacitating. I needed to get to hospital, but I wasn't going to die yet.

Stars flickered briefly in front of my eyes.

*No.*

*You're not going to die.*

I edged around the boy's body and stepped out onto the decking. The world in front of me starred over again, the wall of trees sparkling in the darkness. Very slowly, the crystals in my vision dissolved away. When they did, the sound was much louder than before, and it was definitely some kind of vehicle. An engine gunning in the distance.

Definitely inside the compound now.

*Okay.*

I was at the bottom of the steps, stumbling slightly as I hit the turf. I hadn't made a conscious decision to move. It just seemed to have happened.

The garden. I headed round the side of the house.

*Ally*, I thought.

*I'm going to find you.*

# Chapter Thirty

This was not her farm.

Standing at the corner of the fence, Hannah was certain about that. She had images – memories – in her head. And if her father's story had been a lie, then those images must have come from reality. They didn't match this place. Even with the memories distorted, surely she would recognise the terrible place she'd grown up in? If not from sight then from the clenching in her chest.

But still.

There was *something* wrong with this place.

Standing in the field, she could hear the gentle *putt-putt* of a generator coming from somewhere on the other side of the fence, and it was obvious it was electrified. Not only could she see the links in the chicken wire, and the cable snaking off between the trees, but she could see dead birds lying on the ground.

Which was an elaborate set-up for a normal farm.

A short distance further down the trail from the corner of the fence, there was what looked like a gate. It was made of the same chicken wire, and presumably just as dangerous to the touch, but she could see a pole and hinges. It was sealed tight. A gate, probably operated by remote control. There was no sign of the red van that had driven down this way. She guessed it was already inside.

And that Neil Dawson was as well.

When the van had turned down the dirt track, without even indicating, it was lucky for Hannah she'd dropped far enough behind to sail past the entrance without drawing attention to herself. There was a car parked a little way back down the road, which she guessed was Neil Dawson's, so she'd driven a short distance on, then turned around, driven back and parked up behind it.

By the time she'd walked up to the dirt track, the van had disappeared and the field was dark and silent. She'd tried phoning Neil Dawson's mobile and got no answer. It just rang and rang. Presumably he'd ignored her advice and gone down there. She'd deliberated a little – nervous – but what else could she do? And so she'd made her way down the edge of the treeline on foot, keeping a wary eye on the dark, apparently empty fields to the left.

She glanced around again now, out across the pitch-black land. There was nothing to see. The land that way even *sounded* empty. Listening to it was like holding your ear to a seashell. And yet, despite gripping the baton, she felt exposed, endangered.

Something was wrong.

Hannah turned back to the fence.

*See if there's another way in.*

That meant going into the wood. Holding the baton in her left hand, and using the trunks for balance with the right, she moved into the undergrowth there. Beneath her feet, the discarded branches cracked softly. She moved slowly, keeping away from the fence, trying to stay quiet. After a minute, she reached an old felled tree, propped up at an angle between the others. Someone had whacked it repeatedly at the base with an axe and sent it tumbling, but only halfway to the ground. It was still attached at the edge of the base by enormous, stretched tendons of wood, like a half-snapped stick. The chicken wire cut across the top of the stump. The tree had just been half chopped down to make way for the fence.

She crouched and moved underneath. A little further on, she could see more trees laid out in huge piles in a break in the forest, properly felled this time, stacked like hay bales and tethered together with dirty rope.

Hannah stepped into that clearing, smelling the old, wet wood. On the other side of the fence, there were trees still standing, but she thought she could see something else between them, a little further away. It was hard to make out in the darkness. Was it corrugated iron? Like the back of a factory, or perhaps a barn—

Hannah heard glass smashing.

She flinched, ducking down out of instinct. The noise was distant and muffled. It had come from somewhere inside the compound, and in the silence that followed, her heart thudded solidly and her skin began tingling.

And then someone *shrieked*.

It wasn't in pain, but in rage. She stayed crouched down in the undergrowth, stunned by the horror of it. It was barely even a human sound, more like the howl of a wild animal. Shivers broke out all over her; her skin went cold. And she knew for sure.

This wasn't her farm . . . but somehow it was.

She was back home.

Round the back of the house, my vision starred over again. The pain in my stomach had seemed bearable only minutes ago, but it was flaring brighter and brighter now that I was properly moving. Every step I took made the world shimmer. Facing out across the land behind the farmhouse, I forced myself to stop and rest a hand against a rough wooden strut.

*Deep breaths, Neil.*

Long, slow, deep breaths.

A few seconds later, the world began to resolve itself. The sparkling crystals of light in the air faded away.

This was the end of the compound. Twenty metres ahead of me, there was a long row of apple trees, and I could just make out the chicken-wire fence between them and the black woods beyond. On the right, halfway between the house and the trees, there was what appeared to be a concrete bunker, pale as a skull.

I stumbled down and across towards it, and had to put my hand out to stop myself as I reached it. Up close, I could see it was made of breeze blocks, each one pasted tightly in place. I leaned my shoulder against the wall and patted my way down the side, one foot crossing the other, barely able to stop myself tripping.

'Ally?'

I said it too quietly, but I was terrified of making any noise. From the far side of the house, I heard a car door slam: an abrasive, grating sound, reverberating through the underwater pulsing in my ears.

I rounded the corner of the bunker, glancing back up the garden as I did. Just as someone screamed. It was a man's voice. A cry of horror and loss and *rage*.

And then something shattering.

*Come on, Neil.*

I forced myself down the side of the bunker, the house out of sight now, the concrete blocks scraping against my shoulder. There was a door up here. A way in. I had no idea if Ally was in here, or even if she was still alive, but there was nowhere else to go anyway. I was holding my stomach with my left hand, and could feel blood seeping and sticking between my fingers. The centre of me was blazing hot, but everything else seemed to be growing cold and shivery.

Nowhere else to go.

Nowhere else I would get to anyway.

The door was made of steel, flush with the wall of the bunker.

There were rivets around the edge and solid cylindrical hinges bolted onto the concrete at the far side. A metal strip had been soldered on nearest to me, stretching over the edge of the breeze blocks and fastened to a protruding iron ring. The padlock there was enormous. The metal loop arching from the top was as thick as my finger.

I reached out and pulled it. It barely moved.

'Ally?' I whispered.

There was a window a little past the door. I moved towards it, again nearly falling. It wasn't really a window: just a square cut out of the concrete with three black, metal bars running down. No glass. I peered through, trying to make out something – anything – inside. The walls and floor seemed to be covered with white tiles, lined in-between with grime. It looked like a place you'd slaughter cattle.

'Ally?'

The bunker sounded cavernous inside, like putting your ear to a shell and hearing the sea. For a moment, my words echoed around and there was no reply. Then I heard a scraping noise.

And a whisper:

'Neil?'

Even through the stars in my vision, the pain in my abdomen, relief flooded me. A burst of energy. For a moment, my skin even felt warm again. And I could see her too. She was right there, standing in the shadows beside the window.

'Ally,' I said. 'It's me.'

Her hands shot out between the bars: small white fists that I gripped, and which unfolded and gripped me back.

'Oh my God,' she said. 'Oh my God, oh my God.'

'It's okay.'

She wouldn't let go of my hands. She couldn't move her own out any further because they were bound at the wrist with thick black tape.

'You're bleeding,' she said. 'Oh God, you're bleeding.'

'It's not mine,' I said, even though it was, and I could tell there was far more of it now. I'd been shot and I was bleeding, and I was finding it harder and harder to stay standing. But I squeezed her hand. 'I'm all right, I promise. Are you hurt?'

'No. Not really – is it safe now? Are the police here?'

Her voice was suddenly full of hope, and it made the energy I'd felt evaporate. This whole time, she wouldn't have understood a thing about where she was or what had happened to her; she'd probably been convinced she was going to die, maybe even accepted it. And now here I was. Now, she thought, it was going to be over.

'The police are on the way,' I said.

I had no idea whether that was true any more. I reached for my phone – gone. I remembered the tumble down the staircase. From back at the house, I heard another smash. Shouting.

I took her hand again. 'It won't be long. In the meantime, we need to stay calm, keep quiet.'

'Oh God.'

'It'll be all right.'

'Can you get the door open from out there?'

'I'll try.'

She let go of my hand, and I moved back carefully to the door. It was a pointless exercise though; there was no way of breaking the padlock with my bare hands. I wouldn't have been able to do it with the garden fork, even if I'd thought to pick it up again. But what else was there?

For a moment, I just stared at the lock stupidly.

What the fuck was I going to do?

And then I whipped my head round, distracted by a new noise: *whump*.

*Whump.*

*Whump.*

*Whump.*

And suddenly, the back garden was flooded with glaring light. I winced, blinking from the shock of it. The man at the house must have turned on the lights through the compound. He was preparing to come and search out whoever had killed the boy.

And yet all I could do was stare at the sight in front of me.

At the garden that had been revealed.

Hannah remained crouched at the edge of the clearing, listening. There had been no other noises since the scream.

She didn't know what to do. It was as though she needed someone to take her hand and lead her. Any exhilaration was long gone: that had been a weird illusion, one she could no longer remember now that this was *real* and she was actually *here*. What she wanted to do, more than anything else, was be anywhere else in the world than this place.

But right now, she didn't even dare to move.

Then:

*Whump.*

*Whump.*

*Whump.*

*Whump.*

Somewhere close to the corrugated iron structure, a floodlight came on. It was pointing inwards, but enough light fell through the fence to illuminate the clearing and it revealed the hundreds of black flowers growing here. Hannah stared down at them in absolute, non-functioning horror. They had spread out here from the compound on the other side of the fence, like an army of ants eating their way steadily through the forest floor.

In her mind, she imagined them chirruping as their petals flicked open and closed – and an image came to her. Not one from her father's story, but an actual memory. A woman buried up to her neck in the ground below a house. The woman had once talked very calmly and told her it would all be okay and they would get out of there together, but now her eyes were rolling, her mouth wailing, and the words coming out of it no longer formed part of any sensible language whatsoever.

*Oh God.*

It was too much. The moment broke.

Suddenly Hannah was upright and moving. Back through the trees. Back towards the path. Mind blank – she had no armour against this. She was just determined to get out of here as quickly as she could. To get as far away from this nightmare as would ever be possible again.

# Chapter Thirty-One

At first, I thought my vision was starring over again.

The whole back field here was open, and every square metre of ground had been dug up and filled in again, so that it was uneven: tufted with patches of grass between ridges of bare, churned earth. All of it glistened under the floodlights, but it wasn't my vision creating the stars at all, I realised, it was the flowers.

Hundreds of them. Black flowers covered the entire lawn, poking up from the ground, their petals fragmented and missing. They looked like baby birds, scrawny necks stretched out, mouths open wide to receive food. Blind and bedraggled and helpless.

*Oh God.*

It was an enormous mass grave, divided into obvious sections. This was where the old man and his family had buried their dead. Cultivated their crop.

A door slammed somewhere back at the house.

I glanced around me, feeling helpless. There weren't any rocks on the ground here at all, never mind one large enough to smash the padlock with. Even if there had been, I doubted I'd have had the strength to lift it. There was nothing to defend myself with.

I stumbled back to the window.

Ally's face was pressed up to the bars, pale and frightened.

'I can't open it.'

'Neil—'

'Give me your hands. Let me try to unpick that tape.'

'There's no point. My leg's chained to this fucking thing.'

'What thing?'

'Some kind of steel table. It's bolted down.'

I pushed myself away from the wall and half fell along the side of the bunker, towards the end closest to the house. Checking the ground as I went. Looking for *anything*. Finding nothing.

I had no idea what we were going to do.

*I'm sorry, Ally.*

Sooner or later he was going to come down here. Probably straightaway. I stopped at the corner: the only plan I could come up with was to wait here. The floodlight was blocked by the bunker at this corner. I could press myself into this sharp angle of shadow and try to attack him as he came round, before he had the chance to see me.

It was a fucking laughable idea. I realised that as an arc of pain went through me. My hands were slippery with blood, and I pictured rainbows of fire, and my stomach full of curling migraine-light. Barbara's words came back to me.

*And the policeman didn't end up being tortured to death on a farm.*

A shadow began spreading down the garden. It seemed enormous, and it rippled over the ridges of earth. His footsteps sounded across: soil crunching beneath his boots, petals crushed silently.

I readied myself. Breathed in slowly and deeply through my nose. For the moment, the stars had faded away again. Now was as good as it was going to get—

Except then the shadow moved sideways a little across the black flowers of the lawn. And when he stepped into view it was several metres away from the corner of the bunker. Too big a distance for me to close, even if I could have kept myself upright without the wall for support. I'd never stood a chance.

So I just leaned there, looking at him. Waiting.

He was a huge man: surely the one I'd seen in the van below my flat that night. Half of him was illuminated by the floodlight at the top of the lawn; the other half was in shadow. The one eye I could see was looking directly at me.

And he was holding a shotgun.

We stared at each other for a few silent seconds before he began walking towards me. As he reached the corner of the bunker, I realised I couldn't stand up any more. I fell down, ended up on my back. And then, a moment later, he loomed directly above me, blotting out the whole world.

*Walk quickly, but don't run.*

*Try* not to run.

Hannah emerged from the undergrowth, back onto the dirt track at the corner of the fence. It was much brighter out here now. There was a floodlight near the entrance, and it cast an angle of brightness over the field in front, a rough, crinkled shadow of mesh across it. But she only looked that way long enough to make sure nobody was coming out. They weren't. She turned and headed immediately back up the path in the direction of the road.

Walking quickly.

Her heart was running, though.

*It's okay*, she thought. It was simple: if she could get back to her car and drive away then it would be all right. Because Neil Dawson was in there, sealed away within the compound, and her old family would take care of him and anything he knew. They'd dispose of his car too. All of it would just disappear. If anyone remembered the message he'd left, she could make up a story about phoning him and it being nothing. Nobody needed to know she was ever here. Nobody would ever have to know anything about this place.

Most of all, she wouldn't have to be *here* any more.

She could do that.

Hannah faltered, but forced herself to keep going. The darkness, the silence, felt like it was pressing tight up against her back, and it was fear that pushed her forward again. Ahead of her, to the right, she caught sight of the pylon: a malformed grid, darker black against the night sky. Already, she could hear it humming ominously.

*You can do anything.*

And again she faltered – this time right on the lip of the hill.

She turned, glancing behind her.

The light through the gate was still visible from here, just smaller and more insignificant, like someone had dropped a torch on its side. But even from this distance she could see the tiny nub of darkness on the field in front. The smallest of shadows.

Someone was at the gate.

Hannah stood there. *You can't go back.* Every instinct in her body told her to turn around and keep going. And she could run now – the car was no more than a minute away. The fields around her were empty and dead. Nobody would know she was ever here.

*You can't go back.*

But that was the voice of a terrified little girl. One who had been brutalised her entire life, beaten down and made to feel insignificant and always scared. Who had never known what *safety* was until its embers had been breathed carefully into life through years and years of love. And maybe Hannah was that girl, but she was also another one entirely, and all the shades in-between.

*Hannah, you can do anything.*

And before she could think about it any more, she ran back down the hill. The night-time world juddered around her, a green-black haze with a spot of light dancing in front of her, growing larger and larger as she approached.

When she reached the gate, the figure there stepped closer. Not touching it, but coming as far forward as possible to meet her.

A little girl. She was mostly just a silhouette against the light, but Hannah could see enough. She had long dirty-blonde hair, pulled into rough bunches, and she was wearing an old-fashioned dress, and the expression on her face made Hannah pull up slightly. Her heart was thudding, but not from the run.

She got as close to the fence as she dared and crouched down. Her jeans tightened around her thigh.

'Hello,' she said softly. 'What's your name?'

The little girl didn't reply, but lifted her head slightly.

Hannah said, 'Can you let me in?'

For a moment, there was nothing. After a few seconds, the girl looked away to one side, then back – right at Hannah – and nodded. She whispered back, and her voice was so small and frightened that Hannah understood what a risk she was taking, even considering trusting this stranger. And yet there was something else there too. A sense of determination beyond her years.

*Fierce little thing.*

The little girl said. 'Will you help me?'

Hannah nodded.

'Yes,' she said. 'I will.'


After he'd opened the padlock and the door, the man dragged me into the bunker with one hand – just grabbed a handful of my jacket, hefted me inside, then threw me down in the opposite corner from Ally. The collision jolted me so badly that I blacked out.

The next thing I knew I was coughing so violently I was nearly being sick, almost choking. Aside from the pain, I had no real idea where I was or what was happening. The white tiles beneath me were shockingly cold. When I opened my eyes, I saw my own hand pushing violently against the wall beside me, leaving smears of blood. There was a shadow over me, and it felt like my stomach was raging with fire.

Ally was screaming. *Shrieking.*

I rolled my head quickly to the side and saw her through the gloom in the cell. She was over by the window, one foot chained to the leg of a steel table, and she wasn't screaming because she was being hurt. She was screaming at the man I realised was standing with one foot pressing down on my ruined stomach.

'You *bastard*!' She was spitting at him. 'You *fucking bastard*!'

He took his foot off me and moved towards her instead. Immediately, she fell silent: backed away as much as she could, her bound hands held up defensively in front of her.

'Hey,' I said.

The man ignored me. His back was almost wider than the door he'd dragged me in through. Through the pain, I tried to think of something, anything, that would distract him.

'Hey,' I said louder. 'Your father's dead.'

That stopped him moving.

Very slowly, he turned around. In the darkness, I couldn't see his face. He walked back and stood over me again.

'I saw him in the hospital,' I said. 'He's dead.'

He crouched down above me. I caught the smell coming off him. It was awful – he reeked of woodland and freshly dug graves. The anger was beating from him: waves of heat.

'I put a pillow over his fucking face.'

It wasn't hard to get the hatred into the lie, to make it sound convincing. Right now, I wished I'd done it. It would have been something, at least.

He knelt down on my upper arms, pinning them to the floor. The weight of him was pulverising. My biceps felt like they'd just been crushed completely. The pain was impossible to bear, and my body screamed for it to stop, but I couldn't do anything. *Shit shit shit, I can't cope, I can't cope, get away NOW.* All I could do was blink, again and again, and think that if he stayed over here with me then there was at least a chance help would arrive in time for Ally.

The first punch was only a light jab, but it knocked my thoughts off-centre. It took a second to realise it had even happened. Ally began screaming – just plain screaming this time. The man drew his fist back properly.

I looked to one side. Through the open door of the cell, just before he hit me again, the last thing I remember is seeing the flowers growing out there.


Through the open door of his cell, Sullivan can see the flowers that grow in the garden out there. Even in the sunlight, they are pitch-black. They seem to colonise the land like mould, drawing his attention away from the apple trees beyond them. Without the flowers, and what they are, it would be a curiously idyllic scene – he can hear birds singing, for example, and they sound happy. They are oblivious to what's happening to him in here, tied to this chair.

The man hits him again. The chair rocks onto its back legs for a moment, and everything blurs.

The view through the doorway gradually swims back into view, and he remembers where he is. He blinks away blood and hears a rasping sound, then a hock. The man has just spat onto the grimy white tiles of the bunker floor. Sullivan's head lolls to one side and sees it there, then turns loosely back to the man, who is standing before him, wiping his mouth with the back of his hand.

They lock eyes – as best Sullivan can anyway.

Behind his hand, the man starts giggling to himself.

Sullivan isn't even sure why. Perhaps he has seen the damage he's inflicted, which Sullivan himself can only feel, numbly guess at. It's so much that it doesn't even matter any more. The man has hit him a lot – always in the face, because that is where true sadists concentrate their attentions. Our faces are important to us because they define our identity, which is why torturers disfigure them in particular. Partly because we fear it beforehand, and partly because others fear it afterwards. And yet perhaps that is at odds with what is occurring here. Because this man does not intend to let him live for others to see. And because Sullivan understands that there is more to a person than what he or she looks like to others.

His head rolls again, his vision turning back towards the open door and the black flowers out there, incongruous in the sun. As the man begins beating him again – harder now, perhaps determined to get this over with – Sullivan's mind is knocked free. The black flowers, he thinks. Once the seed is planted, it's inevitable the flower will bloom. He thinks about Clark Poole and what he did to little Anna Hanson, and how everything, really, comes back to that. He wonders at how the structures that grow from such terrible ground can become so elaborate, so strange.

And then he realises he can see her.

He thinks it's a dream at first. Or worse. His thoughts have become detached by the constant stream of blows and perhaps he is being visited by ghosts or an angel. Perhaps she will grip his hand in a moment and take him away with her.

But no, he does see her. She is there.

Anna Hanson. No, of course, not her. Charlotte. She is standing in the doorway of the bunker, blocking his view of the garden now. The man hasn't seen her – he is still at work, exhausting himself. But as Sullivan's head is knocked back and forth, he sees her. Every time he faces that way, she has moved a little closer to the shotgun the man has leaned against the wall by the door.

Closer.

Her expression is full of terror. Despite that, he would smile if he could. She is so brave doing this. It must be enormously hard, because he knows how badly she is scared of this man, and she knows what happened the last time she dared cross him.

Closer.

Nobody has any right to expect her to be brave again.

But she is.

Sullivan closes his eyes, almost losing consciousness altogether. The last thing he remembers seeing is the little girl picking up the shotgun and raising it quickly. Anna Hanson. Charlotte Webb. In his mind, there is no longer a difference. It no longer matters.

And then, before Sullivan can think anything else, the world explodes in crimson and black.


Hannah lowered the shotgun.

It had been a controlled shot. She'd aimed, tightened, squeezed. The stock had juddered against her shoulder, jarring her, but not badly. It was the noise that was worst. The explosive bang seemed to have sucked all the other sounds out of the world, and her ears were ringing emptily now it was gone.

As the ringing subsided, the screams returned.

Hannah glanced across at the woman on the other side of the bunker – little more than a girl, really. Dawson's partner. She was crouched down by a steel table, hands tied, and appeared to be trying to clench herself into the smallest ball possible, while still peering over her arm at the sight across from her.

'It's okay,' Hannah said.

It was still hard to hear her own words, and she wasn't entirely sure whether she was shouting or whispering.

The man that must once have been her brother was lying in the far corner of the bunker now. His head was gone, along with most of his left shoulder. The force of the shot had blown the rest of his body clean over the man lying on the floor. Hannah presumed that was Neil Dawson. It was hard to tell – he was on his back, entirely still, and his face was a mask of blood.

Hannah stared down at Dawson for a couple of moments, then at her brother's body. At the moment, she felt blank. But as bad as this was, it wasn't so bad, she thought. There was an odd sense of things slotting into place out of sight, things she didn't understand but felt right – as though it would always have come to this eventually, and that it had needed to.

She cracked the shotgun to one side, and the spent cartridge clicked backwards through the air. She knelt down beside

Dawson, made sure his airways were clear, and gently rolled him onto his side.

And then she stepped back out into the garden of silent black flowers, and called an ambulance.

# One Year Later

# Chapter Thirty-Two

It was an ordinary day, with no hint of magic to it.

Certainly not for the people braving the promenade in Whitkirk, anyway. Many of them were taking late holidays here, and the early September weather had not been as kind to them as last year's. It was bitterly cold, the rain whipping across, stinging the road along the seafront. Behind the wall, the waves were turbulent and wild. They crashed angrily against the great stone blocks, and occasionally even cascaded over onto the promenade itself, landing with a hiss and a spatter.

In the moments when the wind stopped roaring, Hannah could hear the sound of the amusement arcades. The machine-gun *chatter* of success; the *whoop-whoop* of failure. Up ahead, she could see The Fisherman's Catch. A waitress was leaning over a table inside by the window, her elbow working at an angle. Opposite the café, on the promenade itself, a woman was standing.

She was wrapped in a coat, her dyed-black hair twirling in the wind like ribbons, and, even from a distance, Hannah could tell she was very beautiful. But there was also something spectral about her – something indefinable, or even supernatural. Standing there, clutching her handbag, she might almost have been a ghost from some old movie, or a flickering, sepia memory of the seafront itself. As Hannah walked towards her, a line from *The Black Flower* drifted into her head.

It is as if the world shifted in its sleep, and one of its ideas escaped and became real.

Something like that, anyway.

Except this woman wasn't a ghost, and nor was she a sepia memory or an idea. She was a real person of flesh and blood, albeit one whose identity was constructed from lies so efficiently that she might as well have been a work of fiction. She certainly was on the few days every year she returned here to Whitkirk.

'Hello, Charlotte.'

The woman had been staring out to sea, lost in thought, and hadn't noticed Hannah approaching. She started slightly, then shook her head as she turned.

'I'm sorry?'

'It's Charlotte, isn't it?' Hannah said. 'Charlotte Webb?'

'No.'

The woman feigned confusion but caught unawares, she wasn't half the actor she could be. That name had hit home, and below the surface she was obviously wary, nervous. The wind struck up, and the woman's hair wrapped itself around her face. The hand she used to hook it back over her shoulder was trembling slightly.

'I'm sorry,' she repeated. 'That's not my name.'

'Yes, it is.' Hannah leaned against the wall beside her. 'We both know what I'm talking about. And there are only two of us here, so it doesn't really make any sense to lie, does it?'

She stared at the café across the street. Beside her, she could sense the woman's gaze. Her real name was Suzanne Doherty. Right now, she was probably wondering who the hell Hannah was and weighing up her options. She was curious to see what Doherty would do. Would she deny knowing the name again – perhaps make some quick excuse and walk away – or was she going to admit it?

'I'm sorry.' She managed to sound more adamant now. 'My name is Suzanne.'

Hannah nodded and smiled, but said, 'No, your name is Charlotte.'

'I just told you—'

'Do you remember me?' She turned to look at her. 'We were at the foster home together, although I had a different name back then. That was when *I* was Charlotte. But now my name is Hannah Price.'

'I'm – I'm afraid I have to go.'

And this time, the woman really did try to walk away. So Hannah grabbed hold of her arm, very hard.

'What do you think—?'

'*DS* Hannah Price.'

She waited for that information to settle, and for the woman to realise walking away wasn't going to be an option. When the resistance was over, Hannah let go of her arm and nodded again.

'Sensible decision, Charlotte.'

'Stop calling me that.'

'It's your name, isn't it? Or it might as well be. If you repeat something often enough, it becomes true. That's how stories work. And we both know that's what you did. You stole my story and pretended it was yours.'

Doherty looked as though she was about to deny it again, but then seemed to understand there was no point. Instead, she just stared at Hannah, not blinking, not knowing what to say. Caught out, and scared of the consequences, the trouble she was in. She was almost shaking.

*Good*, Hannah thought.

But at the same time, that brought a twinge of guilt. She didn't actually remember sharing the foster home with Suzanne Doherty – the time she'd spent there was as hazy and indistinct as all her early memories – but, looking at this grown woman, she could easily make out traces of the child she had been. From what Hannah had read in the files, she knew that at six years old Suzanne Doherty had been one of those hollow-eyed, skinny-shouldered children who had never been safe in her home. She also knew that, unlike Hannah, Doherty had been in the foster home not because her parents couldn't be found, but because they had been all too horribly present.

It was natural to feel sympathy for the little girl she'd once been. Normally, as people grow up and commit acts of harm themselves, that sympathy gives way to blame and anger. No matter what has happened to them in the past, adults are culpable. Under different circumstances, Hannah would have had no trouble tearing into Suzanne Doherty for what she'd done but the problem was that little girl was still so readily apparent below the surface. While Doherty had grown older physically, inside she had not.

Perhaps there were other reasons too. Doherty had stolen her story, so their identities were bound together in some ways. And without the intervention of Colin Price, this was the woman Hannah might have become.

Doherty said, 'I haven't done anything wrong.'

That was the child talking. Hannah noted the defensiveness: the almost pleading tone of her voice. No longer denying what she'd done, but still shifting positions to refuse taking the blame. *It wasn't me, it wasn't my fault.*

'That's a matter of opinion,' Hannah said. 'Maybe there was nothing legally wrong in pretending to be someone you weren't, but it had consequences for people, and you know it. You told my story to Robert Wiseman and he wrote about it in his book. That had consequences for him and his wife. It must have been very exciting for you, to have somebody paying you that much attention, but didn't it ever bother you, what happened to him afterwards?'

The woman said nothing.

'And last year, of course, Christopher Dawson died trying to protect you. He was a small man, but he probably bought you enough time to escape into the woods. Which means that he died because of your fantasy. Don't you think that was wrong?'

296

'That wasn't—'

'*Your fault.*' Hannah folded her arms, shook her head. 'I really didn't know if you'd come this year, after what happened last time. Because it must have been terrifying at the time. I suppose you knew it was safe this year, didn't you? After all, you knew the family had been found. So what was there to be afraid of?'

Suzanne Doherty turned away, then took a long, deep breath. She spent a few seconds just looking out over the crashing waves, and Hannah allowed her them. The wind picked up again. It seemed to batter the people walking past, but she ignored it, and eventually Doherty spoke.

'I didn't believe they existed.'

'No.'

'It was enough that other people did. He did. Christopher Dawson. I met him the day before what . . . happened. We arranged to go to the viaduct. I was going to help him research his book. I thought it would be "fun".'

Hannah said nothing.

'I didn't think anybody would know.'

'Well, if it makes you feel any better, coming here today didn't make any difference. I was just curious to see if you would. If you hadn't, I already knew your name and address, and I'd have come to see you instead.'

'How did you find me?'

Hannah shrugged. 'It wasn't so hard.'

If Neil Dawson had died from his injuries at the farm, she wouldn't have known there was a woman impersonating her at all. But, after Dawson had recovered enough to be interviewed, it had been fairly straightforward to put the various pieces together. She knew someone had been pretending to be Charlotte Webb. Whoever that was must have heard the story somewhere, and it seemed they also had a reason to return to Mrs Fitzwilliam's foster home every year. It was reasonable to assume those two facts were connected, and so Hannah had obtained the foster home records for the period she had stayed there. In reality, she had needed only one. The girl was right there in the photograph on Mrs Fitzwilliam's mantelpiece. Even all these years later, it was possible to recognise her. Dawson might have too, if he hadn't been looking at the wrong girl – or rather, the right one.

Hannah said, 'You haven't changed much, Suzanne. The moment I saw the picture of you as a little girl, I recognised you from the photo with Robert Wiseman. And the shot in your adult file isn't so different either. It's as though not much has changed for you at all over the years. That's interesting, isn't it?'

Suzanne continued to stare out to sea and didn't reply.

It wasn't just the physical resemblance either. As an adult, Suzanne Doherty had been convicted of wasting police time on several occasions. She had once been charged with fraud, after pretending to be the victim of a real-life murder, one where the body had never been found. Doherty had claimed she'd actually disappeared and was in hiding from her alleged attacker, and extorted money and shelter from a well-meaning man she'd met in a bar. Those charges had ultimately been dropped at the man's request, but similar activities dotted her case file. False accusations; false reports. The little girl had grown into a woman who lied, personally and professionally, in order to get attention. A woman who had learned first-hand which stories mattered to people and which did not.

That woman sighed now, defeated.

'I remember you,' Doherty said.

'And?'

'You talked so much. Do you remember that? You used to tell your story, over and over again. And that policeman who came to see you, believe me, he never tired of listening. He kept coming back to see you.'

*That policeman.* Her father, of course, the man who had ultimately adopted her. With some trepidation, Hannah had looked into her past and had the relevant files opened. She had

298

read the documents Colin and Melissa Price had made for application of custody, the agency investigations and reports, the evaluations and conclusions. Colin Price was a respected member of the community, and had supporting statements from several equally well-respected sources. Even more importantly, the reports noted he had already established a considerable rapport with the girl then known as Charlotte. One line had leapt out immediately at Hannah as she read the file. It had stayed with her ever since.

> Although traumatised, it is evident that Charlotte has developed a deep, reciprocal bond of affection with Colin Price, and that his presence is reassuring and comforting to her. In her own words, he makes her 'feel safe'.

Amongst her father's papers, she had found the birth certificate they'd given her. She had been adopted as Hannah Price, in a bid to provide a break from her past. To start again and try to forget.

And that was exactly what had happened.

'I was so envious of you,' Doherty said. 'So envious of how much you *mattered* to people. Because I didn't matter to anyone. Nobody listened to me. Nobody ever came to see me. They just didn't care. I mean, do you think someone like Robert Wiseman would ever have written a book about *me*?'

She seemed about to say something else, but the words fell away. She looked back out to sea again and just shook her head.

Hannah watched her for a moment, and thought about all the things she could say. All the *rage* she could unleash on this ultimately inconsequential person – someone who, really, had nothing to do with anything. Just a little girl who had heard a story and seen how it could benefit her. And ultimately, Doherty was right. She had never been adopted, just bounced from foster home to foster home until adulthood. And no, Robert Wiseman would never have written a story about her back then, although he might have done now.

'You don't have to worry,' Hannah said. 'I'm not going to arrest you. I could, and I probably should, but I don't see much point. Everything is closed now, give or take. Nobody even knows for certain you were there that day at the viaduct with Christopher Dawson. Nobody really cares about you at all.'

Doherty frowned. 'But—'

'I just came out of curiosity. Maybe I just wanted to see what had become of me.' Hannah leaned away from the barrier. 'Goodbye, Charlotte.'

'That's not my name.'

'It can be. You wanted it and I don't. It's yours now.'

Hannah pressed a piece of paper into Doherty's hand; it had her phone number written on it.

'If you don't want it either, maybe at some point I can help.'

And then, before the woman could reply, she walked quickly away, back down the promenade. If Doherty wanted to continue her charade then so be it. It didn't mean anything any more. The story was past tense now. You don't have to read anything you don't want to, and if Doherty got in touch then she would try her best to explain why and how.

The end.

When Hannah reached The Southerton, she thought about glancing behind her – but didn't. She had no wish to see Suzanne Doherty standing where she had left her, her dyed-black hair whirling in the wind like tattered petals. She had her own flowers now, growing in the back garden of her father's house. She'd planted them that summer, and they were very beautiful indeed. Reds and blues and yellows, just like she remembered. What she wanted to do now was light a fire and sit inside, and maybe go through to the kitchen occasionally, glance outside, and remind herself they were there.

And she could do that.

**Extract from unfinished document by Christopher Dawson,
retrieved from his laptop**

It's one night, early September, 1993.

He is sitting at home with his wife and they are watching the television – or Laura is. The programme is a documentary about cancer. Years later, this is the disease that will claim her life, although neither of them knows that yet. Watching the programme, Laura keeps expressing small noises of sadness at the accounts of suffering and courage that flicker on the screen. *It's impossible to imagine*, he can hear her thinking, *it's so horrible for the people involved – thank God we aren't going through something like that ourselves*. In the future, when they do, Laura will display levels of resolve and strength equal to anyone in the programme tonight, and he will save his own expressions of sadness and grief for times and places when she can't hear them.

For now, though, he is just sitting beside her, reading. The front room is threadbare (they can't afford better tailoring than this) but at least it's warm and gently lit. The volume on the television is turned down: a low murmur, as quiet as a parent whispering to a sleeping child. Without taking his eyes off the book, he reaches down and runs his little finger over the back of her hand. A gentle tickle, just to remind her he is there and thinking of her.

And that is when someone knocks at the door.

It's three hard *raps* from downstairs, harsh and aggressive. If the noise hadn't stopped, he might have thought someone was trying to break in.

He turns to face the door to the hall. His first thought, of course, is of Neil, who is a light sleeper at the best of times and hard to settle. The noise might disturb him.

The second thought is the hour.

'Late for visitors,' Laura says.

'I'll go.'

He stands up and heads as quietly as possible into the hallway, to the top of the stairs. For a moment, he listens for signs that Neil has been disturbed, but that end of the house remains silent, so he heads down the stairs carefully but quickly, anxious to avoid more noise. There is a square panel of bobbled glass above the old front door, black with night. It makes him uneasy. Laura was right – it is late. And it takes effort to get to their house, the long driveway and steps discouraging casual visitors. As he reaches the front door, he wishes there was a chain he could put on. He has never got round to installing one.

As he opens the door, he hears the burst of cold night air rattle the windows upstairs. Instinctively, he recognises the man in the black suit, standing on his doorstep.

'Robert,' he says.

It is him, and yet he's still taken aback by how much Wiseman has changed since they last met. In his mind, Robert is slick and professional, a cool handler of crowds, very self-assured – everything, in fact, that he himself will never be. The man on his doorstep now might almost have been a different person altogether. His suit is shabby and tatty, far too big for him, and he has lost so much weight that his skull gleams through his skin. His hair is also much longer than he ever wore it in the past: unbrushed and greasy-looking, so the length feels more due to lack of care or interest than to any kind of design.

Of course, he knows from casual conversations that Robert has dropped off the radar since Vanessa's disappearance. The rumours were that he was unreliable, his behaviour increasingly erratic. Professionally, he is damaged goods. Looking at him now, pale and gaunt and sickly, it is obvious that he is personally damaged too. His hollow eyes have a glint of insanity to them.

Robert nods at him and then stands expectantly, hands clasped before him. It looks like one hand is trying to pull off the fingers of the other.

*Of course*, he thinks.

*He wants to come in.*

The night breeze rustles the leaves over by the stone steps, and the sound makes him even more uneasy than this skeleton of a man on his doorstep. He feels the presence of ghosts. Thinking of the warm, softly lit life he has upstairs behind him, he realises he does not want this man in his home. That in fact he will do anything to keep him out.

'What can I do for you?'

'Can I come in?'

'No.'

The bluntness of the response brings a pained expression to Robert's face. 'I understand.'

'I'm sorry, Robert. About everything that happened.'

'Thank you. You were right, though, all along. Everything that happened is my own fault. I understand that now, and I'm going to try to make amends for it.'

'You don't look well.'

Robert nods, as though it's of absolutely no consequence, then stares down at the ground for a moment. There is a carrier bag at his feet. Then he looks up again.

'Vanessa came back.'

'Oh?'

That surprises him; he would have expected to have heard.

'She came back as a flower.'

The words settle. For a moment, he has no idea what to say.

'Have you told the police?'

Robert smiles sadly. 'I can't do that.'

'Perhaps you should.'

'Perhaps.' The smile slips away. 'But you could have done, as well, couldn't you? When you heard what happened to Vanessa. Although . . . you probably didn't know everything. And it's not your responsibility, is it? Not your story. I understand that.'

He shifts slightly. It isn't an accusation, but it feels like one. Because, yes, he had thought of telling the police what he knows. The reason he has not done . . . well, he thinks again of his wife and child upstairs. Regardless of whether it is *his* story or not, it is a dangerous one. He has distanced himself from Robert out of cowardice, perhaps, but not entirely for his own benefit. One can be cowardly on behalf of others.

And from the very beginning, he's felt an instinctive desire to keep this story at arm's length to protect those he loves.

Robert says, 'If I did go to the police, would they believe me?'

'I don't know. They might.'

'Maybe if I had somebody to corroborate meeting her?'

In the cold night air, he convinces himself to stand firm. He puts images of Laura and Neil at the forefront of his mind. And eventually, Robert looks away.

'It doesn't matter,' he says. 'I'm going to write about it. I've got an idea for a new book. A sequel, I suppose. It's about a man who writes a story. Part of it's already real, and the part that isn't comes true. I'm going to call it *Black Flowers* and I'm going to research it properly too. I've figured out how to find Charlotte again. I think she goes home on her birthday every year. I'm going to find out.'

'Is that a good idea?'

'It's an idea, isn't it? That's all we have.' Robert smiles to himself, then picks up the carrier bag. 'Before I go, I've got something for you. I want you to take it. In case anything happens to me.'

'I don't want it.'

'Please. For old times.'

There is something in his face then: that same expression of sadness, but stretched longer, back through time. And, for a moment, he sees his old friend there. The guilt threatens to bloom, turning his life inside out. He wants to help him. He knows he probably should. He presses it all down again, but something still makes him take the carrier bag from someone who had once been his best friend in the world.

'Thank you.'

Robert steps back onto the flagstone path. It takes him outside the stretch of light from the door, leaving merely the pale impression of a skull in the night. He says:

'In another life, Christopher.'

And before he can reply, his old friend is gone.

After he has closed and locked the door, he looks inside the carrier bag. There is only one item in there: a copy of *The Black Flower*. It is a paperback: well thumbed, spine bent, a handful of pages turned over at the corners. As he begins to flick through, the book falls open very naturally near the centre, where he finds a black flower pressed carefully between the pages.

He stares at it for a while. The emotions he feels are impossible to describe, because he knows exactly what he is looking at. *She came back as a flower.* What he wants to do most of all is throw the book away, but he knows that he won't do that – that what his old friend has just given him amounts to a sacred pact. He is its caretaker now, this dangerous story. So instead, he closes the book gently and looks at the front door with its glass square of black night above.

A chain.

He will get around to installing a chain.

At the top of the stairs, he pauses before entering the living room. What should he say to Laura? Instinctively, he wants to keep this from her. Although he will have to tell her it was Robert at the door, he doesn't want to involve her any more than he has to. The book and the flower make that difficult.

'Dad?'

Neil – calling from the darkness down the corridor. He hesitates for a moment, and then turns from the living room and walks down that way instead.

In Neil's bedroom, he doesn't turn on the main light, but walks across and flicks on the more gentle feathered lamp. It reveals his son, sitting upright in bed, looking frightened. He feels the familiar burst of love for the boy, and knows that, whatever guilt he feels over abandoning his old friend, it is worth it to keep his family safe.

'Hey there,' he says softly. 'What's the matter?'

'I heard a noise.'

'It was nothing, I promise.'

'I'm scared.'

He can see that. Neil often is scared at night, when the house is dark and the silence is heavy. Perhaps he should be growing out of it by now – but then again, does anyone ever grow out of that?

He sits down on the chair beside the bed.

'You're safe,' he says. 'There's nothing to be scared of. Mum and I would never let anything happen to you.'

Neil doesn't look convinced by that. Although still afraid of the dark, he is already smart enough to have begun doubting that kind of re-assurance. He amends it in his head now, purely for his own benefit. *I will do everything I can to keep you safe. Whatever it takes.*

'Would you like me to read to you for a bit?' he says.

Neil nods.

'Well, okay then.'

He slips the carrier bag underneath his son's bed, almost without thinking about it. He will figure out what to do with it later. For now, he crosses one leg over the other, and leans back in the chair, con-sidering. They have a book on the go, but he doesn't feel like picking it up.

It is hard to think of anything except Robert. His old friend has filtered down into his subconscious, and he knows that, whatever happens, he will write about him someday. It is inevitable. He will write about the real life story his friend stole, the piece of fiction he made from it, and the effect that had on everyone. Not yet, but some-day. When it feels safe to.

And in the meantime . . . well.

There are only the two of them here.

Christopher leans in closer, almost conspiratorially.

'This is not the story of a little girl who vanishes,' he begins. 'This is the story of a little girl *who comes back.*'

# Chapter Thirty-Three

I don't remember a huge amount about what happened at the farm right at the end, and that's probably a good thing. Afterwards, in the hospital, the police kept asking me how I'd found the place, and all I could tell them was that I'd followed my father's map – the cross he'd drawn in the road atlas – but at that point I still had no idea at all how he'd found it. It was only later, from what other people discovered, that it began to make some kind of sense.

The old man, Cartwright, suffered a second heart attack and died in the hospital, but poor Lorraine Haggerty, along with the three children born on the farm, had been able to tell the police a certain amount. Cartwright had been obsessed with the idea of transformation. *We are all made of stardust* – that was what he used to say. *Nothing ever really dies.* In his mind, he and his macabre family had been involved in a grand experiment on Ellis Farm. They received visitors there, and those visitors stayed for a while before being sent home again, changed into something else. In his mind, his victims remained alive, just different. In much the same way that wine was different from the grapes it was made from. Or champagne, as Robert Wiseman might have said.

At some point, Cartwright had happened across Wiseman's novel. The title alone would have drawn him in, never mind the synopsis, and obviously, when he read it, he would have recognised the story of his missing daughter all too clearly in its pages.

But there had been more to it than that. One thing I do remember, all too clearly, is the office I saw inside the house – where the pages of *The Black Flower* had been plastered over every available wall. Cartwright came to see the author as a kindred spirit. Because Wiseman, in his own way, had done precisely the same thing as he did: taken people's lives and transformed them into something new. And something that, in his case, would truly live for ever. Stories don't die. Books might, physically, but not stories. They take root in people's minds and bloom there. They wait to be told and to grow, like seeds.

The old man had become obsessed by the book. As he saw it, Wiseman had turned his life into a story. Ultimately, he'd returned the favour. He'd taken the fictional parts of Wiseman's story and made them real.

Which was how my father had found the farm. He hadn't.

Robert Wiseman had based the description of the farm in his book on Ellis Farm, which had been owned by his parents when he was a child. He'd mentioned it in the interview with Barbara Phillips. His mother and father were long dead, of course, and the farm had changed hands several times since. Its fortunes had fallen and then failed altogether. But at some point after the publication of *The Black Flower*, the man described in its pages had bought it and moved there. He'd read the description in the book, and he'd wanted to continue his work in that exact same environment.

He'd made Wiseman's story come true. From the layout of the house, it seemed likely that a small bedroom in which Robert Wiseman had laid dreaming in as a little boy had, years later, become a shrine to his words.

The man who had handled the sale was Andrew Haggerty, who had been an estate agent in Thornton at the time, and who now no longer had to wonder what it was he'd done to be targeted. The answer was nothing. He'd just crossed paths with the wrong person and perhaps that's all it ever really comes down to. Even now, the police were still attempting to track Cartwright's previous residences, to see exactly where he'd been performing his experiments and for how long. How many were there? How many victims? How long had this been going on, and for how many generations? Right now, there was no clear answer to any of those questions.

My father, planning to write about his old friend, had simply wanted to see the real-life location he'd based the farm in his bestseller on. A little background colour. From the question marks on the calendar, he hadn't even been sure he would call in at all. Except Wiseman had stolen so much of his story from other people's lives that I guess my father was curious to see one part he hadn't. And so he'd gone there.

I might never know what happened: how much he'd seen, and what kind of reception or conversation had taken place. But whatever it was, it had been enough for them to start following him. All the way to the promenade in Whitkirk. All the way to the viaduct afterwards. And then all the way to me, through the story I'd written and sent.

Thinking it was harmless – just a story, after all.

Imagining it was safe.


'You're safe,' I say.

It's not really true, of course, but it doesn't matter. The way I see it, if you repeat something enough times, it might as well be.

My son, lying in his cot, isn't massively convinced by the sentiment. He's not actively crying, but his arms and legs are going, and he's nowhere near being settled. Obviously, at five months old, he doesn't remotely understand the words or what they mean, but it's not the content, it's just the sound of my voice, the silence being filled.

I rest one hand very gently on his stomach. In my other, I'm holding the sheaf of papers, which I can just about read by the small lamp on my father's old desk. That's the one bit of furniture in the room Ally and I haven't got round to replacing yet, though we will. But Chris is only just big enough for his own cot and his own room, and there's no rush. At least the rest of it is perfect. The new carpet is nailed down at the skirting boards. The shelves of my father's books have been transferred to the back of the living room instead. The walls are freshly papered. The camera for the video monitor sits at the end of the crib, glowing orange.

I clear my throat, and then keep my voice as gentle as possible as I read from the printed papers in my hand. This is the one single piece of my father's planned book that he'd managed to complete. A solitary file I found on his laptop. He was still researching his subject matter, but he'd written what I think he intended to be the beginning: Wiseman turning up with the book and the flower, and the short section afterwards that I'm reading from now. It's rough, of course. I'm not sure it would even have made it into his second draft, never mind the final one. But still. When I read them, they make me feel a little closer to him.

'You're safe,' I tell my son. 'There's nothing to be scared of. Mum and I would never let anything happen to you.'

After my son has gone to sleep, I head back through to the front room.

I take it slowly. I'm mostly back to normal, but my stomach is still tight, and sometimes it hurts if I straighten up too quickly after scrunching. Ally is sitting on the settee and watching a very quiet television programme, but she glances up and gives me a smile as I open the door. She looks exhausted. We probably both do.

'Well done,' she says.

'Thanks.'

I sit down. The video monitor is on the coffee table in front of us. Our son is sleeping peacefully in grainy black and white on the screen, both hands pressed to his mouth.

We watch the television for a bit. I'm not even sure what's on, but it doesn't really matter. The peace and calm is what's important. After a while, I move my little finger over the back of her hand.

Maybe one day I'll write about all of this myself. I'll look at the section Dad wrote and re-work it a little. I'll look at *The Black Flower*, and think about what Wiseman would have said in his sequel if he'd been given the chance. And the story I sent by email too. They're all part of the same story, after all, and so I'll tell *my* version of it, one that stems from all of them. I can't see it yet, not properly, but at least I have an idea for an opening line.

*Sometimes,* I'll write.

*Sometimes it happens like this.*